MW00366627

THE KING'S SWORD

Also by C. J. Brightley

Erdemen Honor:
A Cold Wind
Honor's Heir

A Long-Forgotten Song:
Things Unseen

THE KING'S SWORD

C. J. BRIGHTLEY

SPRING SONG PRESS

THE KING'S SWORD. Copyright 2012 by C. J. Brightley.
For information contact info@cjbrightley.com.

ISBN 978-0-9891915-0-0

Published in the United Sates of America by Spring Song Press, LLC.

www.cjbrightley.com

Cover design by Ivan Zanchetta

For Stephen

ONE

I crossed his tracks not far outside of Stone-haven, and I followed them out of curiosity, nothing more. They were uneven, as if he were stumbling. It was bitterly cold, a stiff wind keeping the hilltops mostly free of the snow that formed deep drifts in every depression. By the irregularity of his trail, I imagined he was some foolish city boy caught out in the cold and that he might want some help.

It was the winter of 368, a few weeks before the new year. I was on my way to the garrison at Kesterlin just north of the capital, but I was in no hurry. I had a little money in my pack and I was happy enough alone.

In less than a league, I found him lying face-down in the snow. I nudged him with my toe before I knelt to turn him over, but he didn't respond. He was young, and something about him seemed oddly familiar. He wasn't hurt, at least not in a way I could see, but he was nearly frozen. He wore a thin shirt, well-made breeches, and expensive boots, but nothing else. He had no sword, no tunic over his shirt, no cloak, no horse. I had no horse because I didn't have the gold for one, but judging by his boots he could have bought one easily. There was a bag of coins inside his shirt, but I didn't investigate that further. His breathing was slow, his hands icy. It was death to be out in such weather so unprepared.

He was either a fool or he was running from something, but in either case I couldn't let him freeze. I strode to the top of the hill to look for pursuit. A group of riders was moving away to the south, but I couldn't identify them. Anyway, they wouldn't cross his path going that direction.

I wrapped him in my cloak and hoisted him over my shoulder. The forest wasn't too far away and it would provide shelter and firewood. I wore a shirt and a thick winter tunic over it, but even so, I was shivering badly by the time we made it to the trees. The wind was bitter cold, and I sweated enough carrying him to chill myself thoroughly. I built a fire in front of a rock face that would reflect the heat back upon us. I let myself warm a little before opening my pack and pulling out some carrots and a little dried venison to make a late lunch.

I rubbed the boy's hands so he wouldn't lose his fingers. His boots were wet, so I pulled them off and set them close to the fire. There was a knife in his right boot, and I slipped it out to examine it.

You can tell a lot about a man by the weapons he carries. His had a good blade, though it was a bit small. The hilt was finished with a green gemstone, smoothly polished and beautiful. Around it was a thin gold band, and ribbons of gold were inlaid in the polished bone hilt. It was a fine piece that hadn't seen much use, obviously made for a nobleman. I kept the knife well out of his reach while I warmed my cold feet. If he panicked when he woke, I wanted him unarmed.

I felt his eyes on me not long before the soup was ready. He'd be frightened of me, no doubt, so for several minutes I pretended I hadn't noticed he was awake to give him time to study me. I'm a Dari, and there are so few of us in Erdem that most people fear me at first.

"I believe that's mine." His voice had a distinct tremor, and he must have realized it because he lifted his chin a little defiantly, eyes wide.

I handed the knife back to him hilt-first. "It is. It's nicely made."

He took it cautiously, as if he wasn't sure I was really going to give it back to him. He shivered and pulled my cloak closer around his shoulders, keeping the knife in hand.

"Here. Can you eat this?"

He reached for the bowl with one hand, and seemed to debate a moment before resting the knife on the ground by his knee. "Thank you." He kept his eyes on me as he dug in.

I chewed on a bit of dried meat as I watched him. He looked better with some warm food in him and the heat of the fire on his face. "Do you want another bowl?"

"If there's enough." He smiled cautiously.

We studied each other while the soup cooked. He was maybe seventeen or so, much younger than I. Slim, pretty, with a pink mouth like a girl's. Typical Tuyet coloring; blond hair, blue eyes, pale skin. Slender hands like an artist or scribe.

"Thank you." He smiled again, nervous but gaining confidence. He did look familiar, especially in his nose and the line of his cheekbones. I tried to place him among the young nobles I'd seen last time I'd visited Stonehaven.

"What's your name?"

"Hak-" he stopped and his eyes widened. "Mikar. My name is Mikar."

Hakan.

Hakan Ithel. The prince!

He looked a bit like his father the king. It wasn't hard to guess why he was fleeing out into the winter snow. Rumors of Nekane Vidar's intent to seize power had been making their way through the army and the mercenary groups for some months.

"You're Hakan Ithel, aren't you?"

His shoulders slumped a little. He looked at the ground and nodded slightly.

He had no real reason to trust me. Vidar's men would be on his trail soon enough. No wonder he was frightened.

"My name is Kemen Sendoa. Call me Kemen." I stood to bow formally to him. "I'm honored to make your acquaintance. Is anyone following you?"

His eyes widened even more. "I don't know. Probably."

"Then we'd best cover your tracks. Are you going anywhere in particular?"

"No."

I stamped out the fire and kicked a bit of snow over it. Of course, anyone could find it easily enough, but I'd cover our trail better once we were on our way. A quick wipe with some snow cleaned the bowl and it went back in my pack.

He stood wrapped in my cloak, looking very young, and I felt a little sorry for him.

"Right then. Follow me." I slung my pack over my shoulder and started off. I set a pace quick enough to keep myself from freezing and he followed, stumbling sometimes in the thick snow. The wind wasn't quite as strong in the trees, though the air was quite cold.

I took him west to the Purling River as if we were heading for the Ralksin Ferry. The walk took a few hours; the boy was slow, partly because he was weak and pampered and partly because I don't think he understood the danger. At any moment I expected to hear hounds singing on our trail, but we reached the bank of the Purling with no sign of pursuit.

"Give me your knife."

He gave it to me without protest. He was pale and shivering, holding my cloak close to his chest. I waded into the water up to my ankles and walked downstream, then threw the knife a bit further downstream where it clattered onto the rocks lining the bank. Whoever pursued him would know or guess it was his, and though the dogs would lose his trail in the water, they might continue downstream west toward the Ferry.

5

"Walk in the water. Keep the cloak dry and don't touch dry ground."

"Why?" His voice wavered a bit, almost a whine.

I felt my jaw tighten in irritation. "In case they use dogs." I wondered whether I was being absurdly cautious, whether they would bother to use dogs at all.

He still looked confused, dazed, and I pushed him into the water ahead of me. I kept one hand firm on his shoulder and steered him up the river. Ankle-deep, the water was painfully cold as it seeped through the seams in my boots. The boy stumbled several times and would have stopped, but I pushed him on.

We'd gone perhaps half a league upriver when I heard the first faint bay of hounds. They were behind us, already approaching the river-bank, and the baying rapidly grew louder. I took my hand from the boy's shoulder to curl my fingers around the hilt of my sword. As if my sword would do much. If they wanted him dead, they'd have archers. I was turning our few options over in my mind and trying to determine whether the hounds had turned upriver or were merely spreading out along the bank, when the boy stopped abruptly.

"Dogs."

"Keep walking."

He shook his head. "They're my dogs. They won't hurt me."

I grabbed the collar of his shirt and shoved him forward, hissing into his ear, "Fear the hunters, not the dogs! You're the fox. Don't forget that."

He stumbled and twisted a bit in protest, but I kept my hand firm and pushed him forward again. Gradually we made our way upriver, keeping the water always above our ankles. The princeling was trembling, and I didn't let go of his collar, afraid he would fall.

"I don't think I can go much farther." His voice shook.

The baying of the hounds had grown no closer, and I relaxed a little, but we were hardly safe yet. "The crossing isn't far."

He said nothing else, and I kept us going until the ford. The crossing itself took only a few minutes, but the water came up over our knees. I kept us in the water for half a league up the other side of the river before finally moving us away into the trees.

My feet were a raging ache of cold and I was shivering almost uncontrollably. But I didn't trust the boy to keep steady, so I pushed him ahead of me for another hour through the growing darkness. Finally we reached an ideal shelter, a grand old tree that had finally been conquered by time and fallen, leaving a broad trunk stretched out on the ground.

The boy collapsed to sit with his back against the tree while I gathered wood for another fire, this one small and subdued. A few hills would hide the light from anyone at the river. It was dangerous if they were close behind us, but we'd both lose our feet if we didn't have a fire soon.

We sat by the fire in silence, the heat stinging our faces. He glanced at me from time to time. I was content with the quiet, and he spoke first, as I was preparing the last of the tubers to roast. I should have been hunting as we walked, but I'd been too cold and too intent on listening for pursuit.

"Please forgive my curiosity, but I've never seen anyone like you before. Where are you from?" His voice had the soft lilt of the highborn.

"Llewton." I smiled at his look of confusion. "I'm Dari. There aren't many of us in Stonehaven. The Dari are from the east, and the few in Erdem are mostly near the eastern border." He waited, watching me, so I added, "I was a foundling in Llewton. I served under your father until about four years ago."

He leaned forward in interest and I handed him the bowl of kiberries and the first steaming skewer.

"I've never seen a Dari before."

I grunted and when he flinched back I laughed. "Do I frighten you?"

"Should I be frightened?" He flung the question back with a bit of fire and I smiled.

"If I wanted to hurt you, I would have done so already."

He smiled then. "Thank you for your help. I haven't thanked you properly, and I do apologize. Normally I have better manners." He tucked into the food with good will, studying me closely.

I couldn't blame him for his curiosity, but I admit it made me self-conscious. We Dari are much taller than Tuyets and much darker. Dark brown or black eyes are normal, but an unfortunate few of us have green eyes. I am uncommonly tall even for a Dari. For all my looks, I have lived among Tuyets all my life and speak Darin only haltingly.

NORMALLY I WOULD have wrapped up in my cloak close by the fire and slept soundly, one hand on my knife in case of trouble but unworried and relatively comfortable. To sleep with one eye open and yet rest well is an invaluable skill for any warrior.

The boy offered me my cloak. I shook my head, and he looked relieved, with a quick, almost embarrassed smile. He wasn't suited for harsh weather, and it was less trouble to simply give it to him than be slowed if he became ill.

The night was long and cold, the wind cutting through the trees. My wet breeches didn't dry much. I amused myself by trying to identify the animals in the darkness by the sounds they made. Once I heard the far off cry of a wolf, and much closer the sudden sharp cry of a rabbit dying, probably caught by an owl, and the soft rustle of rodents in the leaves and snow. I tried once to lie down, but the ground sucked the warmth right from my bones, so I spent the night pacing round the fire, feeding it wood when it got low.

Hakan slept the sleep of the dead, only a shock of yellow hair sticking out from the end of my cloak. My eyes were gritty by the time the sky began to turn grey. I left him and went hunting, taking two purflins and a dove in less than an hour. I wanted to get an early start, but when I returned the boy was still asleep.

I cleaned the birds, roasted them for our lunch, and wrapped them in a bit of cloth before finally waking him.

"Up with you now, we'd best get on."

He rubbed his eyes blearily. "It's early."

"Do you want to be in town with a warm bed tonight?"

He nodded.

"So do I." I slung my pack over my shoulder and started off.

He followed me, my cloak still wrapped around his shoulders. "You didn't sleep?"

I didn't answer. He could hardly have made the night warmer, and he needed the rest more than I did.

"I'm sorry." He sounded genuinely apologetic and I smiled a little.

"We'll reach Four Corners by late afternoon. Do you have any money?"

"Why?" His voice was cautious.

"It makes paying for things like beds and dinners easier." We walked in silence for some minutes before I questioned him. "Are you going to explain why you were fleeing the palace?"

"My father died last night. I mean, the night before I left. Yesterday morning Tibi woke me early and told me to leave immediately. He gave me money and told me not even to stop by the stables because they were too easy to see from the windows. I snuck out through the kitchen." He sounded very young, a slight tremor in his voice.

"Who's Tibi?"

"My tutor, Tibon Rusta." A childish nickname, then.

"You trust him?"

"Yes, of course."

"You left then?"

"Yes. I went out the eastern gate and through Stonehaven."

Rusta might have paid dearly for that warning, but there was no point in bringing that to the boy's attention. Or perhaps it had been convenient for Rusta to send Hakan out to his death in the snow rather than to open himself for accusations of assassination.

"What are you going to do?"

He was silent, as I had expected. I wondered how much he knew of the coup we had all expected.

Vidar had been positioning himself to take over for months, and nothing had been said about the prince. The boy had been almost forgotten in the palace, his father taking no great pains to give him responsibility, to let him earn the respect of the people.

The king's health had been declining for several years, but in the last few months he'd grown much worse. Vidar, the seneschal, had assumed more responsibility each day, and by many accounts he had been competent, though rather harsh. But he wasn't the heir, nor was the prince young enough to require a regent to rule before he came of age.

"Do you have any friends who would shelter you?"

There was a long silence, and finally he said quietly, "Perhaps some might, but they're all in Stonehaven. I'm not sure enough to ask them."

11

I cursed inside. He had no friends, no plan, no sword, no horse, and no idea how to survive alone. It would have been so simple to leave him to fend for himself. I might as well kill him myself; he'd be lucky to last a day.

I wouldn't last much longer without a cloak, either. My lungs stung from the frigid air. My hair and shirt were damp from the snow and my back ached from the constant shivering.

The throne belonged to the prince by right. With the support of the army, removing a usurper should be easy. I wondered what the army would do, whether they would cast their support behind the seneschal or whether they would hold out for the prince.

My soldier's oath was fulfilled when I was honorably discharged from the *kedani*, the corps of foot soldiers. I could have walked away. But when I served the king Hakan Emyr, I did so for love of Erdem, not for love of the king. Every soldier swears allegiance to the kingdom, not to the king's person.

The hereditary rule of the king is well established, but there's logic in it. The army supports the heir because the heir is trained from childhood to be the best possible leader for the country.

This had been the system in Erdem for generations, but it began breaking down with the king Hakan Emyr, the boy's father. He didn't earn the respect of the people and, at least when I served in the *suvari*, the horsemen, and then in the kedani, there were serious doubts about his leadership. Discontent. Distrust. Fears of Tarvil marauders from the north had begun to rise, and questions of

12

border security had become much more pressing as the army dwindled. There was little money to pay soldiers, and many simply retired, took their pay and left to find better jobs. Disillusioned. The word wasn't strong enough.

"What will you do?"

"I don't know." His voice was miserable, and I waited for him to explain. "I don't know if I want to be king."

Odd that he questioned it. I would have assumed that, being born to the throne, he would have accepted the idea. "Why not?"

Again he was silent, this time for long that I stopped and turned around to face him. "Why not?"

"The job of a king isn't easy."

"So you only want to do easy things?" I didn't bother to hide my scorn.

"No!" He frowned. "I don't know if I can do it well. I wouldn't be the only one to suffer for it if I'm not a good king."

"Yes. The position carries responsibility. You'd shy away from that?"

He hesitated. "I assumed the threat came from Nekane Vidar, my father's seneschal. If he seizes power, perhaps he'll be better for Erdem than I will."

"Why?"

He flushed and stared at the ground. "You should know. He's a warrior, battle-tested, with a good grasp of strategy and tactics. We've heard reports all winter that Tafari is preparing to invade. I don't have any experience, and I'm not good with a sword. I would think it would be better for everyone if he was in charge of our defense."

I turned around and began walking again. Right enough, Nekane Vidar the seneschal was battle-tested. I'd served under him distantly, when I was not long out of training. I hadn't spoken to him, of course, but I knew him by sight and reputation. At the time, at least, he'd been respected, though not well liked. Harshly demanding and quite competent.

I'd believed him loyal to the kingdom and to the king himself. He was wellborn and served as a suvari officer before he had been appointed in the king's ministerial staff, rising to the rank of seneschal some five or six years ago. I hadn't particularly liked him, but I wouldn't have thought him likely to send assassins after anyone. He was more direct than that. But perhaps I was wrong. I wouldn't rule out anything yet.

Two

I filled my canteens at a small creek and gave Hakan my second one. He'd need his own soon. The forest was filled with the immense silence of winter, but small sounds punctuated the stillness. The snow squeaked sometimes beneath my boots and once I heard a fantail hawk.

"Where are we going?" His voice followed me.

"First to Four Corners for supplies. Then northeast, to the hills. I know them well and there aren't many patrols anymore." I set a quick pace and could hear him panting behind me, but it didn't stop his questions.

"You served in the army?"

"In the suvari for the first four years, then I was transferred to the kedani."

"Why?"

"There was a shortage of qualified officers."

Many had been killed in the long foolish campaign to the northeast against the Tarvil. It had gained the king nothing and cost him many of his best men. I'd been transferred to a position above many men with years of experience on me. I was fortunate they were willing to recognize my skill and forgive my relative inexperience. My talents for tactics and strategy had then earned their trust, but not every young officer is lucky enough to be given that chance.

"How long is the term of service?"

"Volunteers have the opportunity to retire or reenlist every three years. Foundlings like me serve for twenty years to repay the king's purse for our education and training. We're not slaves; we're paid, though it isn't much."

"Twenty years! That seems harsh." He was breathless now, and I slowed a little and shrugged.

"When you're king, you can change it as you see fit."

"You don't think it was unjust?"

"In what way? I received a good education, though I remain lacking in some subjects. Most officers come from orphanages."

In fact, many orphans and foundlings eventually command volunteers with more exalted positions in life, since we begin our training as children. The army generally rewards merit and talent over the status of one's birth. It can result in odd tensions, but for the most part, it's accepted, for we've had much success even in badly conceived actions.

He ran up beside me and looked up at me, almost falling over a rock as he took his eyes from the path. "Honestly, you don't feel that your misfortune at birth was used against you? That you were taken advantage of?"

"What good would that do?" I shrugged again. "I've no complaints, but if you would seek my counsel once you have your throne, I could probably find in myself some suggestions."

That was the most I'd said in several months, and I clapped my mouth shut to press on. He followed me in silence for some time, but I wasn't surprised when he eventually thought of another question.

"What age does a foundling enter the king's service?"

"Normally sixteen." I knew the question that would follow.

"Normally?"

"I entered the king's service on my fourteenth birthday."

"Why? That's so young."

"Because I was very good. Besides, I was nearly as tall as any Tuyet man by then."

"Into combat at fourteen?" His voice sounded incredulous.

I wondered if he thought I was lying, and decided I didn't care enough about his opinion to be offended. "Skirmishes, yes, but my first real battle wasn't for another year."

He was quiet a few moments. I heard the trilling call of a mountain lark. We'd left the trees to follow the spine of a low hill toward the northern spur of the great forest, and the wind was stronger

17

in the open. My damp shirt stuck to me and the ice flakes felt like little knives on my face. Hakan would have to get his own cloak at the first opportunity.

"How long have you been out of the army?"

"I was discharged four years ago, but I've served as a mercenary on occasion since then." Would he require an explanation of that too?

"But that would mean you're thirty-eight years old. You can't be."

"I'm thirty-three. I was discharged five years early."

"Why?" The boy might have been an interrogator for the courts, he had so many questions.

"Because I received this." I turned to face him and pulled the neck of my shirt and the strap of my pack aside.

I watched him flinch at the sight, then look closer. The wound had healed rather well, considering what it had looked like at first, but I couldn't blame anyone for their initial shock. If I'd been a light-skinned Tuyet, the scar wouldn't have been so noticeable. It had faded from the livid red of the first few months to a sickly greenish white, which stood out stark and ugly against my dark olive skin. It was a ragged circle a few inches below my collarbone on the right side, none too small, sunken a bit below the curve of the muscle, like a shallow crater.

The one on my back was worse, though I didn't see it often, a larger scar that only matched the neat circle in the front with a bit of imagination. It was much lower, at the bottom of my shoulder blade. It would have shattered the bone, but I'd had my arm stretched upward when the javelin hurtled downward from a high arcing throw. It had knocked me off my feet with the force, the javelin driving into the ground beneath me.

"What happened?" I was gratified to see that after the initial horror his face had become curious rather than disgusted.

"I was on the wrong end of a javelin near the end of the campaign against the Tarvil. It wasn't a large battle, but we were badly outnumbered. We were ambushed."

I felt my throat getting tight at the memory. He looked up at me, waiting for more details, and I surprised myself by continuing.

"There were about forty of us and maybe one hundred and fifty of them." I lost my friend Yuudai in that battle. A stupid battle, one that never should have happened at all. It was pointless, a waste of good men.

"Did you kill any of them?" His eyes were wide.

"Aye, some fourteen or fifteen, I don't remember clearly." Yuudai's blood had come bubbling out his throat. I don't remember much after that aside from the pain of the wound itself.

"How did you live?"

I took a deep breath. Patience.

"I was left for dead, the javelin pinning me to the ground. A scouting party found me the next day, and against all predictions I lived. I was honorably discharged upon being able to stand upright without support, given two weeks' worth of food, and sent on my way."

19

I did resent that. I thought I'd earned a bit more compensation, at least a month's recovery time. If not for the injury itself, for my fifteen years of service and the many men I'd trained. It stung to be thrown aside because I was no longer useful. Not least because I might have served my country again, if the army had only waited another few months for me to heal.

The wind carried a hint of heavier snow in the next few hours. Soon we would be in the trees again, but at our pace we would not reach town before nightfall.

"Does it hurt anymore?"

"When it's cold. Why?"

"You can have your cloak back. I'm better now."

"Keep it." Patience. Discipline. Self-denial. Consider it training, I reminded myself. "Come on." I started off again.

We didn't reach Four Corners that night. I had to slow my pace for the boy. I had the opportunity to practice self-denial again that night, alternating pacing about the fire in the cutting wind and sitting huddled close to the flames as I grew colder. The snow petered out around midnight and I dozed a little, but again the grey light of morning was more than welcome.

It was late morning when we finally reached town. There was a light snow falling and I shook the flakes from my head as I entered what I guessed was a general store. I couldn't read the letters carved on the sign, but the rough painting of a bolt of cloth and a barrel of flour was clear enough for me. The room was deliciously warm, and I let out a sigh of satisfaction as I moved toward the back, Hakan trailing behind me.

The wonderful heat was coming from a cheerful fire around which were gathered some seven or eight men. Two were playing a game at a low table, but most were just talking. I studied them a moment before stepping forward, wondering who among them ran the store. Several of them looked up at me in surprise, glancing at my sword and smiling nervously.

"Can I help you?" One man stepped forward, wiping his sweaty hands on a well-used apron.

"Aye. We want some supplies and lodging for the night."

He nodded and glanced back at the group. "Come then, show me what you want and I'll tally it up. It's a bad winter to be out. There's a boarding house just down the street."

I was reveling in the warmth, but he shivered as we approached the front door.

"Phraa, it's cold up front. Now then, what do you want?"

"First a heavy cloak."

He pointed down one of the aisles.

"Naoki, pick the one you want." I caught Hakan's eye as I called him by his new name. Naoki means honest or righteous in Kumar. It wouldn't do to call him Hakan so close to Stonehaven, and Mikar, the name he'd given me, made his noble accent all too obvious.

"A length of rope. Some salt." A scoop of rough salt went into a carefully wrapped leather bundle. Soap. Some string. A new pair of woolen socks; mine had holes in the toes. Then things for

21

Hakan. A canteen. An extra bowl. A spoon. His own soap, a sharpening stone for the knife he'd need, other supplies, and a pack to put them in. Of course he wouldn't know what to buy, so I chose everything.

"Peppers." Dried hot peppers were an extravagance, at least for me, but they reminded me of my time campaigning in the south, which I had mostly enjoyed.

"Not so many, I don't have that much money. A good knife, about so long." That was for Hakan. It was no longer safe to go about the countryside with nothing for protection; the king's law hadn't been enforced consistently for some years.

He shook his head. "I don't sell knives. You'll need to go to Ursin, the blacksmith. He's just down the street." I thought it was a good name for a blacksmith. It's from *urseo*, Common for bear.

I nodded. "A flint."

I could find a flint for Hakan, but with all the snow on the ground and heading into the mountains, it would be worth the expense to not have to look. But that was perilously close to the end of my money, considering the cost of a night in the inn and a good knife. Not to mention the sword he'd need eventually. Hakan had some money, but I didn't know how much. I nodded at the shopkeeper and went back to find Hakan still fingering the cloaks.

"What's taking so long?"

"They're all rough."

"Aye, like mine." What did he expect, silks? I ran my hand down the ten or twelve cloaks hanging neatly.

"Here, this one is the heaviest." I pulled it out and examined the cloth, holding it up to him. Too short for me, of course, but quite long enough for him, with a heavy hood as well. Perfect.

"Get this one. Give me your money." He hesitated, but pulled the small bag from inside his shirt and handed it to me.

The gold inside was heavier than I'd expected, and I wished we were in the sunlight so I could admire it. I've always loved gold, but not for its value. I'm happy enough with what most people might call little. I love gold for its beauty, the warm glow it has, the fine detail in well-worked designs, the way it's like the sun captured within the metal. I picked out one small coin and handed the bag back to him. Good. Lodging wouldn't be a problem then. "Put it away."

His coin was enough for all his items. I paid for my own things, and the shopkeeper watched me curiously as I handed Hakan's change back to him. I shrugged into my cloak and Hakan wrapped his new one around him as the shopkeeper gave me directions to the blacksmith and to the boarding house down a side street. Then it was back out into the snow, this time much more comfortably.

The smithy was also warm, fires roaring as the blacksmith worked on something in the back. I called out to let him know we were there, and a boy came running. When he caught sight of me, his mouth dropped open and he turned right around and ran back into the shop, shouting for his master. In a moment, the blacksmith himself

23

appeared, paling as he saw me. They're always afraid of me.

I spoke politely. "I was told you could sell me a good knife."

He nodded. "I sell knives. You'll have to judge the quality for yourself." Honesty. I like that. I followed him around the corner to the storeroom.

"How much do you want to spend?"

"Let me see the quality and I'll decide."

He nodded and pulled out several wooden trays, knives neatly aligned one beside the other. I picked out seven of the best with plain hilts but good blades. I tested the balance, but three were completely off, and I discarded those.

"Do you make all these yourself?"

"No, I buy and sell them too. I make tools mostly. Knives are a sideline."

I nodded. Someone who knew what he was doing would never have made these so inconsistently.

"Naoki, hold this one." Good, the hilt was not too long for him, the blade clean and straight. "We'll take it."

He nodded and named the price, seven bronze eagles.

"That's a bit high." I frowned. Hakan glanced at me, and I thought he looked a little surprised. Of course he wouldn't know how much a knife should go for.

Ursin hesitated and glanced at my sword. "Six then. For a soldier."

Hakan slipped his hand in his pocket, but didn't pull out his money yet. There was a long silence. The price would have been fine in Stonehaven, but we were only in Four Corners. I thought about turning away. I hate bargaining, though everyone does it. Tell me the price straight, and I'll decide. Once a little girl selling fruit in the market in Stonehaven was so frightened of me that when I frowned at the price for a skewer of roasted apples, she shoved it into my hand and started crying. She was probably too young to even understand why I frowned. Her father turned around to scowl at me, though he too looked a bit unnerved. I paid her high price to assuage my guilt.

Ursin licked his lips. "Five."

I nodded curtly. Hakan paid and bent to slip the knife into his boot.

I was turning away when the blacksmith asked, "What's wrong with these three?"

"The balance is off."

"Can you show me?"

I stifled a smile. "Did you make them yourself?"

He nodded unhappily. "Aye, and everyone who knows what they're about rejects the ones I make, but I don't know why. I can't improve my work if I don't know what's wrong."

"Right then. Naoki needed a blade for his boot, self-defense, a fine thin blade as long as my hand with excellent balance, light. These two, the balance is too far forward, you see? The blade is heavy. That's fine for butchering, but not for fine work. This one, the balance is in the hilt, which makes it quick to move but hard to control, since the hilt is round and can slip in your grasp."

He nodded, studying each knife in turn.

"Why didn't you consider these?" He gestured at the other two trays.

"Those are too small, they're children's knives."

He looked at me in disbelief. "They're not! I've seen many a man carry one of those."

I shrugged. "If you prefer, say my friend needs something more serious. Those are for show. I'm not made of gold and cannot pay for ornamentation. This one will do quite well."

He nodded again. "Thanks. If you have the time, could I ask your advice on some I'm making now?"

"We need to be going. It's almost noon, and I wouldn't keep you from lunch."

"If I offer you lunch and dinner, would you lend me your expertise for the afternoon?"

I hesitated. Food that someone else prepared would be a luxury I hadn't enjoyed in some time, but I didn't want to stay too long and attract attention. "I'm no armorer."

"But you know knives!" He was eager. "If you must go, thank you. But consider my offer."

"Naoki?" I turned to Hakan.

He smiled broadly. "Why not? I'm hungry."

I shrugged and nodded.

"Good, good! We'll have lunch first then. Did you just arrive in town?" He bustled about, taking off the thick leather apron and putting back the trays of knives.

"Aye."

"Where did you come from?"

"East. Do you have any news from Stone-haven? I've heard vague rumors but nothing more."

Hakan glanced at me but said nothing. Of course, we'd come from southwest, but Ursin didn't need to know that.

"Aye, some strange news indeed. Some say the prince is dead."

"Really?" We followed him as he went to the back and spoke to the bellows boy a moment, then out into the swirling snow and down the street. The wind whipped his breath away, and he didn't continue until we entered an inn just a few doors down.

He called out toward an open door in the back. "Bread and whatever you're serving today." Then to us, "It's Nonin, isn't it? Good. It's pork pie day. You'll like that, just the thing on a cold day like this."

I nodded, hoping he would return to the news.

"Of course all the rumors contradict each other. We don't get any real news, though Stone-haven isn't really so far away."

"What are the rumors?" *Get to the point.*

"The prince is dead. The prince is missing. The prince is ill and won't be seeing anyone. Not that I'd be seeing him anyway, but you under-stand. That the prince has been crowned and is sitting on the throne already. That one doesn't have much credibility, since there's no word of any coronation celebration."

I glanced up to see a young girl coming out of the kitchen with a broad platter of food. She saw me and her mouth dropped open before she scurried back into the kitchen, and I scowled at the table.

Ursin flinched back. "What's ailing you?"

"Nothing." I growled. I took a deep breath. "Do you think Vidar is planning to take power?"

Ursin nodded, and a man came out of the kitchen carrying the tray of food. He stared at me a moment before cautiously bringing the food over. I nodded curtly to him as he set down the bread, plates of rich pork pie, and cool mugs of ale.

I wished Ursin would tell me more, but he was cautious and unwilling to speak too freely to a stranger. He said business had been slow, and he wanted to test for the elite armorers who supply the army. Anyone can make a knife or a sword, but standard issue weapons are made to criteria set by the crown. Officers' weapons are works of art. It would be good steady work, and pay better than blacksmithing in a farming town. I thought his chances were slim; an armorer's apprenticeship begins young. But he seemed bright enough and willing to work for it, and I'm not the sort to fault a man for trying.

URSIN WAS A BETTER blacksmith than armorer. The smithy was blissfully warm after my three days with no cloak. I could feel my hair and shirt drying as I stood close by the great fire. The bellows boy eventually peeked out from behind a wall and studied me as Ursin plied me with questions that never seemed to end.

Hakan was quiet, sometimes listening to us and sometimes wandering about the blacksmith's shop. He smiled at the bellows boy, who finally gathered his courage to chatter at him, pointing at me every so often. Hakan laughed and shook his head, letting the boy lead him about the shop. I think it was a change for him, for he didn't strike me as one to enjoy the company of children.

I sketched different blades for Ursin on parchment, showing the proper ratios of width and length, the best cross section for strength, for flexibility, for speed and maneuverability. I cannot work metal myself, but I know what makes a good blade. The strong curve of a scimitar, with its leading edge hardened and sharp, the back edge softer to catch the blade of an opponent. The bold straight blade of a longsword, the fuller nearly to the end, narrowing just a bit through the length. The short triangular blade of a falsehand, three fingers wide at the base and short enough to be concealed easily, narrowing to a precise point at the end. An assassin's weapon, but also good for women to protect themselves. The leaner longer blade of a bootknife. Then of course there were other weapons I'd trained with, but he didn't need to venture into those.

Finally the blacksmith was satisfied, or perhaps overloaded with information. He took us to his home for a simple dinner. His wife didn't join us as we ate, though she stared at me from time to time. Her eyes had widened when she first saw me, and she clutched at her husband's sleeve to speak to him in a frightened whisper when he invited us in to sit in the cramped room. He'd shaken his head and muttered something to her, and she'd backed away to stand over the fire. He was freer with his words after several glasses of ale.

"I wish the prince was found safe. No one wishes him ill, not as far as I've heard. But with the problems we've had, we can't afford another king like the last one."

Hakan twitched as if he would speak and I shot him a look that for once was meant to look dangerous. He quieted, so I suppose it worked.

Ursin continued unaware. "Taxes have gone up, but the roads are worse. We've had all sorts of vagabonds passing through here, and just last week one of the farmers, I didn't know him well, was murdered on his way home from market. Robbed. It wouldn't have been tolerated when I was young."

"And you think Vidar will fix it?"

He nodded. "I hope so. We need the roads, surely you can see that. We have get to market, and my wife's family lives an hour away if the weather's good. Travelers have to worry about bandits more than they have for years, and we've heard the rumors from the border."

"What rumors?" I'd heard many rumors, but I wanted Hakan to hear what the people heard every day.

"That the Rikutans are getting bolder in their raids. Of course, the Tarvil are getting bolder too; everyone knows that. I say it's because we don't have enough soldiers anymore. You should know that, you're a soldier, aren't you?"

"I was."

"Then you've seen how the posts were abandoned. So what do we get for our higher taxes then? Nothing! I'm as loyal as the rest, but surely you can see how we need a change."

I glanced at Hakan, who had his mouth tightly shut, his face very pale. "What would you do if the prince was found?" I asked.

It was a bold question, and he didn't want to answer it, tipping back his mug to gain a moment to think. Finally he said, "I suppose we'd all have to choose, wouldn't we?"

Hakan's mouth opened slightly, and I skewered with my eyes to prevent him from speaking.

"No doubt. I'm for the prince, if he does turn up. But I suppose we'll make do with Vidar, at least for now." I finished my own glass of ale. "Thank you for dinner." I would have smiled my thanks to his wife, but I didn't want to frighten her more.

"If you're short of money you can stay here for the night," Ursin shifted in his chair.

I raised my eyebrows. "Where?"

He glanced back at his wife, who reddened and moved away from the door.

"She's frightened of me. We can go."

"If you like. But you're welcome in the smithy if that would do."

I nodded. It would be warm and dry, and no one else would remember our presence. "Thank you. We'll do that. I want an early start tomorrow."

We walked back across the street to the smithy and he opened the door for us, leaving it unlocked. I splashed a bit of water on my face from a bucket and wrapped myself in my cloak on the floor near the fire. My boots steamed by the hearth and my feet soaked in the warmth. I was nearly asleep when Hakan spoke.

"Kemen, do you think Vidar will strengthen the army?"

"Aye." I stifled a yawn.

"Why are you helping me?"

Sleep tugged at my brain. Two nights with no sleep, two and a half days of walking, all in the frigid cold. I spoke with my eyes closed. "I fought under Vidar once, though I didn't know him well. He's a good man, or so I thought." I had to concentrate to form the sentences. "I don't see why he'd want to have you killed. He has the trust of the people and the respect of the army. If he wanted to influence you, I'd think you're young enough and smart enough to take his advice."

I heard him taking off his boots and fumbling with his cloak as I drifted toward sleep in the delicious warmth of the fire.

"I would've taken his advice. I don't understand why I was warned away."

"Do you know how your father died?" I opened my eyes to see him frowning up at the ceiling.

"No, I suppose not. He'd been sick for years, though. We weren't close, he didn't tell me how he was feeling." He didn't sound as if he grieved much.

I was nearly asleep when he said, "You didn't say why you're helping me."

Patience. I didn't snap at him, though I came close. The frustration helped me formulate my thoughts. "Merely having a strong army does not make one a good ruler. Vidar is a decent man, but there is something more here. Either he's changed, or someone else is threatening you. Either way, it's underhanded and doesn't befit a king. You're young and have much to learn. Nevertheless, I hope you'd put the lives of your people before your own wishes. Unlike your father. Either Vidar is false, or he doesn't have the grasp on power he thinks he has, and so his honesty means little." Then I had to think. "Is there anyone else who could be behind the threat?"

He hesitated. "I don't know. I didn't like some of his ministers, but I couldn't accuse them of anything without proof."

Fair enough. "Then go to sleep. We can't solve the riddle tonight."

He sighed and rustled around a bit more, but I was asleep in minutes. Whether he slept after that, I don't know.

THREE

I must have been more tired than I realized. I didn't wake until I heard the door scraping open the next morning. I was on my feet in a moment, but it was only the bellows boy, who watched me cautiously as he edged around the room to approach one of the tables. He left the door open behind himself, and the clear blue light of morning filtered in. I prodded Hakan with my toe before pulling on my boots. They weren't quite dry, but much better than before.

I turned to the bellows boy, who was apparently hoping I wouldn't see him as he crept closer to the fire. He froze, staring at me with wide eyes.

"Do you know where I could buy two horses?"

He shook his head. I sat down, hoping that would make me less intimidating, and nudged

Hakan again. The boy scurried in front of me and threw the wood in the fire before running off to get more.

"Naoki, get up. It's time to go."

He groaned and sat up, rubbing his shoulder. He was probably accustomed to a softer bed.

In a moment we were ready. The bellows boy collided with me as we were walking out the door, and I caught him by the arm as he nearly fell, his arms full of firewood. He looked up at me in terror. He was quite young, maybe eight or nine, and I suppose I couldn't blame him for his fright. I dropped to one knee in front of him, still taller by at least a head but not so towering, keeping a hold on his sleeve so he wouldn't run before he heard me.

"Tell your master Ursin we're grateful for his hospitality." He nodded, and I smiled as kindly as I could. "Don't be so hasty to judge people. I mean you no harm." I let him go and stood as he scurried around me. Hakan looked at me oddly as we strode away.

We found a stable in town, but by the look of the horses going in and out, we wouldn't find good quality there. It would be better to walk. Hakan needed a bit of toughening anyway. He'd been complaining most of the day before about his feet hurting.

As we passed the stable, a man stopped in the middle of the street and stared, his eyes on Hakan. I put my hand on Hakan's shoulder and pushed him along. "Naoki, get on!" My voice was rough and loud.

He nodded, but looked up at me questioningly.

The man strode toward us and I kept my hand from my sword hilt only by conscious effort. He smiled as he drew nearer. "Your Royal Highness was not expected here. Have you just arrived?" His face was open and friendly, and he sounded as though he was trying to speak correctly rather than with the simple farmer's language that came more naturally to him.

"You're mistaken, sir. This is my friend Naoki. He's in training for the kedani."

The man glanced between us, then addressed Hakan again with a clumsy half-bow. "Your Highness, I saw you once, in Stonehaven. I was there with my friend Curanil. He was taking a petition to the King's Court of Justice. You attended with your father." His voice was not loud, but another man passing by had already hesitated and looked back at us.

My stomach tightened with frustration. He seemed friendly enough, but even a friendly rumor could bring Vidar's men down on our heads.

Hakan frowned. "I don't know what you're talking about. I'm from Dorferto, and the closest I've ever been to Stonehaven was training last week in Kesterlin."

I tried to conceal my shock. He'd spoken with a perfect northwestern accent, with the clipped Ts and sharp hard vowels.

Another passerby stopped at the man's wave and came to stand beside the farmer, who now looked confused, shifting from one foot to the other. "You look very like the prince Hakan Ithel."

I tried to look bored rather than worried, and Hakan sighed as if irritated.

"Really, we do have to get on. I'm Naoki, I'm from Dorferto, I've never been to Stonehaven, and I'm on my way to Darsten for more training."

"The prince is missing." The man spoke to his friend, who also looked hard at Hakan.

Hakan nodded. "I heard last night. Good for him." He smiled quickly before turning to me. "Come on. We're already late."

I glanced back at them as we were leaving town. They appeared to be talking to each other, I saw one shrug, and then they walked away together. I couldn't tell whether that meant their curiosity was satisfied. Would they tell everyone they saw the prince? Would they believe he was only a soldier in training? I could not guess.

I'd wanted to use the roads as long as we could to speed our travel, but it was risky. Still, Vidar's men were probably some distance behind us, for I'd seen no sign of any pursuit yet. I took that risk, and perhaps I was foolish.

The road north was well marked and well enough maintained, and we covered quite some distance before noon. The roads were better there near Stonehaven and on some of the major transit routes across the country. They're a relic from the glorious days of the Second Age, the Golden Era. Some of the oldest and best of the bloodlines for the royal warhorses can be traced to that time, though some younger lines are also quite good. Erdemen history is long and rich; it was my favorite subject in school, even more than fighting.

That winter when I found Hakan, Erdem was entering its fifty-seventh year of the Famine, which began some three hundred years into the Third Age. Of course, not all those years were true famine, but between the famine, the epidemic of plague that cut down half the population, and the resulting lack of labor to bring in the pitiful crops, it was a difficult time. We hadn't seen an outbreak of plague for over twenty years, and things were getting better. But Erdem's glory was tarnished. The great roads that crossed the country carried few travelers, trade had dried up like grass in summer, and the exquisitely ornate palace in the great capital of Stonehaven was only partially used.

Any good study of warfare includes a detailed survey and analysis of history. We must understand the past. What other men have done, what the consequences were, what could have been changed or prevented.

I'd nearly forgotten Hakan was with me as I walked happily through the snow thinking of history, turning the great battles of the past over and over in my mind, until I heard the metallic sound of a horse's bit moving in its bridle. There was no one visible behind us yet, but our tracks betrayed us quite well enough.

"Hakan, go into the woods out of sight and wait. If I don't find you in an hour, go east through the mountains to Rikuto and seek protection from Tafari."

If he made it that far. He nodded with wide eyes and started into the woods. I brushed away his tracks with the edge of my cloak and made sure he was out of sight, then ran back along our tracks a little, so it wasn't quite so obvious that one set of tracks had just disappeared. If they wanted, they could find him in minutes, but I could think of nothing else. I cursed my foolish confidence, thinking the road was safe. The sounds belonged to a group of six suvari who surrounded me in a moment. I made no protest, standing quietly as they jostled a bit. I didn't recognize them, but the voice of the one who spoke was familiar.

"Sendoa? Kemen Sendoa?"

"Aye." I nodded and bowed politely, the way one bows to a fellow warrior.

"Hayato Jalo." He jumped down from his horse and bowed to me formally before we clasped elbows in the soldier's gesture of friendship. Hayato, Kumar for falcon, and Jalo, noble or gracious. He was older than I by a few years, but I served with him in the suvari the last year before I was transferred to the kedani.

"You don't look like a dead man." He drew back and looked me up and down.

"Am I supposed to?" It had been nearly thirteen years since I'd seen him, but I'd followed his career. He'd been a good man, brave and honorable. I wondered what he was like now. People change.

"I heard you were dead. Four or five years ago up in the northeast, in the campaign against the Tarvil." He frowned seriously. "I'm glad to see the rumors were wrong."

"Close enough. I was discharged for injury."

"I see you're healthy now?"

I nodded. "What are you doing out here? It's cold."

"I might ask you the same. Come, let us talk." He pulled me away from the group, motioning for them to stay at a distance. "What have you heard about what's going on in Stonehaven?" He looked worried, tense.

"Not much. Why?"

He took a deep breath, and let it out slowly, studying my face. He glanced back at the group and lowered his voice still further. "We're sent out to find a boy. We have sketches and a detailed description. I think it's the prince, but no one can confirm it. I've never seen him for myself, so I can't be sure... but who else would it be? We're to bring him back alive or dead. Supposedly the orders come from Vidar, but that doesn't sound like him, does it?"

I remained carefully neutral. "You don't think he'd want the prince found?"

"I don't think he'd specify that dead was perfectly fine. Come now, Kemen, you can't believe it of him. He's power hungry, yes. We all know that. He's gotten a little too ambitious the past few years, but I can't believe he'd order the boy killed. Between this and the rumors that the prince is already dead, we've quite a bit of unrest in the suvari."

"Who do they support?"

"The prince, of course, if he's alive. We don't know him, but I should hope he's better than his father. Vidar would..." he hesitated and glanced quickly back at the other suvari. "Well, he does have credibility, I'll give him that. But the last few months he's pushed the limits. It's not his throne. The suvari for the most part would support the prince if he claimed his right. It's the kedani that's a bit more questionable. They've seen Vidar and worked with him, you know, and he's respected, if not popular. They also haven't heard the new orders to bring back the prince, so they have nothing to tarnish his image aside from his ambition."

I nodded. "What of the men with you?"

He spat in frustration. "No one's sure what to do. We're riding about following orders, but we're all hoping we don't find the prince. We're loyal, you know that. We do what we're told. But we're no murderers."

"I assume there are other groups out looking for him as well?"

"Aye, hundreds. We're spreading out all over the country. I can't say how hard we're looking, but we all have orders."

"What about those in the palace? Any word about how the prince disappeared?"

He shook his head, and I debated for a moment before speaking. "Hayato, thank you for the information. I'll be passing through Ravenson in a couple weeks. If you pass through, or hear anything really interesting, particularly about the orders, will you let me know?"

He nodded.

"Leave a message at the inn for me."

He nodded again. "I won't ask what you're doing, since you seem to be in no hurry to say. But it's good to see you again, Kemen." He held my gaze very seriously. "I hope you know you can trust me. Let me know if you need anything. I'm still out of Rivensworth."

I nodded. "I will. Thank you. Safe riding."

He nodded and turned away, but turned back around in a moment. "Say, what are you doing walking? Don't you have a horse?"

I shrugged. "I'm not in the army. I don't have one issued to me anymore."

He laughed, but asked more quietly, "Do you need money?"

Good man. I shook my head. "Thank you but no. I want news more than anything."

He nodded. "Right then. I'll see what I can do."

We smiled, and it was much like any night before a battle, when two friends nod curtly to each other because there is nothing to say. With that he was off, hurrying the others down the road without a backward glance. Of course he couldn't know about Hakan, couldn't know we were traveling together. But he knew, and I knew, that we stood on the same side of the conflict that was inevitable. Vidar, or whoever had ordered the hunt, did not mean to let go of power.

I watched them until they were out of sight, then followed Hakan's trail into the woods. He was not far away, sitting on the snow-covered trunk of a fallen tree behind a thicket. He stood quickly.

"Who was it?" He fell in behind me as I made my way back toward the road. I led him on a path parallel to the road rather than actually on it. I was inclined to trust Hayato. But I didn't know the others with him, and I wouldn't risk meeting another squad on the road.

"A friend. I hadn't seen him in years." Since Hakan was four. Suddenly I felt very old, though I had never considered thirty-three old before. "They were looking for you." I glanced back at him. He was pale, but whether from cold, fear, or something else altogether I wasn't sure. "My friend and many others in the suvari support you over Vidar."

"What would they do if they found me?"

"Their orders were to bring you to Stonehaven, dead or alive. For his part, Hayato isn't looking for you very hard."

Again there was silence except for his puffing as he tried to keep up with me. I slowed my pace a little. It is easy for me to forget that not everyone moves so quickly.

THE NEXT MORNING we started early and walked all day. I hunted as we walked, took a rabbit in a clearing with the little bow, supplemented with burdock and kiberries. I took him farther off the road that night before I finally made a fire, over a low hill that should have concealed the light.

We were both tired from the cold and the long day of walking. I retreated into silence, but the princeling complained. His feet were wet. His fingers and ears were cold. He was getting a blister. He was hungry. I would quiet him with roasted pheasant if he would only wait until it was ready, but until then I glowered at the fire in morose silence.

I heard a murmur off in the woods, sounds that resolved into distant voices. "Hst." I motioned at Hakan, who sniffed irritably.

"When is it going to be ready?"

I stood silently, half-crouched, and slipped around the fire beside Hakan.

"What are you—"

I clamped my hand over his mouth and listened.

Yes, voices. And the sounds of several bodies moving through the underbrush toward us. They were trying to be quiet, and I'd barely heard them over the faint hiss and crackle of the fire. My fingers tight over Hakan's mouth, I bent to whisper in his ear, "Be silent and don't move." He stared at me with wide, confused eyes, and I caught my pack up and slipped it over my shoulder. I pushed the glowing logs apart and threw handfuls of snow and wet leaves over the still-glowing coals. It wouldn't hide the signs we'd been there, but it doused the flames; the light wouldn't be as obvious. I left the half-roasted pheasant in the coals and turned to Hakan, who still stared at me.

"What are you—" he started again, and I put my hand over his mouth again, none too gently this time.

"Silence, I said," I hissed in his ear. I pushed him into the darkness ahead of me. He suddenly thrashed, and I heard a distant shout from a different direction. How many of them were out there? I twisted Hakan's arm up painfully behind him and heard him whimper, suddenly compliant. I muttered in his ear, "People are hunting you. When I tell you to be silent, I'm trying to save your neck."

He nodded hurriedly, and I let his arm down. "Now follow me." I listened a moment, but didn't hear much, and so I led him deeper into the woods away from the road, northwest of our fire.

The moon was new, and the starlight was faint and unreliable. Even with snow on the ground, the darkness was thick, and I picked our way slowly. Silence was of greater importance than distance.

At last I judged we had left them behind, and I told Hakan to sit down behind a tree with my pack and not to move until I fetched him. I crept back carefully through the darkness, listening for every sound. I heard voices near our fire, and edged closer so I could see more clearly. Five ke-dani stood around the smoky coals, the ruined pheasant covered in ash and grit. One of them was poking at the coals.

"Hasn't been long. Think it's him?"

"I doubt it. You think he could make a fire?" The leader frowned thoughtfully and nudged the pheasant with the toe of his boot. "Should be able to hunt though. Could be."

The others stared off into the darkness, eyes scanning the trees, and I tried to read the insignia on the leader's sleeve. One of them shifted and I slipped closer, my steps slow and careful. The Second Division Kedani. They were out of Kesterlin. Were they still under Commander Basajaun? If I'd been sure, I might have approached them, asked why they were bothering lone travelers, asked for news. But I thought Koray Basajaun had been transferred. Not that it mattered much; his men wouldn't know me, even if he did.

45

"Tracks here."

Phraa. I had brushed at them, but only enough to conceal that there were two sets... the broken snow was obvious. I started toward the fire, letting my steps crunch on the snow and twigs beneath. "Who are you?" My voice was hard, rough. They startled and edged around the fire toward me, uneasy, and I frowned more menacingly.

The leader drew himself taller and answered, "Commander Neel Orjado. Who are you?" He was tense, nervous. "And why did you flee?"

I looked him and the others over, scowling. "Why did you barge into my campsite?" I glanced at the pheasant and glared at them again. "Can a man not camp half a league into the woods in peace?

The leader narrowed his eyes. "What are you doing half a league in the woods?"

I knelt and picked up the pheasant by one thin leg and held it up. "Trying not to have to share my dinner with beggars." I tossed it at his feet and stared across at him. The commander was young, and perhaps had never even seen a Dari before. He was intimidated, though I had been careful not to say anything overtly threatening. Nothing to provoke a fight, just to make them uncomfortably aware that I wasn't afraid of one.

He glanced at one of the others and finally said more agreeably, "Have you seen this boy?" He pulled a parchment from his uniform, but I didn't look at it.

I growled, "I've seen no one. That's why I'm half a league into the woods. Didn't want to see anyone."

"No one?" The commander held out the parchment and I glanced at it and shook my head.

"No. Convict?"

"No. Just a boy." He shifted uneasily. "Safe travels then."

I grunted and bowed slightly, the bow of a commoner to a soldier, and they returned the courtesy, albeit hurriedly. I watched them leave, and finally slipped off into the darkness to find Hakan. I found him shivering where I left him, and pulled him silently after me farther into the forest.

WE STAYED OFF the road after that, and it slowed our progress. The snow was fluffy and knee deep in places, and it took us over an hour to work our way to a ridge. The wind was worse there but the snow was much less and we made better time. I pulled kiberries off the branches as we walked. I love the woods, the fluttering thud of snow falling from the trees, the quiet shrill shriek of cold wood, the smell of pine. It wasn't until late afternoon that Hakan spoke again.

"Are we going to have lunch?"

We hadn't had breakfast either, so eager had I been to put distance behind us.

"Aye." I stopped and slung my pack to the ground. "Here. We'll make a fire tonight, but for now chew on this." It was the end of bread that Ursin had given us the night before. I should go hunting.

47

He was chewing on some berries as well, looking a little green. "Thanks. Do you like these?" He put another berry in his mouth.

"Aye. Don't you?" I took a swig of water from my canteen. In truth I should have noticed earlier, but he'd been walking behind me. When I actually saw what he was eating, I struck the remaining berries from his hand.

"Here, drink as much water as you can and then vomit. Now."

He looked up at me in shock. "Why?"

"Those are lushenberries, not kiberries. How many have you eaten?"

"I don't know. A couple handfuls maybe."

"Then drink! Quickly."

He did, tilting his head back and downing the entire canteen.

"Now make yourself vomit."

He looked at me in disbelief.

"It's now or later. They won't kill you, but the more you get out now the less you'll suffer. Here, drink this too."

I dug his canteen out of his pack and handed it to him. It was the last of our water, but there was plenty of snow to melt. The water would make the berries come up more easily. He drank again, suddenly heaving about halfway through. I grabbed the canteen from him before he spilled it, and he vomited a little water.

"More. All of it, if you can."

He was feeling it a little, and leaned his hands on his knees. I rescued the bread still clenched in one hand. He'd want it later to settle his stomach.

"Go on."

If it had been me, I would have stuck my finger in my throat to save myself the suffering later. I had to do it once before battle, when I'd eaten something bad. Better to suffer in camp than be ill in battle, when a moment of inattention could cost your life.

"If you touch the back of your tongue with your finger, you'll vomit soon."

He shook his head in refusal. We waited. He stood and walked around, then bent to vomit water and lushenberries into the bushes. Then again, with less water. After several times, he was shaking and unsteady on his feet, and I helped him to sit on the trunk of a fallen tree.

"Is that all of it?"

He shook his head.

"Here, rinse your mouth. I'll be back. I'm going to get dinner."

If he had any left in him, we would be here all night, and he wouldn't be vomiting. Phraa. There was little I could do for him, and I cursed myself for not paying better attention. I should have known he wouldn't know the difference between kiberries and their poisonous cousins lushenberries, but I wasn't used to having to attend to a boy who didn't know anything about the forest.

I placed traps on several rabbit trails with bits of thong and bent saplings, then took out my little crossbow. It was very small, made for birding, with delicate blunted darts and exquisite accuracy. The design was a modification of the short bows used by the suvari archers. The kedani was just starting to use larger crossbows, forming new groups of crossbowmen, but it was slow going.

The larger ones had a different system of stringing that was not entirely worked out yet, and they were suffering problems with accuracy.

I had larger, razor pointed arrows for hunting deer as well, but I didn't see any that day. I took three purflins. I also saw a beautiful golden hawk, but of course you can't shoot a golden hawk. The stillness of the forest crept into my heart, and I breathed easier in the clean sharp scent of snow and pine needles. The crisp dry air made me feel fresh and alive.

Only one of my traps had taken a rabbit; they hadn't been out long. I killed it and took all the traps down and made my way back to where I had left Hakan.

He was sitting, pale and unhappy, on the same tree trunk where I had left him.

"How are you feeling?"

He shook his head. "Not good." His voice was choked and miserable.

Poor boy. The fault was mine more than his.

"Take care which leaves you use to wipe yourself. Don't use those." I pointed at some poisonvine across the clearing.

He nodded. In a few minutes, he stood shakily and walked into the woods to squat miserably.

He came back for dinner, the fire warming us as the temperature dropped. He shivered unhappily, but I think he felt too wretched to complain. He spent much of the night squatting in the woods, and I was glad the cold stole away the smell of the foulness. I ate lushenberries once. It's a mistake one only makes once.

When I woke in the grey dawn, he was finally wrapped in his cloak, sleeping fitfully. I let him sleep, remembering my own misery. I got up and fed the fire, laying my cloak over him before moving off into the woods. Another three purflins were easy to find, and good clean snow to melt for water. Tubers, kiberries, onions, and a few mushrooms rounded out the meal, smelling delicious as they roasted over the fire. I'm not an especially good cook, but fresh roasted purflins and mushrooms always taste wonderful in the morning. The air promised a clear day, the light cold and bright.

Hakan rose in the late morning, shaky and very pale.

"Can you walk today?"

He nodded hesitantly, and I smiled. Good. Now that he had something to complain about, he was a little braver. When he ate, he had the finicky manners of a nobleman. He wiped his mouth between every bite and held the skewer between the tips of his fingers delicately, as if it was made of silver rather a slim branch of birchwood. He looked a little green still, but when we started off again he made a good attempt to keep up. My estimation of him rose a little, though that isn't saying much.

I had to keep reminding myself to slow my pace, but I didn't let him stop until we ate a late lunch. An empty stomach would be no bad thing for him, and the exertion would help soothe the fever and its clammy sweatiness. He ate lunch well enough, and I showed him the differences between kiberries and lushenberries.

Lushenberry poison is vicious. If he didn't know that, he probably didn't know anything else about the forest either. He had much to learn, but I'd try to make the other lessons more pleasant.

I hadn't decided yet what to do with him. When I was discharged from the army, the freedom was disconcerting, almost uncomfortable, but in those last years I'd enjoyed it. Solitude. Peace. I might have resented the sudden responsibility for the prince's life, but in truth I didn't mind it much. I would have helped any innocent boy in fear of his life, though Hakan was perhaps more irritating than some.

But after that? I didn't know whether I should try to help him regain his throne, or try to get him safely over a border into Rikuto or Ophrano. He'd be able to claim refuge there, though he'd have to learn some sort of trade to earn his living. The alternative, helping him in some attempt to regain his throne, was less than enticing. Vidar had credibility for good reason. Hakan would have to give me reason to believe in him before I risked either of our necks for his throne.

"Where are we going?"

"Northeast, to the hills." The same place we were going before, though I'd taken us north of the road, no longer paralleling it.

"You served in the suvari, didn't you?"

I nodded.

"Why didn't we buy horses when we were in Four Corners? Horses would make travel much faster."

"Aye. But you need to walk."

"What? Why?" He was insulted and took no pains to hide it.

"You're soft. If you want to take back your throne, you must earn it."

"You would punish me for being born a prince instead of a foundling?" The words were flung at my back angrily.

"There's no punishment intended. Vidar has earned the people's trust, but he doesn't have the right to the throne. You have the right, but no one's trust. You must be worthy of that trust if you expect people to accept you."

"I was born to be king! I was trained for it."

I wondered where his doubt had gone. His voice sounded just as I might have imagined the voice of a spoiled prince would. Petulant and irritable. Superior.

"Aye, by your father, no doubt."

"What's that supposed to mean? Of course by my father!"

"Your father squandered the trust we had in him long ago. You cannot rely on that."

"Now you would insult my father as well?" I could hear his anger.

"It's the truth, and none of my doing that he lost the people's trust. No doubt you have many good qualities, but no one can judge that until you show them." I didn't want to be unfair. In the palace, it would have been difficult for him to see his father's failures or the struggles of the common people. Not to mention the problems in the army that served Erdem so steadfastly.

"What will they expect of me, then?"

53

Good, he was rational enough to control his anger, to ask for information, and hopefully to use it.

"From Vidar they expect protection from Rikuto and the Tarvil. That's why they'll accept him. He earned their trust through honorable service in the kedani. If you would take your throne, you must also be able to provide that protection. They must *believe* you can provide it." The ability to protect the people and the people's trust in that ability are two entirely separate things.

"I've studied my father's leadership of the army. He made many mistakes, no doubt, but he wasn't aware of the extent of people's frustration." His voice was no longer angry. Frustrated, perhaps, and proud, but not angry.

I smiled a little. "I don't ask you to justify your father's decisions. You're only responsible for what you do and the decisions you make."

We walked in silence for some time, until we were confronted with one of the many rocky outcroppings that run west to east through the forest from the hills at the base of the Sefu Mountains. The rockface wasn't very high, only four times my height, but I didn't trust Hakan not to fall since I doubted he'd climbed much before. I knotted the rope about his hips and through his legs to form a harness.

"Did you learn this in the army too?"

"Aye, in the kedani."

He frowned. "I thought you would just knot it around my waist."

"That's a good way to injure yourself."

He watched me tie the other end loosely around my own waist. "What about you?"

I smiled. "I'm just taking the rope up with me; there will be no weight on it. You'll follow me, and if you fall I can catch you."

He nodded, and I began climbing.

There were many flat shelves for my toes and fingers. I reached the top in only a few moments and called back to Hakan that he could start up after me. He climbed well enough, but I hadn't realized how much easier my long arms and legs made the climb. He struggled for handholds where I'd simply reached farther to the next easy shelf. He finally made it to the top, panting and red-faced, and we started back on our way.

It was only an hour before we reached the next outcropping, and again we climbed. It took Hakan nearly twenty minutes to reach the top, but he didn't fall. I gave him a hand when he got close to the top, hauling him up the last few feet. He lay on his back breathless for a few minutes, flexing his fingers.

"What happens if you fall? You don't have a rope." He asked as we started back on our way. It was nearly time to stop for the evening if I wanted light to cook dinner.

"I fall." I hadn't proven that by experience, but it seemed a reasonable assumption.

He frowned a little and nodded thoughtfully.

We walked in silence for some time before I found the place we would stop. It was a sizable clearing, the soil rocky but mostly covered with moss or ragged clumps of grass. I built our fire close by one end, and Hakan watched me work.

He would have to begin helping me the next day, but for that night there was little else to do. He spoke as I was preparing a rabbit to roast, carrots and tubers sitting ready.

"You think I need to be a warrior to earn the people's trust?"

I'd been thinking about the question much of the afternoon, and so my answer was more ready than usual. "You need to be disciplined and steady. Courageous. Willing to suffer for what you believe in. Willing to die if necessary. You must have a plan that the people believe will actually succeed. No, you need not be a warrior, but you need many of the traits of a warrior."

He hesitated, looked away. He fiddled with a small stick, methodically breaking it into tiny pieces as the silence drew longer.

Finally he asked, "Will you teach me?"

I blinked in surprise, and the silence drew out again as I thought. "To be a king?" I was hardly qualified to do that.

He licked his lips. "To be a leader. To be worthy of the throne."

I smiled. That I could do, if he was willing to learn. "It will not be easy."

He nodded.

"Aye. I will teach you. We'll start tomorrow."

We fell into silence while the food cooked over the fire, a more comfortable silence than we'd enjoyed thus far. In my heart, I had not committed myself to his throne, but what I intended to teach him would do him good whether he ever became king or not. Courage. Perseverance. A bit of skill with a sword. Woodcraft. Things to keep him alive, should he need to fend for himself.

He was a boy, one I was growing to tolerate a bit more easily and even beginning to like, but only a boy.

A king must be a man.

In those days, Erdem had need not only of a king, but a wise and strong leader, a man who would rebuild our country and protect it, care for the Erdemen people and love them. If Hakan showed promise of being that sort of man, then I would give everything to regain him his throne.

He began to eat, watching me as I poked at the embers. "You've been in many battles?"

I nodded.

"Just in the campaign against the Tarvil?"

"No, in the south too, against the Ophrani."

"I've never been to the south. What's it like?"

"It's hotter."

He picked up a small stick and toyed with it a minute before throwing it at me. I blocked it instinctively and stared back at him in surprise. What did he mean by that?

"Come on. I thought every soldier had stories to tell. I've read about it, but I've never been to the south. My father didn't send me out to learn about my own country. What's it like? What are the people like? I know they farm, but what do they grow? What about the Senga? How are they different?"

I blinked at the onslaught of questions. "It is hotter. The southeast coast near the mountains is lush and very green, cool at higher elevations, much like here. They raise a lot of sheep in the mountains and lower down there are orchards.

Some places are wet enough to grow rice and the hills are terraced. The central part is drier, plains and rich farmland. Very flat and not many trees. Good for grain. It would be hard to defend if you ever had to fight the Ophrani again. Most of the good farmland is north of the border, and the border itself is mostly desert and badlands, but there are stretches of better soil. The coast is rocky near the southern border, but there are several good harbors if you wanted to use them."

He blinked at me. "You think like a king. I thought you were a soldier but you're already planning development."

I shrugged. I was speaking to a prince, and I'd said what I thought he might find useful. "What else do you want to know?"

"What are the people like?" He leaned back on his hands, settling in as if I were a lecturer in a class on strategy or history.

"The Senga?"

"All the races."

"You know Tuyets. I'm Dari, but I'm no authority on Dari culture. There are few enough Dari in Erdem, and those that live here are mostly near the southeastern border in the mountains." He nodded, and I turned back to the fire. "I've never been there. In Erdem the Senga live all along the southern border except in the coastal areas. Have you ever seen a Senga?"

He shook his head. What had he learned in the palace, then?

"They are smaller than Tuyets, slightly built. Their eyes are almond shaped and they generally have straight black hair, very fine. Their skin is mostly pale like Tuyet skin but with a more yellow or golden cast. I've heard they tan dark in the sun but Senga women try to avoid it because they think lighter skin is more beautiful. Many of them are farmers, growing grain in the wide plains north of the border. There are a few nomadic tribes that cross the desert regions. Their culture is very different, defined by their lifestyle rather than by which side of the border they are on."

I handed him a second skewer of roasted meat and vegetables, but I didn't take a second one myself. I was getting fat and soft from lack of training. An empty stomach, a light meal, would remind me of the rigors of army life. Self control. Discipline.

"How so?" He ate with his eyes on me, as if at any moment I was going to say something vital to his presumed future reign.

"They're nomads. They raise sheep and goats and desert horses very different than our suvari mounts. They follow the rains, and they value independence above all. They count no man as king, and they are more loyal to family than to any country. But they're good men for the most part. If you're a guest in a man's tent, his life is yours, and he will sacrifice his own life and all he has, including his children, to protect you, because your safety is his honor.

"When they fight, *if* they fight, they fight a running battle of attrition rather than pitched battles. Their tactics have been influential in refining Erdemen army strategy, though we do not completely subscribe to the same ideals. The women are not well treated, but they have a unique kind of power because they represent wealth. A man

59

raises his daughters harshly to burn them like gold into purity so that they may honor their father and the man he chooses to grace with them in marriage."

Hakan stared at me in the growing darkness. "What about the Ophrani?"

"Ophrano has both Senga and Tuyets, and presumably also some few Dari, though I have never seen them. Each has their own culture to a certain extent. The Senga have always had a gift for music, though the nomadic tribes indulge it differently. I do not know their culture in Ophrano itself or how much it is different than that of Erdemen Senga. The Tuyets of Ophrano are like Erdemen Tuyets physically, but Ophrani culture is different. Their courtesy is different. The peace treaty signed ten years ago was partly facilitated by a greater understanding of our different languages of courtesy. A word may be translated clearly but have different meanings within that culture. Appearances are more important in Ophrani culture than they are here. Learning of knowledge is not as highly prized, but they hold their elders in very high respect."

I forestalled further questions. "It's time to sleep. We'll be up early tomorrow for your training." He rolled up in his cloak with a sigh but he must have been tired for I heard his breathing slow into the rhythm of sleep soon.

Four

I t took me several hours to make the wooden swords the next morning. They were quite simple, but I wanted to make sure the weights were approximately right before he began training. He watched me curiously, studiously.

I tried to be patient, but it made me self-conscious.

Finally I looked up irritably. "What do you want? I'm not done yet."

"I'm just watching."

I grunted. "Go gather wood for the fire tonight. And bring back some kiberries and onions."

He didn't move.

"Go on then."

He stared back at me. "No."

I put down the wooden sword. "What do you mean, no?"

He shook his head. "No. I don't want to."

Spoiled brat. Until then he must have been too afraid of me to argue. I felt anger rise, but such a reaction was not fitting. Finally I shrugged and leaned back against the tree, closing my eyes as if to take a nap.

"What are you doing?"

"Nothing." I shifted into a more comfortable position and yawned.

"Aren't you going to make the swords?"

"Why should I?" I smiled to see him frowning angrily. "Boy, hear this now. You may be a prince, and you may have been pampered and coddled all your life. But I'm no nursemaid, and I will not cater to your every whim. If you don't have the courage and the will to take back your throne, Vidar deserves to keep it. You will act like a man and pull your weight, or I'll leave you here to fend for yourself."

He stared at me with wide eyes.

"If you show me you deserve it, I'll shed every drop of blood I have to get back your throne. But if you don't, I've no call to waste any more time on you, and I'll be on my way." I stood and brushed off my breeches.

"Stop." He stood too, and I looked down at him, hiding a smile. "I'll go get the wood. You don't have to threaten me."

I laughed. "I wasn't threatening you. I was informing you. I'm a soldier, not a servant. I'm hardly treating you as one either. We'll work together, or we'll go our separate ways. It's your choice. Right now, we need wood for a fire, we need kiberries, roots and onions to add to the doves for dinner, and we need to finish these swords so you can begin your training. You will pick one or more of these things to do, but you will not sit and wait for me to do all of them, as I've been doing for over a week. If you won't, then I bid you farewell. Do you understand me?"

He looked a little shocked but he did nod. "I'll go get the wood then."

I nodded and began to work on the wooden sword again. He disappeared into the woods, reappearing every few minutes with a handful of kiberries or onions or an armful of wood. He worked diligently, amassing a sizable pile of wood, until I finally finished the second sword.

"That's enough. Let's have lunch."

We ate in silence. I would be dishonest if I said I didn't question my decision to teach him, but I hoped we wouldn't have a contest of wills over every small task.

I handed him one of the swords hilt first.

He grasped it uncertainly, holding it out as if he thought it was a keen blade rather than a simple wooden practice sword. "I..." he hesitated. "I'm not very good with a sword."

"That's why I'm going to teach you." I felt a twinge of sympathy. His grip was good enough, but that might be the end of his skill. "You have trained before, haven't you?"

He nodded.

"Then I'll attack slowly, and you defend yourself. I want to see what you know."

I stepped back and bowed formally, sweeping the wooden longsword back and to the side as if we were beginning a true duel. He smiled nervously and dipped his head, letting his eyes drop to the ground for a moment. That would have to be corrected, of course. His stance was passable, though not good, and I swung the sword very slowly, watching him parry. He had some of the basic parries, but though I left myself deliberately open and vulnerable on several occasions, he never attacked.

I pushed him a little harder and studied him. He stood in one spot like a tree, not using his feet to give him greater reach or carry him away from my attacks. His movements were jerky and awkward, his shoulders high and tense, shortening his reach. He kept his eyes on my blade rather than on my body, so he was fooled by every feint.

I rapped him on the shoulder, and he flinched, though it wasn't a hard blow. After only a few minutes, he was slowing, sweat beaded on his forehead despite the chill, his arms shaking a bit as he parried.

"Attack!"

He flinched away and then lunged at me awkwardly.

I parried the blow easily, but smiled. "Good. Again, when you see I'm open." I pushed him a little and then gave him an opening that I thought was obvious, but he didn't take it. Then again, and he slashed at me clumsily.

"Good. That's enough." I swept my sword to the side and smiled at him as I bowed again.

He was thoroughly winded and collapsed to lie on the frozen ground. The wooden swords had held up well, and I was pleased with my handi-work. I glanced over at him while I sharpened my knife before preparing our evening meal. There was a bit of suspicious moisture on his eyelids, and I looked away.

Finally he sat up. "I suppose you're disappointed." He stared at the ground. "You're not even tired."

I shrugged. "I have a bit more practice."

I could have beaten him when I was ten years old, but it was no time to bring that up. It was clear he would never be a good swordsman. Yet he'd have to improve if he would take the throne. Vidar wouldn't give it up easily, and I couldn't imagine that Hakan wouldn't need a little skill with a sword if he hoped to oppose Vidar.

The boy rubbed his shoulder where I had hit him.

WE BEGAN HIS true training the next morning. I drilled him on the basics of swordplay, the essential parries and strikes, footwork, and strengthening exercises. He worked hard, watching me closely. He was an intelligent pupil, his attention to detail much better than his coordination. The day passed easily enough for me at least, though Hakan threw himself on the ground in exhaustion when we halted for dinner.

We continued on our way early the next morning. It was some ten days' walk to Ravenson through the woods, for I knew several smaller roads that sped our travel.

One night I made stew for us, which took longer than roasting the rabbit but I thought we'd both enjoy the warm comfort of rich stew. "Do you like hot peppers?" I glanced at him.

He was sitting close by the fire, rubbing his feet and grimacing a little. "What kind of peppers?"

"Hot peppers." I repeated. I'd never heard a name for them.

He looked at me as if I hadn't answered the question, and his voice sounded very disrespectful. "Sevara peppers? Pharan peppers? Ikoa peppers?" He raised his eyebrows.

I shrugged and tried to push away the irritation. "Hot peppers, from the south. Try one and see." I dropped one in the bowl of stew I handed him.

He sniffed it cautiously, then took a bite of the stew that did not include the pepper. He chewed thoughtfully. I poked at the fire, then pulled off my own boots so they would dry. The warmth of the fire crept through my woolen socks, and I stretched my shoulders. I felt tense and irritable. He was cold. His boots were wet. His feet ached. He was hungry. Did he think I was not cold, or that I had not walked at least as far as he had? And hunted and fed us both. I tried to keep from scowling. I pitied him, yes, but I did not want to listen to him complain.

He coughed, and I looked up to see him red-faced, tears streaming down his cheeks. He almost overturned the bowl as he put it down, then gulped from his canteen. He glared at me and coughed again, gasping, wiping at his eyes. "You meant to do that!"

"What kind are they?" I almost laughed at him, but I kept my voice even.

"I don't know!" His nose was dripping, and he wiped his face on his sleeve. "You don't actually eat those, do you?"

Good. I wouldn't have to share. They were expensive anyway. I reached over to pluck the remaining half of the pepper out of his bowl and ate it myself. I smiled at him, feeling rather more lighthearted. "I like them."

He glared at me again.

The weather that winter had been viciously cold, and we were both glad when we sighted Ravenson in the distance. We reached town in the afternoon of the twelfth day of Nalka, the first month of the new year. The inn was easy to find, and we ate a very late lunch at a battered table. Hakan's head drooped in the warm comfort next to the fire, so I told him to go upstairs and rest while I spoke with the innkeeper, a greasy looking fellow named Blin. Blin showed Hakan to a room with two rough beds, cheap accommodations. I didn't want to use much of Hakan's money. Who knew how long it would have to last?

Hayato had not left me a message, and indeed had apparently not yet reached Ravenson. I sat in a corner of the dining room as it slowly filled for the evening, trying to remain as inconspicuous as possible. A group of suvari arrived, and I hoped Hayato would be among them, but I didn't see him. They ate by themselves. Though they didn't appear to be too concerned with scanning the faces of the crowd, I was glad Hakan was already upstairs.

The food and drinks were served by a pleasant looking young woman who smiled at me kindly and didn't flinch away when I smiled back.

Women make me nervous, uncomfortable, because so often they show their fear of me openly. I liked her for her smile, and because she didn't notice, or didn't seem to notice, that I let my eyes linger on her more than was strictly necessary. Many of the other men also liked her, apparently, for she laughed and smiled at everyone, taking their compliments and demands for more ale with good grace and an even temper.

I listened quietly to the conversations, and finally the room filled so completely that men sat right next to me, though with a bit of caution.

"We can't rely on Stonehaven to do anything. You know as well as I that the raids are getting worse."

"Aye, I heard so from my brother last month. He lives in Daison, you know."

"Rhophin was murdered last month on his way home from market. Bandits. Everything of any value was stolen."

"Phraa, and to think how safe the roads were when we were young. The wife doesn't want to send our boy to Creekmill on market days, but I can't go myself."

From another table. "There were suvari out this week on the road to Farthinsworth."

"Why?"

"They asked if we'd seen a boy. I think it's the prince, but they wouldn't say. He's been missing for a few weeks now, haven't you heard?"

"No, I thought he was dead."

"Well, I thought they were looking for the prince, but could be anyone I guess. I wonder

THE KING'S SWORD

though. You don't think Vidar would try to kill him, do you?"

"I don't trust any of them in Stonehaven. There's been no good out of there in years. Better to keep your head down and hope for the best."

Then just by my ear, "Would you like a drink?" The serving woman smiled at me warmly, and I felt like the sun had come out of a cloudy sky.

I ducked my head, a little embarrassed. "Aye. Ale, please."

She went laughing on her way, stopping to banter with a group of men as she passed into the kitchen. When she returned, and gave me the mug, her fingers brushed mine and she didn't draw back. I almost thanked her for that kindness.

I spent much of the evening sitting there, listening to the crowd, but finally I went upstairs as well. The room was cramped but clean, warmed by the fire below. I locked the door and opened the window to let in a bit of cool fresh air before climbing into my own bed.

The next morning I woke to the sound of Hakan putting on his boots, though he tried to do it quietly. I blinked the sleep from my eyes. It was early, but Hakan had been sleeping since the late afternoon. "Do you feel better?"

"Yes." He was bleary eyed. "I'm hungry. Is there food downstairs?"

"Aye."

He waited while I pulled on my boots and I led the way downstairs. The dining room was deserted. I knocked at the kitchen door loudly, and

C. J. Brightley

the serving girl opened it with a smile that quickly disappeared and a small gasp of surprise.

"Could we get some breakfast?"

She nodded, and I backed away to sit at a table. Now with the daylight streaming through the windows she was more frightened of me. Perhaps she could see me better, and last night of course I'd been sitting, so she hadn't seen my great height, my hair nearly brushing the rafters. But when she brought us our food, rich bread, butter, jam, boiled eggs, ham, and hot tea with milk, she smiled again. A cautious half-smile at me, and a larger one for Hakan, but kind enough nonetheless. The day was already more pleasant than I had expected.

We were nearly finished when there was a clatter of horse hooves outside. Hakan's back was to the door and I was facing him. I never sit with my back to a door. It is a mostly unconscious habit, though Yuudai used to tease me about it. Then the sound of boots on the steps and a sudden stream of light. Suvari.

The first two I didn't recognize, but the third was Hayato, followed by another three men. The others sat immediately, calling for food, and the girl disappeared into the kitchen. The innkeeper was apparently her father, for he came out and bantered with them while she served them breakfast. I suppose he was keeping an eye on them, letting them know by his very presence that the girl was not unprotected. Of course, if they'd been bandits, dishonorable, determined, he could have done nothing, but out of respect they restrained their comments to compliments and not suggestions.

70

Hayato saw me almost immediately. "Kemen, I'm glad you're here." He nodded quickly at Hakan, eying him with interest but making no comment as he slid into another chair.

"Our group has found nothing, of course. One of the squads sent southeast was a bit more zealous. They burned a homestead just east of Darsten. The father and son were killed by the suvari, and one child was burned to death in the cabin. Apparently the fire was something of an accident, but the men took no great care to stop it. The mother and the youngest child lived. The squad thought the boy was the prince sheltered by the family, but he was their eldest son. The woman and her brother are on their way to Stonehaven to make a formal protest and request for compensation to Vidar." Hayato was solemn, voice low.

"I thought they weren't looking very hard."

He looked grim. "You're right, most of us aren't. But there are a few who are. I went back to Stonehaven while my squad searched, and right glad I am to find you here, for you'll be interested to hear this. The search orders didn't come from Vidar, though they were given in his name. They came from Ryuu Taisto."

"Taisto! Really?" He was the Minister of the Military Affairs, the official title for commander of the suvari and the kedani, the highest military officer in the country. Of course the king, and perhaps in this case Vidar, would have the final say, but as far as operational specifics, he made the decisions.

"Aye. Taisto. One of my friends, Siri Andar, is in the king's personal guard. Do you know him?"

The Royal Guard was a position of honor and generally easy work, a reward for good service, for until recently the kings had been rather popular. I shook my head.

"Now they're guarding Vidar until told differently. Taisto of course will be the one to tell them, unless Vidar himself overrules him. Siri says Vidar ordered Taisto to find the prince and bring him safely back to the palace if at all possible. Note the word 'safely.'"

"So the specification that the prince's death was perfectly satisfactory did not come from Vidar but from Taisto?" I asked.

Hakan looked back and forth between us seriously.

Hayato nodded. "Right."

"And the suvari?"

He smiled a little. "They make me proud to be a suvari. Aside from that one incident, regrettable though it is, they've been mostly trotting about the country eating in inns and enjoying the lovely winter weather, with their helms deliberately pulled over their eyes."

I grinned, for it was a typical statement from him. It had been cold with a cutting wind for weeks. Hayato had always been ironically positive, and I was relieved to find that this hadn't changed.

"What about the kedani?" I wished I knew myself, but I no longer heard the rumors that flew about the army so quickly.

"They are as yet undecided. Vidar promised better pay and better training, with no such stupid maneuvers as that foolish campaign that retired you. He's made some internal changes that I can't evaluate yet. I don't have enough information. Promoted some people, demoted others. I don't know any of them, but I'm sure he has reasons. I imagine he's planning on strengthening the borders as a preliminary move. That's been needed for some time. Tafari is getting bolder."

I spoke very quietly, eying the group behind Hayato to make sure my words did not carry. "Hayato, as you can see, the prince is alive and quite well. You know well enough where I stand. If Taisto is the one behind this rather than Vidar, we'll need much more information. I know little of him. Do you stand with us?"

He nodded with a quick glance toward Hakan. "Aye, you know I do. I'll see what I can find, but I'll need to be discreet."

I nodded. "We're going to the eastern border, probably to Senlik."

Hayato tapped his fingers rapidly on the table as he thought. "I know a man in the kedani, Katsu Itxaro."

I liked the name. Katsu, victory or triumph. Itxaro, hope.

Hayato continued. "He commands the division out of Rivensworth, so we work together sometimes. I'll see what he can find out about the mood in the kedani, and if he knows anything about Vidar and Taisto. He's in Stonehaven more often than I am.

"I also found something else. The rumors of your death weren't just rumors. You're counted as dead in the official records." Hayato frowned seriously at me.

Somehow it didn't surprise me. The mistake seemed to fit with the rest of the tragic affair.

"Do you have any enemies?" Hakan asked.

"No." I shook my head.

"Yes," Hayato said at the same time.

I looked at him with raised eyebrows. "Who?"

"Baris Eker, for one. He'd love to see you dead."

I sighed. "He's not behind that."

Hakan looked at me. "Why doesn't he like you?"

"I beat him wrestling." I took a drink and glanced over Hayato's shoulder at the suvari.

Hayato blew out his lips. "That's not what I heard." He grinned. "I wish I'd seen it. I heard you wiped the ground with him, made him eat dust."

I shrugged, frowning at my mug. Eker had been angry, no doubt, but I still didn't think he was responsible for having me recorded as dead. It didn't make sense. Our match had been several years before my final battle, and I'd barely seen him in that time. His anger had simmered, I knew that, but I'd had no further dealings with him.

"What happened?" Hakan was still curious.

Hayato grinned again. "What I heard was this: Eker was a braggart and a fool, and he challenged Kemen to a wrestling match."

"I should have turned it down," I muttered. I'd thought it was all in good sport, at least at first. Wrestling matches are a common way to let out a little energy in the slow times between skirmishes. They keep you sharp and loose enough to fight.

"You did nothing wrong! Eker had a reputa-tion to uphold and he bet stupid amounts of money on the match. I heard Kemen pinned him in the first round faster than your heartbeat, faster than thought. The judges wanted to call the whole match, it was so beautiful. But they went two more rounds, and Kemen let Eker test his strength, get a few good holds, and then pinned him twice more."

I protested at that. "Not exactly. He was good; it wasn't effortless." Eker was a big man, not quite as tall as I am but heavier. We were well matched in strength, but I was faster and more skilled. I could have pinned him more quickly, but I wanted to be mindful of his pride.

"I heard it looked effortless, as lovely a match as any of the judges had ever seen. Afterwards, Kemen gave him a hand up, the judges called him the winner, he turned away, and Eker lost his temper and slashed at Kemen with his bootknife. Going for the hamstring, trying to cripple him."

Hakan gasped and glanced at me. "What happened?"

Hayato looked at me as well.

I shrugged. "The judges didn't care for it too much, and neither did the rest of the soldiers. He barely escaped hanging. He was demoted, fined two months' pay, and spent a month in prison."

Hayato frowned. "That's all? Should've been hung, I think. He's always picking fights. With you he just picked a fight he couldn't win. He's a snake, and I'd bet he's the one behind this. I wonder what happened to your pension money."

I frowned at my mug again. "Fine. He's an enemy. But I don't think he had the authority to affect my pension or record me dead."

"What about to have you sent out to that ambush?" Hakan asked quietly.

Hayato frowned thoughtfully, but I shook my head. "No. Besides, the orders came from the commander at Blackburn. He was a good man." Dead soon after, though. I'd never thought about that coincidence before.

Hakan chewed his lip. "They *appeared* to come from him."

Hayato was still thinking about the wrestling match. "I wish I'd seen it."

WE LEFT EARLY the next day heading northwest. After a week on the road I took us north again through the country to avoid Iskara; it's not a large town, but it's on the route to several border posts and I didn't want to meet any suvari looking for Hakan. We found a clearing ideal for his training after another week, well off the road and with flat ground for us to work.

We stayed there over a month, and I drilled him every day. Hour upon hour of swordplay, back and forth, around and around the clearing. I was much kinder than my instructors had been, but I did push him.

I rapped him on his arms, his shoulders, swiping at his knees, barking his shins with the end of the sword to remind him to move his feet. Jabbed at his gut, carefully, because a blow even from the dull point of a wooden sword can be fatal with enough force. I was easily strong enough to drive it through his thin body and out the other side, and I had to exercise care. Care also when I rapped his head, for I wouldn't want to drive out whatever learning a prince receives to prepare him for his rule.

"Guard your head!" I finally snapped.

That day he had been particularly slow and clumsy, and though he'd improved since we had begun our lessons he remained thin and wiry, slow to block, his arms weak and tiring quickly. I was impatient, frustrated. Perhaps unfairly so.

"I am!"

I rapped him smartly on the side of the head. "Not well enough."

He flushed and sniffled, eyes wet.

"Again. This time guard your head."

We went through the motions again, and again he left his head open. I rapped it again, and he put his hand to his head angrily.

"Guard your head." Again.

And again.

Finally he threw the sword down in frustration and turned away.

"Hakan, you cannot turn away from an opponent."

"I don't care! I'm not practicing anymore."

I would indulge my own need to practice then, instead of wasting time on him. I tossed my own sword off to the side and kicked his after it. My knife also came from its sheath in my boot.

A few deep breaths in the ready position and I was relaxed. Then the moves carried me, kicks, trips, jumps, a roll, punches, a grab of an imaginary opponent followed by a smashing blow to the throat, then back up into the air for a whirling series of kicks. Not so useful in combat, of course, but excellent at refining balance and testing a man's strength.

I love the regularity, the predictability, the beauty in the perfection of the movements. The efficiency, the devastating power that can come from one small part of a body properly trained.

Balanced on my hands I lifted my feet high in the proper form, shoulders tight and perfect. I've always been good at that move, despite my long legs that should have been a disadvantage. I was the only one, aside from Yuudai, who could push directly from that position into another flip that carried me across the clearing and nearly into the trees. My long legs and arms again, that time more of a challenge.

A deep breath, then another. Peace. Breathe. I was sweating, and I threw my tunic off to the side. It needed washing in any case. Breathe.

Then again, the same sequence, the most difficult one I knew, my favorite, for it tested me every time. By the end of the second round my chest was heaving, and I leaned my hands on my knees a moment before taking the position again.

Again, the same sequence, my arms trembling a little in the balance position, but I pushed off and finished well.

Then again, blinking sweat from my eyes, muscles burning. It felt good to push myself.

A final time, and I nearly thought I wouldn't have the strength for the balance move, the pushing of my entire weight vertically, the taut line from straining fingers up to toes high in the air. But I did it, the tight arcing of my back, the spring into the flip with kicking feet and head skimming the ground, for I nearly didn't jump high enough, and then the deep finish, one leg far back and straight, the other knee deeply bent, head up and shoulders straight in the last punch.

I stood for one moment out of pride, then collapsed to lay flat on my back with my arms spread wide. I wished it was snowing. Every inch of me was burning with heat, waves rising from my chest and face. My eyes were closed, and I could hear nothing but the pounding of my blood in my ears. It's a pleasant sound, one I've grown to love. It means I've pushed myself hard.

A shadow fell over my face, and I opened my eyes to see Hakan sitting a few feet away, staring at me.

"That was amazing!" His eyes were glowing with awe.

I blinked in surprise and nodded. What is one supposed to say to something like that? I sat up, thoroughly wearied but unwilling to look up at him from such an awkward angle.

"Will you teach me to do that?"

I laughed, though I suppose I shouldn't have, for I could see the hurt in his eyes. "It takes many years of practice. But yes, I'll teach you to fight barehanded as well." It was nearly dusk. "Do you want to start today?"

He nodded eagerly.

"Right then. You'll have to start at the beginning, and it won't seem very interesting at first."

He nodded and I pushed myself up.

"This is the ready stance. Feet apart, toes pointed straight forward, knees slightly bent.

Hands relaxed, held here. Shoulders back, look forward."

I felt oddly light-headed, and shook my head slightly to clear it. I should not have lain down so long. I stepped forward to correct his form. "That's good. Are you comfortable?"

He blinked.

"The position is comfortable, like resting. You're prepared to move, but relaxed."

"I am."

"Now step forward, like this. Feet a bit wider apart than your shoulders, nice and deep. Drop your hips, sit into the stance. This stance is for power. Bend your knee more. Your shin should be vertical. In this stance, your hips will be either square forward, like this, or back, like this." I demonstrated again.

"More square. Straighten your back leg, knee toward the ground. Your back foot should be pointed forward, at least at this angle, more if you can get it." I used his belt to position his hips correctly. He kept his eyes lowered, and I wasn't sure whether it was to check the position of his feet or because he felt awkward so close to a Dari.

"Don't look at the ground. The ground is not your opponent. Look at your opponent in front of you. Now step forward into the same stance."

He stepped forward, bobbing up from the deep stance and sinking back again.

"Watch me. The back foot comes into the middle to meet the other before moving forward. Both knees are bent in the middle, as your weight shifts to the foot that was in the front. See, this foot can move freely now." I kicked out with my right foot.

"You'll develop the balance for that in time. Now you move it forward, sweeping out. Don't let your head bob up and down." I demonstrated a bad transition, up and down, up and down with each step. It's a common mistake, but easy enough to correct, especially if we started early.

"There are the two positions for your hips, square or back." Actually there are more, but I didn't want to confuse him. "Now step forward again. Your feet are too narrow. Good. Step. Now your stance is too short. Lengthen, move your front foot forward. Good. Step. Too wide this time." I stepped with him, letting my mind wander. Back and forth across the clearing.

"What do I do with my hands?"

"We'll do another stance first. It's easier that way. Put your feet as wide as your shoulders, toes pointing forward. Now double the width."

He moved awkwardly, toes turning outward.

"Then a bit more, you have long legs for your size. Toes forward."

He grimaced as I bent to point his toes more forward.

"Aye it hurts a bit at first, but you'll get used to it. The muscles need to be developed. Bend your knees more, sit deeply into it. Shoulders and hips square. Very good." I assumed the same position facing him. The moves are as natural as breathing to me; most of them I don't even remember learning. In the kedani, I taught many of the soldiers, including some of my superiors, because I gained a reputation as a fighter. We'd all received the same training, of course, but even at fourteen, when I entered the king's service, I was more formidable than many of my commanding officers. Then, I wasn't quite the height of most Tuyet men, though of course now I'm much taller.

My skill comes from attention to detail. When others went through the motions, even with dedication, I studied them, deconstructed the techniques, turned them inside out in my head, finding the reason and the art and owning each move. The simple punch is the most ignored and one of the most beautiful moves in its brilliant simplicity. The forces are awesome if used correctly, though most soldiers, even with training, don't find the full beauty in them.

"Do you know how to make a fist?"

He stuck out his attempt and I smiled. "It's a start. Tighten your hand. Straighten your wrist to make a straight line from elbow to the ends of these bones, in the knuckles here. You hit with the first two knuckles."

He nodded.

"Pull back your hand, so your fist is on your ribs, the inside of your wrist upward. Lower." Again, a common mistake, but easy to correct.

"Put your left hand out."

He straightened his legs for a moment, wincing.

"Back in your stance. It hurts now, but it will get easier. Punch like this. The front hand moves back and twists so that the inside of your wrist is upward. The punching hand moves toward the center of your body, twisting at the very last instant." I demonstrated several times. "See? Twist at the end. It gives greater power. Always keep your wrists straight unless you want to break them. You try it."

He moved his hands slowly back and forth, frowning in concentration. It made me smile a little to see him trying so hard.

"Good. Keep your shoulders square and don't lean forward. Power comes from your hips, not your shoulders. We'll work on that later." It was nearly dark. "Keep your weight low in the stance. You should feel strong, the tension arcing across the outside of each leg to support you."

He nodded. "There's plenty of tension. Now what do I do?"

"Practice. Those two stances and the punches are enough for tonight."

He nodded and punched several more times. I stood in front of him and placed his outstretched fist on my stomach. If I'd been his height, it would have been on the soft spot just below where the ribs join together with the breastbone, since his stance was nice and deep. It was a good height for him to practice.

"Punch."

He punched halfheartedly, his fist scarcely touching my skin. He glanced up at me, a split second of bright blue before he swallowed and looked away. I wondered if he felt uncomfortable touching my dark skin, whether he thought I was dirty because I was a Dari. I was sweaty no doubt, but no worse than any man after a hard practice.

"Again." As I had thought, he was punching off to the side, his right hand veering right, left hand veering left. "Punch to your centerline. Imagine a line down the center of your body and punch to that, not off to the side. A punch from your left hand or your right should land in the same place." The next punch was better, though he was still scarcely touching me. "Now, punch like you mean it."

He glanced up at me again.

"Go on."

He punched harder, but he didn't drive through his target, his knuckles barely grazing my skin.

"Do I disgust you?" I stepped back.

He looked up at me, looking very pale in the growing darkness. "What?"

"Does my dark skin offend you? Do you not punch me because you don't want to touch my skin, or because you aren't used to the idea of striking anyone?"

He drew himself up in righteous indignation. "Have I ever said anything unkind about the color of your skin? I have many flaws, but this is new! I think you are being unfair this time." His voice rang out clear and high with anger.

I smiled. "I was only asking. Forgive me if I've offended you. You wouldn't be the first to be disgusted." Far from it.

He spat, a most unbecoming act for a future king, but I didn't bother to hide my smile.

"I've never met a Dari before you, but I've never considered Dari less than Tuyets, or Senga, or any other race. I am not in the habit of punching people. Is that so strange?"

"No, it isn't. But it's a habit you may have to develop. Consider it a gesture of friendship then, as we punch each other in practice."

He laughed for nearly the first time since we had begun our training. "I hope you'll take into account that I'm not used to being hit, either."

I bowed with a smile. "Of course."

"I'd like to practice a little more tonight."

I nodded and took up my position in front of him again. "Don't be afraid to punch me. Here is your target." I made a circle with my hands and put it in front of my stomach.

"Punch."

He did, a little harder but not much.

I shifted a few inches closer. "Again."

Again he scarcely touched me.

"Punch through me, not at me. Your target is three inches into my belly. Again." That was better. "Again." Better still. "Keep going. I'm too close for you to shorten your punches and maintain good form. Punch through me."

He looked up at me, then concentrated. The next few were better still, though hardly powerful; he was learning.

I stepped away. "Keep punching like that, through your target. I'm going to practice again." I moved to the center of the clearing and assumed the balance position from earlier. Up and down, arced into the leap and the flip. Good. Then again. And again. Then the sequence of kicks. My foot had been out of place on the same kick the last two times I'd done the whole sequence. Sloppy.

85

FIVE

"I'm out in four months. I've done my time. I want to see my children. Every day, not just for a week twice a year." Mikoto speaks to me quietly.

"That's understandable." I try to push down my envy. A wife. Children. I would give almost anything for those joys.

Yuudai is the first to realize we have a problem. He shouts to warn us. The scouts must have been killed already. There are Tarvil everywhere. They are among us before we can organize. Our formation is ragged, but we are well trained, and we pincer the Tarvil among us as we close ranks.

They have archers. They outnumber us. Badly.

We make them pay dearly for their victory, but we are lost.

Blood spatters across my chest, Yuudai's blood. His throat is open, but even fallen to his knees, he brings

up his sword with his last strength to block a blow
meant for me.

Sword brothers.

We will die together.

My chest blooms into brilliant pain, searing. I am
staring along the length of a javelin at the sun-streaked
sky.

I woke with a jerk. My chest hurt, a heavy
ache, and I sat up, hunching forward to rub the
scar with my left hand. The pain was in my mind
more than my chest. I tried to calm my breathing.

"Are you well?" Hakan was up on one elbow
looking at me.

"Fine." I closed my eyes again. Phraa. It still
felt like the shaft of the javelin was grinding
against my ribs with each breath.

"Do you want a drink or something?" He
sounded a little frightened.

"I'm fine." I lay back down and stared up at
the stars. Out of the corner of my eye I saw him
stare at me a minute longer before settling down
again. It took a long time for my shoulders to relax
and to sleep again.

"DO YOU DREAM of battle often?"

"Sometimes." I didn't want to talk about my
dreams.

I could hear him breathing hard behind me as
we hiked up a steep hill. We'd moved on northeast
that morning from the clearing where we'd
camped for weeks.

He didn't question me much that day. I set a
quick pace, and I suppose I looked rather grim,

C. J. BRIGHTLEY

because when we stopped for lunch he glanced at me a few times and ate in silence. Dinner was the same.

The next day we started early but stopped while there was still good light left so I could practice. I hadn't been training much while I concentrated on Hakan's training, and I didn't intend to let myself get too far out of practice. He threw himself on the ground and watched tiredly as I began.

Deep breath. Relax. The sequence I had done before, the hardest one I knew. Three times, then again. Then the strengthening exercises. The balancing move, again, over and over, and yet again. Jumping into the flip, legs extended in proper form. Always proper form. Often people forget how important it is; they get sloppy and lazy. But the form was designed to be the most efficient, the most effective, the best possible way to move for the given goal. The flip, again and again.

I wonder sometimes how much of my success as a warrior is because of my great size and strength, for which I can take little credit, and how much is attributable to my need for perfection, the insatiable desire to do it better, the willingness to sweat and bleed in training, to train longer and harder and not to rest until I have done it right.

Afterwards I was spent, and I lay in the growing darkness with the calls of insects and birds surrounding me in a trilling roar. The exhaustion was soothing, comforting. It took my mind off the dreams, the loneliness, the sorrow. The sense of failure. It would have been impossible to know about the ambush, but that didn't stop the memories from returning. Just as it was impossible for me to earn my place in Erdemen society.

Finally I stood, almost shaking with fatigue. Hakan had gathered some wood, and I prepared our dinner in the vibrating air of a spring evening, when everything with a hard exterior rubs its legs against its body, calling for its mate. Or two or three mates, as the case may be.

I heard the flap of a night hunting bird above us and the soft rustle of small rodents in the leaves well back from the fire. We ate in silence, and I rolled myself in my cloak for the night. Hakan too rolled up in his cloak, but after some time I heard him sit up and move closer to the fire. It was quite dark, the embers glowing faintly under a layer of ash. He sat near me, behind my back but within reach. I could feel his eyes on me, though I did not open mine.

I half-expected a knife blade between my ribs, the knife I'd chosen for him. I had not been especially kind to him that day; I'd been irritated by his grumbling. His complaints had diminished in the past weeks, and he'd helped me with the simple work of provisioning ourselves. Though he was no great hunter, he would gather firewood, roots and kiberries, and I'd showed him how to make a simple stew from dried or fresh meat and whatever could be gathered in the wood. I'd taught him how to shoot the crossbow and how far to lead his target when shooting something small like a dove or purflin. He did not have the gift of good marksmanship, but he showed more patience than I'd expected. I'd taught him to aim for the lungs when shooting deer with the larger arrows, and how to clean his kill afterwards. How to roast meat, and how to wrap it so it would stay fresh for several days.

Yet that day he'd complained about the food, the walking, the heat of the sun and the cold of the water when we waded through a small stream. Then it was his wet boots. He was a boy yet, but would perhaps someday be a king. He tried my patience. At eighteen, I was an officer in the king's suvari, commanding men twice my age. Complaints about wet boots would not have been tolerated.

I waited, my breathing even and very calm.

Finally I asked, "What do you want?"

He spoke very quietly. "You don't like me, do you?"

"What?"

"You don't like me very much, do you?"

I answered with my eyes closed. "Does it matter?"

He was very quiet, poking a stick into the embers. Finally I rolled over and looked at him. He turned his face away and brushed angrily at his cheeks, though not quickly enough to hide the shiny streaks of tears. I sat up, feeling guilty and awkward.

"I like you well enough." I could see his jaw clench in the dim light. "What do you want me to say?"

He shook his head wordlessly, stabbing the stick into the ashes. I waited, my eyes drifting closed though I still heard him clearly.

"If you don't like me, if you don't believe in me, then who else will? And who's to say you should? Maybe you're right. Maybe I'm not good enough, and it would be better if I left. Better for everyone."

I put one hand on his shoulder, feeling more guilty when I realized how thin he was. Maybe he wasn't eating enough. "You're not ready yet, but when the time comes, you will be." I cursed my lack of words, my inability to speak more kindly.

"Do you think I'm a coward?" His words were very quiet as he stared into the feebly glowing embers.

"I think you'll need to exercise your courage more now than you have in the past."

He choked out a short bitter laugh. "You mean, 'Yes, Hakan, you are a coward.'"

"Nay, I think not. I think you haven't been pushed until now. Being pushed isn't a comfortable thing, Hakan. I wouldn't expect you to be happy with it." I squeezed his shoulder a little, hoping it was a comforting gesture. The bones shifted beneath my fingers. I fed a small branch into the embers. It blackened and then a tiny puff of flame started its burning. "What did you study, in your education as a prince?"

"Trade. History. Diplomacy. Military strategy. Mathematics. How to manage the various ministries. Languages. Common, Kumar, Modern High Tongue, archaic High Tongue, Rikutan, Ophrani. A little agriculture. Riding. Swordplay, though you've seen how badly I failed at that."

"All those things are necessary for a king. Swordplay is not, though it may be necessary as you regain your throne. But it is a good way to exercise your courage. Later you'll have the entire army to do your fighting for you, and it won't matter if you're a bit slow in your strikes. It's earning your throne that counts now, Hakan, not your skill with a sword."

He looked at me, eyes glowing oddly in the orange light of the fire. "Why do you push me, Kemen? I don't even think you like me, but you make it sound as though you would make me king. Why? If you don't think I would be a good king, why do you bother?"

I must have been harsher than I'd realized, for in truth I was warming to him, despite my frustration that day. "It's your right. You've been trained for it. I believe you'll be a good king." I phrased it as a certainty that he would become king, though we both knew it was still a question.

"I think only a few things are lacking in your education, and they aren't things I'd expect you to receive in the palace. Courage. You have it in you, but courage grows by exercise. A willingness to work hard without complaint. The job of a king is often a thankless one, open for much criticism but little gratitude. As a prince, you were pampered and spoiled; it isn't your fault you haven't worked hard until now. But as king, that will not continue. Best to learn to work hard now, rather than when your nation depends on you. An awareness of the problems that those outside the palace face. This you will learn as we near the border. I imagine it will help you form your policies as king, and perhaps even show you how to regain your throne." I clapped my hand on his shoulder again.

"I don't think it matters much whether I like you or not. But if you care, I do. We need a king as we haven't had since before the Famine began, and I see the promise of that great king in you. I'm doing my part to help you grow into that role, for it is a large one and challenging. If I didn't believe you could do it, I wouldn't push you so."

I don't know how encouraging my words were, but that was all I could think to say. "Now get some sleep."

He poked the fire for another moment, looking very thoughtful. Finally, he turned away and rolled up in his cloak, and I did the same.

Did I believe he'd be a good king? I'm not sure what I believed, but the words had come to me. I am not given to untruths, so I suppose deep inside I must have believed it.

Six

The rustle of the breeze in the leaves above us the next morning sounded like a rushing stream, cool and fresh in the crisp spring air. Hakan's voice followed me. "What would you change about the army if you could?"

I thought for several moments before I answered. "The army bases that used to guard the borders have been weakened by lack of men. Too many good, experienced soldiers are retiring, or have been killed in stupid campaigns like the one to the southwest against the Ophrani and the one to the northeast against the Tarvil. Men aren't an inexhaustible resource, even for a king. Soldiers must have faith that their sacrifices are worthwhile. We're not afraid to die, but no man wants to throw his life away needlessly."

"What else? Anything in the training? In the pay?" Every question was followed by another.

"The training is very good, but it suffers as the best men retire. That's what has given Erdem such strength. We have the numbers, the rigorous training, and the intelligent leadership to use our men well. Every soldier will say they would prefer to be paid more, but in truth the pay is fair enough. If you wanted to attract more volunteers, it would have to be raised."

"The army is supposed to reward merit rather than birth. Is that true?"

"For the most part, yes." They were good questions, and I was glad to hear him ask them.

"Good. That is good to know. What's it like, being a Dari in Erdem? What is different for you than for a Tuyet?"

That one was harder, and I hesitated. "I've never been a Tuyet, so my perspective is limited."

"Of course. And I know what the books say. But what have you seen?"

We had reached a small stream and I took off my boots and rolled up my breeches to wade across.

"In the army, I didn't stand out as much. Soldiers have traveled around the country and most have seen Dari in the southeast and Senga in the south, so they aren't as put off by my appearance. Civilians often fear me. Some of that is because I'm a soldier and there aren't as many about the country now as there were in the past. Some of it is because of my dark skin and my size." Some because of my green eyes, but not all Dari have that affliction. The stream came nearly to my knees, and I rolled my breeches up further before continuing.

"What else? I know the Dari used to have a hard time of it in Erdem. How is it now?"

The Dari were never slaves, not as a race anyway, though slavery has existed in Erdem sporadically throughout history. Dari were prized as warriors, especially in the dawn of the Third Age and the Steeling, when their fighting prowess helped the tribes jostling for resources. The tribes were defined more by location than by race, and the Dari played a role larger perhaps than their numbers would justify.

But they were always viewed with a bit of suspicion by the Tuyets, and never fully assimilated into Tuyet culture. Most still live in Joris, in the southeastern mountains, where they don't trouble Tuyets and Tuyets don't trouble them. There has always been tension, perhaps a bit of disgust, on the part of Tuyets toward Dari. Our dark skin does not wash white.

I answered carefully, thinking about my words. "It's not so bad, but better in the army. A man can earn respect by his deeds, and then he's fully accepted regardless of his race. But outside among civilians, it's different. Dari aren't scattered about the country, so most Tuyets have no experience with Dari that they know and trust. There's lingering aversion and fear in most areas, but no outright hatred. At least I haven't seen any. The Dari are partly to blame for this too. They don't mingle with Tuyets much to give Tuyets better memories to judge them by." I wanted to be fair, but in truth this had stung me deeply.

"What about the Senga? Are they treated the same way?" The ground on the far side of the stream was rockier as we made our way slowly toward the hills that skirted the mountains.

"They are not seen as..." I hesitated again. I didn't want to be unjust. "Tuyets generally see lighter skin as more beautiful. Senga have light skin, though it tans easily, and so despite their differences they're more accepted. Dari are seen as ugly and dirty, which doesn't help the persistent fear that Dari seem to inspire in Tuyets." I took a breath. "But this is only one soldier's limited experience."

"Of course."

He walked behind me in silence so long I nearly forgot he was there.

"What do you do when you're not training or fighting?"

"What?" My mind was leagues away, in the southern deserts among the nomadic Senga. Their culture fascinated me, and someday I wanted to go back and learn more about them.

"For fun. For amusement. What do you do?"

I blinked. "I train."

"I mean when you're not training. Don't you do anything for fun? What do you like? Do you like to read the old legends of heroes? Do you like to sing?"

I had no real answer for him. "What does a prince do for amusement?"

He laughed. "My father didn't give me much time to amuse myself. I studied a lot. I ride. I like to sing. Tibi and I sang together. Father thought it was stupid, of course, but Tibi said we were good.

If I hadn't been a prince, I might have enjoyed being a bard. I like to read, especially history."

Good. A king needs to know what mistakes others have made in the past, so he does not make them himself. History defines the people he rules and the challenges he faces. I hoped he understood what he read.

"You don't do anything for fun then?"

I shook my head. "I train. I enjoy resting afterwards."

The things that give me the most pleasure are things I cannot describe. The feel of wind on my face. A woman's smile. Exhaustion from training, followed by the gradual slowing of my heartbeat, knowing I'm faster and stronger than the day before. The perfection of the moves, every muscle working together in exquisite coordination. The sound of water flowing over and around rocks in a river. A good meal after several days of an empty stomach.

WE STAYED MOSTLY off the roads, but after a week in the woods I took to one of the smaller roads cutting northeast through the great forest. It had been paved, but in long stretches the paving stones were broken or missing, and the dirt was deeply rutted. I pulled several small trees that had fallen across the road off to the side so carts could pass, but it was still cold for most people to be traveling.

"Haven't these roads been maintained at all?"

"Not much. Money ran out."

"My father said the roads were the 'cords of commerce' across the country. He would have found a way if he'd known it was this bad."

"This one is relatively good. They're worse farther from Stonehaven."

"I didn't know there were any Dari in Llewton. Do you know if you were born there?"

The boy had an endless supply of questions. I would have preferred silence sometimes, but I tried to be patient.

"There aren't now. Probably my mother was only passing through. No one remembered when I was old enough to ask. There was some tension between Dari and Tuyets then and I was told I should be glad I wasn't left to starve."

I glanced back to see him smile.

"Well I'm glad. Was that when plague broke out there?"

I was surprised he knew of it, since it wasn't a large outbreak. "Yes, the year before I was born and then for two or three years after. I don't remember it, of course."

I had been accused of bringing it though. I'd been eight years old. Quite suddenly in the market a woman spit on me and shouted that I was the cause of the plague. When I'd looked at her in shocked terror, she'd shrieked that I'd put the plague on her with my demon eyes. I knew it was absurd, but I'd never forgotten the panic and fury in her voice.

I swallowed. "There were accusations that the Dari brought the plague, though I have no idea if it's true." I'd never told anyone that story, not even my grappling instructor, my favorite at the time.

"What do you know of the Dari people?"

"Not much else. That we are from the east. I don't speak much Darin."

"Temel wrote that the Dari shaped Erdemen history by supporting Kai Txomin over Inaki in the Steeling. Txomin was only able to unite the tribes with Dari help. But it doesn't seem like Dari get much credit for that now. Doesn't that bother you a little?"

I shrugged. "That was four hundred years ago. The plague is a more recent memory." I was a little surprised he'd read Temel. His work was an unusually favorable assessment of Dari influence, and I wondered whether he meant to flatter me or whether he took Temel's words as truth. Or whether he simply wanted to see my reaction.

"My father told me once that he wished we had such patriots now. But he didn't blame the few Dari in Erdem for keeping a low profile; it's only to be expected when Tuyets treat them so badly."

"Badly is a bit harsh. I'd say with caution and sometimes fear."

He ran up beside me and I slowed my pace a little.

"They fear you, Kemen, and you can't blame them. But not all Dari are soldiers. There are myriad reasons that few Dari live outside Joris, and many of those reasons are the fault of Tuyets."

I would have preferred not to dwell on it. It stung me to compare my deep love of Erdem and my sacrifices and service to her with the cautious neutrality, fear, and sometimes even disgust and hatred I received in return.

Unrequited love is a deep sorrow and a great joy.

THE AFTERNOON WAS fading into twilight, and we were perhaps a week's walk from Benoa, the nearest town of any size. The nights were much warmer, even though we had been gradually climbing in elevation. That morning we'd seen one of my favorite sights of the foothills of the Sefu Mountains, a small valley painted with an astonishingly vibrant carpet of bluecaps.

I heard Hakan behind me again, humming. I'd heard him before as we walked, but that time it was a little louder, cheerful despite his weariness.

Finally I said, "You can sing if you want." He'd said he enjoyed it, but I'd never heard him sing.

He fell silent, and after a moment I turned around to face him. He flushed bright red and looked at the ground. "Sorry," he muttered.

"I said you can sing if you want."

He glanced up at me. "You don't mind?"

I shrugged and started off again. For some time there were only the sounds of the leaves rustling in the wind, the rocks and dirt beneath our feet, and our own breathing. But then I heard his voice, tentative and wavering with breathlessness.

I'm no musician. I have a terrible voice and precious little ability to tell good music from bad. But even I could recognize his talent. A gift like that isn't given to many.

He sang a patriotic ballad of Erdem's glory, an old song of pride. When he finished, I realized I was smiling, almost grinning, as I walked. My heart was lighter than it had been in years.

SEVEN

I stared at Hakan across the fire. "You know more about your country than you let on at first."

He shrugged a little. "I wanted to know what you thought. All my knowledge is from books, studies, reports from provincial governors. I haven't actually seen much of Erdem. It's good information, but what people perceive is their reality. I want to know how others experience Erdem."

We sat in silence for some time. It was reassuring to know his years of study had not been utterly wasted.

Finally I asked, "What do your books tell you of the campaign against the Ophrani ten years ago?"

He smiled. "That it was an unmitigated success, a shining example of the strength and honor of the Erdemen army. Were you there?"

"Aye." At his expectant look I smiled a little. "I commanded a kedani company in 356, then I was promoted to deputy regiment commander in 357."

"One hundred men are in a company and five hundred in a regiment, right?"

I nodded.

"I read that the terrain and the weather were more challenging than the Ophrani forces. Is that true?"

"Aye. It was very hot. We lost many horses to the heat, and men too."

"Which battles were you in?"

"A great many. The largest was at Dorvale, in the autumn of 357."

His eyes widened. "You were at Dorvale?"

"I commanded the right flank." I smiled a little.

"That's right." He blinked. "Kemen *Sendoa*. You received the Iron Shield for that, didn't you? Didn't the right flank win the battle?"

"Not without the center and the left holding their ground."

He nodded. "All the same, that's something to be proud of. My father the king took note of your skill."

Not enough to allow me to stay on after I'd been wounded. I swallowed, and the taste of bitterness was in my mouth.

"WHAT DO YOU know of the Tarvil?" Hakan asked.

"They're barbarians." I spat in disgust.

There was a moment of silence, then he asked, "That's it? Anything else?"

I scowled. "They steal Erdemen livestock. They kill Erdemen men and rape Erdemen women. They smell like rotten meat." I spat again to emphasize my words. "*And* they don't respect the parley flag."

I have always thought of Erdem and Rikuto as brother countries, far more similar they are different. But if Rikuto is Erdem's brother country, a nation that Erdem sometimes wars yet generally understands, the Tarvil barbarians are the shadows in the night.

To be fair, Tarvil are not monsters. They are human. But they are different than Tuyets, and not in ways that are easily understood or loved. Where Tuyets are beautiful, their faces made of elegant curves and their hair like finely spun gold, Tarvil are ugly and stumpy. They are small and sallow skinned, with pale yellow brown or ice blue eyes. Their hair is a dirty brown or dusty reddish color, often curly. I've always hated that my hair tends to curl when wet; I'm already ugly enough without that additional fault. Tuyets almost never have curly hair, and when they do, it's somehow forgivable because it's so golden. Tarvil smell different when they sweat, saltier and more sour. Their language sounds like gravel being poured into water, an ugly grinding clamor with a deep liquid undertone.

That's only their appearance, and I, more than most, should be able to look past that. But the

Tarvil give me no reason to. They kidnap border women and girls when they can. They steal from the border settlers. They harass and rob travelers, often for so little money I wonder why they even bother. They have no discipline, and they fight like uncivilized brutes, without care for their own men and even less for the rules of war.

Eight

We skirted Benoa and went on to Miafal, near the base of Mount Teilar. Miafal is a tiny village, but I thought it a good place for Hakan to see the border people before we turned north toward Senlik. He trailed me tiredly as we made our way through the woods.

I smelled the smoke from some distance away, and I didn't think it odd until we were a bit closer, when I tasted the hint of burnt flesh under the stronger smell of burning wood. We hurried then, but there was little to see. Three small buildings were burned nearly to the ground and a few disconsolate villagers were watching and kicking at the embers.

"What happened here?"

"Raid."

"Anyone hurt?" Details. Information. I cannot work without information, and the man appeared to be in shock, staring blankly at the ruined house.

"This morning." Aye, that was clear enough.

He continued, his words coming in fits and starts. "Three men killed, protecting the livestock. Sheep taken, one hundred or so. Several horses. Houses set afire behind us." No doubt to distract the men from the raid.

"This is Mirson's house. Wife died inside. Trying to save the baby."

Hakan gasped beside me.

"He's taken the boys to his mother's house, she's off at the other end of town. They're three and six." The man's voice faded away, and I thought he wouldn't talk again, but just as I was about to turn away, he spoke very quietly. "Mirson's my wife's brother. Like as not we'll raise the boys. Her mother's dying."

What can one say in the face of tragedy? I stood with him a moment as we stared at the embers of his wife's brother's home, the body of the mother and her infant nothing more than ashes and blackened bones hidden beneath the charred timbers. He'd run out of words, picking slowly through the ashes for some little remnant by which to remember the woman. I made my way across to another man who was sitting on the edge of the well, staring at the ground.

"There was a raid this morning? Tell me what happened," I said.

Hakan needed to hear it, needed to know what the people of the border faced. The raids were all too common, the story familiar.

The man looked up at me, blinking as he recognized my sword as that of a soldier, though I was no longer in active service. I didn't wear the standard kedani armor, nor wear the insignia on my breast or the distinctive helm, but I carry myself as a warrior, my weapons well-used and good quality.

"Are you from Stonehaven?" He sat up hopefully.

"Close enough. I'm traveling with a friend, and I can't stay long. What happened?"

"They came this morning. My daughter saw it. Probably shouldn't have fought it, we're nothing but farmers. The sheep are gone. I don't know what we'll do this winter." He leaned forward to place his head in his hands.

Hakan asked, "It's barely spring. Surely the town can recover before winter?"

The man spoke into his hands, his voice muffled. "Some, maybe. The flock was shared by the whole town, we all had a share in it. Tesna found one of the spring lambs with a broken leg on the path already. The others are long gone. We were going to sell them along with the wool. Most of the goats are gone too. We still have the gardens, and the granary was mostly untouched. They couldn't take it with them, I suppose."

It would be a lean winter. By the number of houses there were near one hundred people in the town proper, not to mention those farther out. They'd be hunting for meat rather than eating the extra lambs. The children wouldn't have goat's milk. There would be no goat cheese. Salt would be scarce because it's expensive. That would make meals less tasty, but more importantly it would make preserving the meat difficult until temperatures dropped in the autumn.

Hakan nodded slowly. I paced up the street, hoping to find someone else who would tell me more about the raiders, but everyone was out in the fields. What to do now? I had hoped to remain here for a few weeks before taking Hakan up the eastern border, but it was clear enough they had no food to spare.

I wondered whether it would be more helpful for me to hunt here a while, take a few deer for venison as they tried to rebuild the food stores, or whether we'd be more burden than help. The women would fear me, of course, and Hakan was hardly useful as a hunter, though I could more than feed us both. Clearly we couldn't buy horses to speed our journey.

Finally I returned to the man sitting by the well. "You need food immediately?"

He blinked in surprise. "Near enough. We're short for the winter, and some of the crops were trampled. Anything we can find now will give us more to save for later." He sat up hopefully again. "You can send word to Stonehaven? I hoped the king could help us, though I suppose that's a distant hope these days."

I shook my head. "No, there will be no help from Stonehaven. The king is dead, and Vidar rules now, though I can't say how long that will last."

"What? What of the prince? Who's Vidar?"

Little information had come out here, then.

"Nekane Vidar, the king's seneschal. The king died in late Kylma, and Vidar took power in Nalka. The prince is missing. I've heard rumors he was hunted by assassins." I watched his face and was gratified to see a look of horror.

"Assassins! Sent by Vidar? That's terrible!"

I nodded.

"We don't know the prince, but he is the prince, isn't he? Surely he's trained to handle things like this. I'd hoped that when the king died, the prince would reinforce the borders again. Is the prince dead then?"

I shrugged. "No one knows. I've only heard rumors, nothing sure."

He looked at Hakan directly, though I hoped he saw only a thin young man, tall and quite serious, standing behind me quietly, and not a prince.

"You know things haven't always been like this. We've heard rumors of attacks all up and down the border, but we hadn't seen one until now. Three men dead, you know, and Mirson's wife and baby too. This wouldn't have happened when the king was young. There were soldiers out here then."

Hakan nodded silently, and I waited a moment before speaking. "Aye then. We won't stay long, but I'll hunt if you and the others will share the meat."

The man nodded. "Aye, that would help. I'll tell the others. You'll probably stay with Rawlin, at the boarding house."

He stood, suddenly energized, and stumped off briskly. His head came up scarcely past my elbow, and Hakan looked very tall and almost regal

111

next to him. The people of the mountains live a hard life of much work and meager food, and it shows in their stature.

Hakan stared about the town curiously as we followed the man to the small boarding house, where he introduced us to Birt Rawlin, a round-faced man with a well-used dish towel over one shoulder. Rawlin rang the small bell hanging in the courtyard of the boarding house and we waited while the people gathered.

I wondered what Hakan thought of the people, the town. I'd never been to Miafal, but it was familiar enough. The northern mountain towns follow a similar pattern for the most part. A small boarding house with a bell serves as a little town hall, where the people decide on town matters when necessary. The houses are very small, generally with only two rooms, sometimes only one. They have low wooden or slate roofs, depending on what is available in the area.

The people keep sheep and goats, chickens, and sometimes swine. Sometimes they breed horses for the suvari. There are small vegetable gardens behind each house. Sometimes there are fields of grain, winter wheat, barley, rye, spelt, and teff, depending on the soil and the terrain.

It wasn't long before a small crowd of a few dozen people was gathered to stare at me cautiously. Hakan was mostly ignored, but he didn't seem to mind.

The man seemed a bit at a loss as to what he should say, though he was the one who'd gathered the crowd together.

Priven spoke up. "These men are going to hunt for us. We need to share the meat. Maybe someone can go and tell the Caslins and the Pestars and, well. Hm. They'll need to stay here with Rawlin. So you'll need to give a bit to Rawlin for putting them up." Everyone stared at us, not knowing exactly what to do, and I waited while he searched for more words.

Finally I lost patience and spoke myself. I tried to sound authoritative and reassuring. "I want to know which families lost a man in the raid." They would be in the most desperate need. "Also the families that lost property and livestock. We can't stay long but we'll do what we can while we're here."

The people shuffled their feet uncomfortably, and I wondered if any of them could read and write.

"My friend Naoki here will record the losses if Rawlin will give us a little parchment and a quill."

Rawlin nodded when I glanced at him and we slowly followed him inside. Hakan sat behind a table and recorded the names and losses of each family. Some knew others not present, and we recorded their names though we could not tell what they had lost. It seemed to take hours, but finally the crowd trailed away, leaving us with Rawlin.

I asked if any suvari had come, but he shook his head. "We haven't seen soldiers here in months." His eyes flicked to my sword and then away, and he muttered something about getting us food before hurrying out.

Hakan put down the pen with a sigh, staring at the parchment.

113

I wondered how foolish it was to try to help. Would it make a difference? Rawlin set plates of food before us as we sat in silence and then retired to the kitchen for his own meal.

Hakan pushed the parchment away and dug into the food, not speaking for several minutes. Finally, he looked up at me. "What are we going to do?"

"I'll hunt. Venison now will save their grain for later, or they can dry the meat."

It wouldn't be that much help, for there are only so many deer a man can find, even here in the hills. But often the farmers aren't particularly good hunters, despite the forests surrounding the little towns, for they have to spend all their time making the poor soil yield its scant harvest. Perhaps the hunting would be easy then.

I'd give them the rest of my money if I thought it would help, but I had so little it would do them no good. I couldn't ask Hakan to give his, for who could tell what he might need it for later?

What had I been thinking, to bring him here? I had no plan, only a vague idea that he would somehow earn the respect of the people and thus be able to take back his throne. Somehow. Now it seemed sheer idiocy.

I pulled the knife from my boot and spun it on the table. I like the even sound of the hilt rocking on the wood when it spins. The light from open window reflected on the blade. It helps me think, to see the smooth even metal surface. A knife, the surface of the blade, the sound, they're all predict-able. They follow patterns. Unlike people.

Vidar would surely have a firm grasp on power. It was nearly the end of Kyntaa; he'd had two months already.

I flicked the knife again, watching it spin rapidly, slowing gently, gradually, the blade pointing at me when it finally rocked to a halt. I wondered whether that meant anything. I'm not especially superstitious, though some soldiers are. Brushes with death do make one think. I spun it again, and this time the blade pointed off to the far wall. I supposed that the blade pointing at my chest was no more significant than that.

How could Hakan earn the trust of the people? And what difference would it make if he did? One little village on a distant border would mean almost nothing.

The knife blade winked as it spun again. Did it really matter if the prince regained his throne? Was Vidar that bad? I liked Hakan well enough, but Vidar had credibility for good reason. No man desires power for purely altruistic reasons, even Hakan, as much as I might like him.

Nekane Vidar. The name is in Kumar. Nekane means sorrows or sorrowful. Vidar means end. How was one meant to interpret that? End of Sorrows, or Sorrowful End? Sorrowful end of him or of Hakan? Or me? Though I'm not afraid of death, I wouldn't rush it before its time.

What was Taisto's place in this tangle? Ryuu Taisto. Ryuu meaning Great, taken from the same root as the beginning of Yuudai's name. Taisto meaning Battle. Great Battle. Great in the sense of noble? Great as in victorious? Or Great in the sense of bloody and vicious, causing much sorrow and

115

loss? Or perhaps I was too limited in my thinking, limited by my warrior training. Maybe his name meant a Great Battle of morality, of right and wrong, of public opinion, of trust and betrayal.

For the more I thought, the more convinced I was that Taisto's was the hand behind the attempt on Hakan's life. Vidar was hungry for power, but if it came to bloodshed, he was more likely to thrust the knife in your chest and to look you in the eyes as he did it, not send assassins in the night.

"Aren't you going to eat?"

I looked up see Hakan staring at me over his empty plate.

"Aye." I shoved the knife back in my boot and ate, still thinking.

"Where will we go next?"

"North. You should see the border towns."

He nodded, accepting that as if I knew what I was doing. I wondered if he would accept my leadership so easily if he knew I couldn't read the words he'd written on the parchment. I don't often think of myself as inadequate, but I suddenly felt all too aware of my many failures.

What business did I have trying to play king-maker? I can't even read, and no amount of effort on the part of the teachers had been able to over-come my problem. The letters would not resolve into words as they did for other students, even those I knew had not the slightest grasp of tactics or strategy or anything else that came so easily to me. Even a child, an average child of no special intelligence, could puzzle out the words and their meanings with a bit of instruction, but I could not.

Yet did I have the right to forsake the idea of Hakan's kingship? It was his throne, not mine, to give up. He had received the training for it, and Vidar had not. I wondered whether any of that training was actually useful. A king must make many decisions, and education can only prepare a boy so much to become a man and a king. But surely his training would be of some use as king, if only he could gain his throne. How would that compare to Vidar's experience as a soldier?

I glanced up at him and was startled to see him staring at me. "What?"

He shrugged. "What are you thinking about so hard?"

I stared at my plate. What could I say? Finally I stood.

"You might as well rest tonight. I'm going hunting." I felt his eyes on me as I pulled my crossbow out of my pack. I needed to be outside.

WE STAYED FOR only a week. I went hunting before dawn and at dusk every night. During the day, Hakan and I helped the men repair fences and with other work. He didn't know how to do any of it, but when asked he just shrugged and said he'd never learned. He was willing to work though. The second night I smiled to see that the palms of his hands were covered in blisters from hammering all day. He groaned when he got up the next morning, and said his arms were terribly sore.

117

"You'd best not complain too much. They'll ask questions."

I wondered whether he'd be able to keep his complaints quiet, but I didn't hear anything worrying from the townspeople.

Mirson decided not to rebuild his home yet and instead the men built an extra room onto his mother's house, so he could sleep there and she could keep his two living children while he worked his little plot of land. Hakan and I helped with that too. I enjoyed the work, though I wished it wasn't necessary. Mirson himself was not there often, and I heard his crops had been some of the ones that suffered the most damage. He was trying to salvage what he could, and when he tried to help with the construction, his friends told him not to worry. They'd do everything they could to help him.

I saw him a few times. I couldn't bear the look on his face of absolute loss, grief beyond all comprehension. A wife, clearly beloved, and their infant daughter, were both gone. I wondered what I would do, if I'd suffered such loss. Would I have the courage to continue living alone? A father doesn't have the right to desert his two remaining children, nor to place the burden of their care upon his own dying mother. But I ached for him, though I never knew how to show it.

Once I saw him with his two little boys. They didn't understand, of course, and seemed as carefree as they would have the week before, when their world was simple and whole. No doubt they cried at night for her, but when I saw them they seemed happy.

Mirson showed me courage of a different sort than I'd ever seen before, though he didn't know it. The younger boy, only three years old, ran to meet him from the door of Mirson's mother's house, tripping over his own feet and falling flat on his face in the dust, pushing himself up to run to greet his father with dirt sticking to his cheeks and lips. Mirson grabbed the boy about his middle and threw him wildly into the air, catching him with a laughing smile to hold him close. The little boy had been on the verge of tears, but at this, he burst into laughter and wrapped his arms about his father's neck in childish faith.

In Erdem, warriors like me often believe we have a monopoly on courage. We face death with firm jaws and stout hearts, unafraid of pain. We train through agony and exhaustion, we march through snow and driving rain when necessary. We serve Erdem with our bodies and our hearts, strong and proud. There is a long history of great deeds, of heroism, of honor and courage that demands the same from each warrior down to the youngest volunteer and even the foundling children in training.

Mirson showed me another kind of courage, a courage most warriors would never have to exercise. His was the courage of love, smiling through heart-breaking pain for the sake of another. Many of us would never have the chance to forge such close ties, find a wife and have children, but any man can identify raw pain when he sees it. Mirson humbled me, though I hadn't known I needed it.

We were on our way out of town when Hakan stopped me. "I want to do more for them."

119

I waited.

"I have money. It isn't much, but it might help the families buy food this winter. But I'd like your help in distributing it."

I nodded. "Aye then. How will you do it?"

He turned and began to walk back toward the center of town. "I suppose an equal amount for each family, with a bit extra for those that lost a husband and father. And for Mirson. I imagine a wife performs vital tasks as well. But not all the families are in town. Who should distribute the money for those families?"

I thought for a moment before I spoke. "If it were me, I'd give the money for each family to Rawlin, and let three more men know he received it all. Rawlin seems a good man, and three others should keep him straight if he isn't."

I was surprised when we actually reached the inn again. Hakan pulled out his bag of money and gave Rawlin nearly all of it, along with detailed instructions about how much each family was to receive. I hadn't expected him to give so much; it was probably more than the town had seen all year. In any case it widened Rawlin's eyes. He took it with a bit of trepidation, and I saw no greed in him, though he was more awed by the amount than Hakan had apparently expected.

Hakan spoke to three more men as we again left town, explaining what he'd done and how much each family should receive. The men looked at him strangely, for of course it was unheard of for a commoner to have such a great amount of money. But they didn't question him, accepting the instructions with a grateful nod. In a city, I wouldn't have expected such a plan to work, but in the small towns, everyone knows each other. They wouldn't hide the money, for half the families were connected by blood, and all relied on each other for help in farming every year. It would do them no good to try to cheat each other.

Finally we were on the road north again. I was proud of Hakan, for I think he was changed by that week in Miafal just as I was by watching Mirson. Or perhaps I had underestimated him before. In either case, I was pleased to see this unselfish compassion in him. A compassionate king cares for his people in a special way. Though they did not know him as the prince, much less the king, the people would be well-served by a king who cared for their needs. Though his ability to help them was yet limited, it gave me confidence that he would consider his people's needs when he finally ruled. He would be unlikely to seek out foolish wars, or to exact harsh taxes for little reason.

A king's pride is a good thing, for it helps him ensure his nation's power and prestige in the world. It gives the nation pride. It may help keep the nation safe in peace with its neighbors, less likely to be pushed to war because of its very strength. Other nations will fear it with a healthy fear, for its strength ensures that it may defend itself, while a sober and rational ruler will not provoke other nations to war against his people.

Many kings are proud, but a king should not veer from proud into prideful. A prideful king may become foolishly arrogant, not taking adequate care for his people. Pride should be tempered with compassion for the people. I'd seen

121

plenty of pride in Hakan already. It cheered me to see this compassionate side of him as well.

NINE

We made good time on the road north, though I wondered why I was hurrying us so. Hayato knew to expect us in Senlik in a month or two in case there was news. Hakan was helpful with the work of finding wood each day to cook with and gathering food. He didn't grumble at the tasks anymore, which made my days much more pleasant.

We traveled each morning and generally used the afternoons for his training in swordplay and barehanded fighting. The weather was warming with the spring, but we moved higher into the mountains and the greater elevation ensured that the nights were still quite cool.

I love the mountains, the clean bright air that stings your lungs with its purity, the scent of pine and rich dirt. Rotting leaves and pine needles make a thick carpet that softens footsteps. The snow on the Sefu Mountains has a purple and blue cast in the early morning light, almost silhouetted if you look directly east. It brightens to an impossibly beautiful white in the noonday sun and catches the orange and red hues of the sunset each evening.

When I was discharged from the kedani, I went to the base of the mountains to recover in the serenity of absolute solitude. I grieved for Yuudai there, a few leagues lower down the hills and west of where we walked, and I grieved for my former life. It had been good, though harsh, and I didn't quite know what to do with myself in the odd freedom of civilian life. It was nearly a year before I spoke to anyone, for I lived alone in the woods, and when I finally did return to society I worked off and on as a mercenary.

It was different from formal service, but not bad in the way that some nations view mercenaries. Because of the many retirements in the past decade, mercenaries were well respected, for we performed a vital service. We were paid a bit more than active duty soldiers because the work wasn't steady. Most have army experience and are likeable enough, old soldiers, a few are knaves more or less but most are honorable and good men. Once a soldier, always a soldier. Mercenaries were often used for escort duty, light patrols, sometimes even border security.

I could have taught with my experience, but I didn't want to live in Stonehaven or any of the cities with major military schools. I didn't want to be surrounded by people, and I suppose it pained me to no longer feel a part of that camaraderie. Instead, I wandered around the country, feeling a bit aimless but not sure whether I really minded it.

When I did take a job, I sang with the others, for we knew many of the same marching songs from the kedani. I'd practiced my Dari on the most recent job; one of the other men wanted to learn it, more for the sake of curiosity than anything else. I probably wasn't much help to him, since I've spent all my life around Common-speaking Tuyets, and only learned bits and pieces of Dari by chance. His accent was better than mine, though I knew more words.

Every afternoon I drilled Hakan hard, and he toughened somewhat under my training. He didn't complain as much. His footwork improved, and certainly his blocking and parrying improved. They weren't good, but they were better. Again and again I made him attack me. He wasn't good at seeing openings in my defenses, and when he saw them, he hesitated. He did better with empty hand fighting, though he'd started it later. I wouldn't have bet on him in a fight, but he did improve.

You can see a man's personality in the way he fights, and I grew more fond of Hakan as I taught him. He was intelligent, smart enough to realize his own weaknesses. He was not naturally aggressive, and at first I thought him dangerously passive, waiting to be attacked. But as he learned more, he grew more confident.

One day when we were training with the wooden swords, I made a stupid mistake. I could fight him nearly with my eyes closed, and I let my mind wander. It was late spring by then, an unusually hot and sticky day, and I was wondering whether the Fliscar River, which flowed into the Purling to the south, was one day's walk north or two. I wanted a swim, and I wasn't paying attention at all when he lunged exactly as I had taught him. The sword point caught me hard a few inches below my ribs on the right side.

He cried out in surprise, already apologizing as he stepped back.

"That's exactly what you're supposed to do. Now finish me."

I made him continue and taught him some of the many ways he could finish a wounded opponent. Most of all, I tried to teach him to remain cautious. An opponent is dangerous until he is dead. I had him repeat his successful stroke, fell to one knee, let him approach for a final cut. I brought up my sword for a killing strike, for he was too close and too confident. Too trusting. He nodded that he understood, but it worried me; he didn't expect deception from an opponent. I resolved to focus on that more in the future.

When I stripped off my shirt that night I had a black bruise on my side topped by a bloodied scrape.

Hakan's eyes widened. "I'm sorry!"

I grinned. "You should be proud."

He smiled, still a little shaken.

We bypassed the larger towns as we headed for Senlik. The smaller, more remote village would serve us better while Hakan trained, and Hayato knew this place would be our final destination. I'd never been to Senlik, but I knew the road to it well.

We'd passed by on our way to my last battle, the one in which Yuudai had died.

"STRIKE!"

His lunge was better than the last, but he still wasn't aggressive.

"Hakan, when you're fighting, your opponent is an enemy, not a friend. Losing is not an option."

He nodded.

"Attack again."

He blocked my strike and struck again. I barely suppressed a sigh.

"Kill me, Hakan. Don't fight. Win. If you don't kill your opponent, he will kill you."

He didn't fear me anymore. He trusted, because we were friends. So I attacked.

My wooden blade slid across his throat, not hard but firmly enough to frighten him.

Again. My blade crossed his stomach. It would have gutted him if the blade had been real. A few minutes later, a jab to his stomach that doubled him over, though he straightened in a moment, his face pale and his eyelashes damp with tears.

It worked, somewhat. He clenched his jaw and attacked again, not well but more strongly than before.

"Don't let your anger make you careless." My wooden blade tapped the back of his knee. "That would cripple you. Don't forget to block."

He nodded, his mouth tight.

I gave him the opening because he wasn't good enough to make his own opportunities. But I was pleased when he took it, the wooden point of his sword raking across my stomach.

"Good."

You learn how to strike by striking. When Hakan struck, I let him hit me. Not every time, of course, but when his strikes were good. A man needs to know when his efforts are producing results.

That day was the best of his training thus far. When I stripped that night to bathe in the Fliscar River, I had half a dozen more dark bruises across my ribs. Hakan frowned, and when he tried to apologize again I deliberately dipped my head beneath the water and ignored him.

I train hard and am used to the bruises and scrapes that go along with it. I enjoy teaching, and I flatter myself that I'm good at it, partly because I don't mind the bruises. Every time a student strikes me well, it is more practice, more experience, that may help him when he needs to use his skill. Maybe that last bit of intensity in our training together would save his life.

I've never been good at floating, I'm fit enough that I tend to sink, but I lay on my back in the water and watched the sun set behind the trees. The frigid water was refreshing and my skin felt tight and alive with the chill. Tiny merlkina fish nibbled at my shoulders and I wondered lazily whether they were aware enough to tell that I was salty with sweat, or whether to their little fish minds I tasted the same as a leaf or a waterbug.

When Hakan grabbed my foot, I was so startled I inhaled water and came up choking and sputtering.

"What?" I spit river water and glared at him.

"I thought you were asleep. You were drifting downstream." He looked like he wanted to smile but wasn't sure if I was so angry smiling would be dangerous.

"It's called relaxing. I don't do it often."

TEN

We stayed the first night outside Senlik with a family by the name of Priven, a reference I suppose to their proximity to the river. Names in Common are not as clearly derived as those in Kumar or the High Tongues. They may be taken from a family's location or profession, a physical attribute of some ancestor, or something else, which may be impossible to determine. My name was given to me when I was found, else I would have had a name in Darin. Kumar, the warrior tongue, is my native language, the one in which I was trained. Everyone speaks Common, and I've studied enough High Tongue to indulge my interest in names, but I wouldn't claim I'm fluent.

I approached the man as he was entering his house for the evening. "Sir, I ask your hospitality for the night."

It was a common request in the country, and generally granted. Hospitality is a vital part of Erdemen culture, one I hadn't appreciated until my service in the army took me out of the kingdom. He had the good grace to try to hide his fear of me.

I inclined my head with the proper measure of respect of a warrior to a commoner. Soldiers are in between classes, not nobility, but certainly not common. Courtesy is one of the marks of a warrior, and I've exercised mine more than most to overcome the "demon-child" epithet I heard when I was young.

"Aye then, welcome."

"My friend as well?" I smiled at his nod and waved Hakan to follow me. "We are grateful for your generosity. My name is Kemen Sendoa; call me Kemen. Do you need help with anything before the evening meal?"

"No, I'm finished, except for feeding the horses. You're welcome to come if you wish. My name is Feo Priven." He glanced at me nervously, flicking his eyes toward my sword before hurrying toward the barn. I followed, keeping pace with his quick steps easily. I moved down the stalls, patting a few horses on their noses.

"Your horses are beautiful." It was the right compliment, and a grin split his face.

"Thank you, sir. This one is Hragar, and this Hrana, her foal born just two days ago. Light and purity, of course." Both were bred for speed, probably for suvari use.

131

"She's early."

He nodded. "Aye, quite early. But she seems to be doing well. I think she's strong."

I nodded. The little foal was nursing hungrily, a good sign.

"Then Harpan, Strength, the gelding."

He was a massive draught horse who turned calm eyes on me and nosed my hand gently, hoping for a bit of an apple.

"And this is Phrena, fleet-footed. She's due in about two weeks."

The mare was beautifully rounded with pregnancy, waiting eagerly for her bucket of grain, fine clean lines showing her good blood. Her foal would be valuable.

"Where's the stud?" I asked.

He talked as he finished working. "Both foals are by Hroth, over at Thosin's place. He's a good stallion, strong and very fast. Last year I only had Hragar, but with the money from her foal and some extra I saved up, I bought Phrena. This year I scraped together enough for the two stud fees, and I'm hoping to get a colt from Phrena. If he's good enough, I can keep him for my own stud in a few years."

I nodded. "You're going to sell Hrana then? And maybe Phrena's foal?"

"Aye, certainly Hrana, but mayhap the other one as well, if it's a filly."

They were far too young for Hakan and me, of course, but horses would be necessary soon. "I wouldn't mind buying a good horse or two, if you know who has some for sale. Broken, not foals."

We headed toward the house, Hakan following without a word.

Priven nodded. "Thosin has quite a stable. Come inside. Mira, we have guests!"

I ducked as I passed through the doorway. Doors always seem a bit too short to me, and I had to keep my head uncomfortably ducked as we made our way inside. Priven turned back and smiled at Hakan.

"Ah, this is your friend. What's your name?"

I answered for him. "His name is Naoki."

Hakan smiled and inclined his head, but it wasn't the proper bow for a soldier to make to a commoner. Priven's eyes narrowed in irritation but he said nothing. His wife appeared in the doorway, smiling nervously as she caught sight of me, and I bowed more deeply.

"Thank you for your hospitality, madam." It was a slight promotion from gooduf, the standard greeting for a common woman, and she smiled again cautiously.

"Sit. Make yourselves comfortable." Priven pulled out chairs for us from the table as his wife moved to the stove. The room was small and close, and I was uncomfortably aware that we must stink from our weeks outside. I had bathed, of course, but my bath in the Fliscar was three days before.

Priven and his wife were a few years older than I, maybe forty or so. There were four chairs around the small table.

"Do you have children?" Everyone loves to talk about their children, and it would be useful if they liked us.

C. J. Brightley

Priven smiled proudly. "Aye! Our older boy, Baso, is in service at Thosin's stables. He's sixteen. Neel is fourteen, and he's apprenticed to Mullin. He's the blacksmith."

Only two children. I wondered how many they'd lost. His pride in the children stirred a bit of envy in me. But envy does not suit a warrior, and I stifled it as best I could. Not to mention that I envied him a wife. At my age, I could have had a son nearly Hakan's age, maybe a few years younger. Those pleasures were not for me, however much I might wish it. No woman would want me, and I'd come to terms with that long ago. I realized that I was staring at the center of the table, and glanced up at Priven. He flinched back and muttered something about helping his wife with the food.

I wonder what I look like when I'm thinking. Priven wasn't the first to be unnerved by it. I missed that about the army; surrounded by other warriors I didn't stand out so much. People like Priven didn't remember how the army used to be. It was strong and proud. Honorable. There was no tolerance of abuse of power, nor of looting, nor of any other base behavior. Training was grueling, but I excelled both as a child in training and later as an officer. I'd risen in command and respect very quickly. My downfall was my complete and utter inability to do figures and to read. The letters swam on the page before me, and I could not seem to make them make sense as others did with ease.

It had first become a problem in training. With a bit of effort, I could enlist the aid of other students in reading and writing my work. The answers were easy, the problems and strategies came

134

naturally, but I couldn't put my answers to parchment, and I couldn't turn the mess of cryptic symbols into words. Maps I could read, pictures, but the letters and numbers of soldiers, the logistics of supplying them, I could not manage those. A commoner doesn't need to read, but as an army officer, it was a constant humiliation. I had to rely on a scribe or a friend to even read my orders. Yuudai Urho had been most helpful, and we'd been sword brothers until that last battle. His name fit him. Yuudai means great hero, and Urho means brave, and he was both of those. He was a good friend.

Mira Priven put a plate with some thick mutton and vegetable pie in front of me and another in front of Hakan. Then there was a basket of bread and cups of wine well diluted. She stood nervously while her husband sat down with us.

I nodded toward her. "There's no need to wait on us. Come eat."

She smiled a little nervously but turned back to prepare her own plate. In a moment she was seated and we began to eat.

Priven had apparently gathered his courage again, for he began to ply me with questions. "Where have you come from?"

"South, from Stonehaven." I smiled my thanks at his wife. The food was better than I'd expected, and certainly better than my simple fare. She smiled tentatively.

"What news of the king? I heard he was ill, but we've had no news in months." He leaned forward eagerly. Out of the corner of my eye, I saw

Hakan watching me. I hoped he would hold his tongue.

"The king is dead."

Priven's face showed no emotion. "And the prince is crowned then?"

He was curious, but nothing more. Like as not, nothing in the capital had affected them for years out here. I said, "Nay, the prince is missing."

He stared at me curiously. "Missing?"

"I can only repeat rumors, of course, I have no certain knowledge."

He nodded.

"I heard that Nekane Vidar had sent assassins after the prince. He's taken power for himself."

Priven slammed a fist into the table. "Cowardly bastard!" He glanced at me with sudden fear. "You're for the prince, aren't you?"

I nodded. "I served under the king. He had his faults, but I'd take the prince over Vidar any day."

He nodded eagerly. "Aye, right enough. You know the problems we've had here."

I shook my head, and watched him as I continued eating. Hakan sat quietly, and I was right glad of it too.

"Raids over the border have gotten much worse lately."

"Which border? North or east?"

"Both." His voice was grim. "Rikutans have been over the passes to the east for nearly a year. Last summer I nearly lost my younger boy to them. When I was young, there were soldiers here to control the passes. Taxes have gone up but we don't have soldiers any more, and the roads are falling apart. I want to know what we get for our money!" His voice had risen in irritation, but his wife put her hand on his arm with a look of fear, and he suddenly looked at me. "Begging your pardon of course."

I nodded. "What about the northern border? That's been secure for years." I made a concerted effort to not look threatening. Information is a tool, a weapon if you use it well, and I needed more of it.

"Didn't you know? The soldiers posted there have decreased steadily for the past six years, and just last summer Fort Ilkanao was closed, despite the raids. We're protected, closer to the mountains, but my wife's family lives a bit west and north, not far from Highden near the plains, and they've lost livestock every year. It's hard, and getting harder. They're thinking about moving south if it doesn't get better."

"Raids by the Tarvil?"

"Aye. That whole stretch from Highden to Ironcrest is nothing but a wasteland. They come and steal cattle, sheep, horses. They've killed a few people, but thieving is the goal. They've kidnapped a few girls too."

Hakan spoke up at this. "That's barbaric." His voice was filled with scorn.

"They're barbarians, that's what they do."

Hakan started to rise in anger at Priven's tone, but I put one hand on his shoulder and held him in his seat. "Naoki, sit down."

At the sound of his new name, he clenched his jaw angrily but sat.

I turned back to Priven deliberately, keeping my voice very calm. "We would not take advantage of your hospitality past this one night, though you've been most generous. Yet I would ask you for more information."

He nodded.

"Do you know the mountain passes well?"

"Well enough."

"Do you have any parchment? I'd like your help on a map then."

He hesitated.

"I'll pay for it."

He smiled, a little embarrassed, but moved off toward a chest in the corner. Parchment and ink are dear in the outlying regions, and I couldn't blame him for hesitating. His wife stood and ducked her head respectfully.

"Would you like any more pie?"

Hakan nodded. "Thank you."

She looked toward me, still a little nervous, and I could see a bit of strain around her eyes.

"Thank you, but no. It was delicious though." I smiled as gently as I knew how.

I'd made an effort, those last years since I was discharged from the army, to not seem so frightening, but my success had been limited.

She ducked her head and scurried off to refill Hakan's plate. Control. Self-denial. I had to remind myself because I was still rather hungry. They didn't have much, and I wouldn't take more than necessary.

Priven returned with several sheets of precious parchment, a quill pen, and a small bottle of ink, which he spread out before me. I slid a silver eagle across the table to him. I'd always been good at making maps, though not so skilled at labeling them, and I devoted myself to the task with a will.

There was the capital Stonehaven, and there the great forest that spreads along the length of the country from east to west, north of the great plains just above the southern border. The Sefu Mountains ranged from far in the north to the south and slightly east, forming the border with Rikuto. Sefu is an old word, from a language long lost, meaning sword, taken from the knife sharp edges of the jagged peaks. There are few passages through the mountains during the summer, and none of them reliably passable in winter when the harsh winds rake over the hills and mountainsides and tear away layers of ice and snow to crash down on any foolish travelers who may try to cross.

The three great rivers come from the mountains and flow away west until the northern two, Greentongue and Silvertongue, join not far above Stonehaven, then turn south to join the Rivlin which itself turns southwest and flows to the sea. There are smaller rivers of course, and lakes, but those were the main features.

Hakan sat up. "There, you have the border with Rikuto wrong. Let me do it."

He took the quill from my hand and I let him turn the map to see it more clearly. His eyes narrowed as he studied the map, adding some of the smaller rivers and correcting the southeastern border. He labeled the rivers in a practiced hand, the flowing curves of the letters coming effortlessly.

This was his element, parchment and ink, the narrow planes of his cheeks matching the straight clean lines of the northern border drawn arbitrarily across the flat cold plains. Good. He needed to know this land.

More than that, he needed to know these people. I could see no other way. The people would have to make him king. If they feared the Rikutans enough, they would accept Vidar for the protection he might offer. But if they were not so afraid, perhaps they would support Hakan after all.

"Priven, where are the passes through the mountains?" I spun the parchment around and took the quill back from Hakan.

He marked tentatively on the map. "I don't know them all, of course, but the last raid came from here, just east of town, from the Ising Pass. I've also heard that some have come from here, but that's all I know. We don't get much news here since the soldiers left. Senlik is only half a league north. I go in every week. Thosin is just west of town, less than a league."

Hakan took back the map in the silence, studying it a moment before marking nine more passes. "This one is a good wide road all the way to Rikuto. These two have established trails, wide as roads, though not so flat. Horses could pass three abreast. These six are footpaths, wide enough for one horse at least. The ones you've marked I've never heard of, so there are probably more that I don't know."

Priven stared at him, eyes narrowed. Suddenly Hakan looked at me, realizing his folly, and Priven looked between us suspiciously.

I was cursing inside, but I smiled at Priven. "Naoki studied to be a mapmaker, but he suffered from an insatiable desire for adventure. He's in training now for the kedani, and I'm hoping to bore him out of the idea. We need more good mapmakers, don't you think?" I have never been good at humor, and this time was no better.

Priven stared at me. "No, we need good soldiers. They're in short supply here."

"Do you?"

"Yes." He stared at me a moment longer.

Fool boy should have kept his mouth shut. He could have added to the map later, when we were alone.

Priven leaned forward. "I venture that the town would be happy to put you up for the rest of the summer if you train some of us to better defend ourselves against the raiders."

I looked at him sharply.

"We can't fight them. We don't have the skills or the weapons, and foolish courage in the face of trained soldiers would only leave our wives and children to starve."

Like those men in Miafal who died protecting sheep that were taken nonetheless, wives and children left to grieve in hunger.

I sat back. "Aye, you're right. But mayhap we need to get on our own business."

"Mayhap. It's an offer nonetheless. I'll take you in to town tomorrow if you want."

I stood. "I'll think on it. Thank you for your hospitality. We can sleep in the stable?"

He nodded and stood, leading the way out into the darkness. Hakan trailed after us.

"There's an empty box stall and good clean straw in the back on the right."

In a few moments he left us in the warm smells of horses, hay, rich grain, and manure. It was so dark I couldn't see my hand in front of my face, but I heard Hakan drop down into the straw with a tired sigh.

"I'm sorry, Kemen." He sounded thoroughly subdued.

"Then be more careful."

PAIN.

The Tarvil drives the javelin deeper in the dirt, grinding against the bone. His breath smells of rotten meat. He is missing a tooth.

I can't breathe.

"Kemen!"

I jerked awake.

"Are you alright?" Hakan's voice came out of the darkness.

"I'm fine." I took a deep breath. "Sorry." My heartbeat felt ragged.

I heard him shifting in the straw and one of the horses snorted softly. I was glad he didn't ask anything else, though I know he was awake for some time.

PRIVEN TOOK US into Senlik early the next morning. Word spread that we would be introduced to the town that night at the inn, and in the meantime he showed us about the town, introducing us to the blacksmith, the baker, and others. His son Neel was a good-looking boy with a quick smile, though his eyes widened when he saw me.

A small crowd, mostly of children, slowly accumulated and followed us curiously. We had dinner at the boarding house, served by a young woman who looked at me with a mixture of curiosity and fear. I tried not to look at her, since when I did, she seemed to flinch away.

But she smiled at Hakan, an admiring, hopeful smile. He was probably used to such smiles from pretty girls, and from noble ones at that. The smile of a serving girl was a gift he didn't even see and couldn't appreciate.

I wonder sometimes if Dari women would have the same reaction to me, whether I'm considered ugly because I am Dari or because I'm ugly even for a Dari. Not that it matters.

A crowd had gathered by the time we finished eating, and Priven stood on a chair to address everyone crowded into the dining room. The crowd was mostly men, of course, with a few boys just getting their first beards, and several women in a little clump at the back of the crowd. I could see clearly over everyone's heads, and I studied their faces while Priven waited for them to quiet. Good faces, some simple, some less so, but honest and friendly enough. All curious, all staring at me, though most had the good grace to try to hide it when I met their eyes. I don't like being stared at; it burns inside, as if I have failed somehow, or am about to.

Priven did not have a good voice for addressing a crowd, and I could see some of the men in the back straining to catch his words.

"This is Kemen Sendoa, a warrior of great skill and courage. He's offered to train us to defend

143

ourselves against the next raid. Would you have him do this?"

There was a murmur in the crowd, and I hid a smile. That wasn't exactly how the offer had been made, but Priven continued unabashed. "I think it only fair that for his help, we provide food and lodging for him and his friend for as long as they train us. What do you say?"

A man spoke up from the middle of the crowd. "I would hear from this Sendoa himself. You served in the army?"

I nodded. "Aye, in the suvari for four years, then I was transferred to the kedani."

"We have few weapons. What can we do against the raids?" This from another man.

"It depends on what they want. If they want to kill you, it will be difficult, but there are defensive measures I can teach you. If they only want your livestock, it should be easy enough to remain safe. I'd have to learn more about the raids before I recommend anything."

The men were nodding now, cautious still. "Have you ever stolen anything?"

"Aye, a drink from a horse trough." They mistrusted me, and I suppose I should not have been insulted, but I was. A warrior would never speak to another warrior so disrespectfully, insinuating such base things. But they were not warriors, and I reined in my anger. Courtesy among common folk is of a different kind.

"Can you be trusted around women?"

Now who, if they could not be trusted around women, would admit to it? I felt my jaw tighten in anger, and my words were clipped, though I did try to remain polite. "I have never been accused of anything less than perfect courtesy toward a woman." It was a stupid question, but I supposed it was meant more to gauge my reaction than my words.

"Who's your friend?"

"Naoki." I gave no more details, and though I would not have expected the questions to end there, the crowd seemed to hesitate.

"I would have you train us."

"And I."

Priven put it to a general vote, and no one said nay.

"For now they're staying with me, but tomorrow and after that, they'll stay here at the boarding house." He looked to a flabby man with pale red hair and a large beard for confirmation. Then he continued, "Everyone should contribute for their food and lodging. Haral Twilling, will you keep the records?"

The red haired man nodded again. With that, the meeting was over, though many men lingered, most watching me but not speaking to me. Hakan and I followed Priven back his house and slept in the stable that night.

THE NEXT DAY we began in earnest. The sheepfold was sturdy enough, but the wooden gate was simple and easily broken. I asked Mullin, the blacksmith, to make a lock for it while Adin and I reinforced the gate. The granary got a new lock, as did the stables. In a city, most of the simple measures would have been taken long ago to prevent common theft, but in small towns, there's little need of such care until raiders come.

The blacksmith had no skill in making swords. He could make a blade, of course, but nothing that would stand up to a Rikutan sword. I didn't have the knowledge to teach him, either. Instead, after the basic reinforcements were completed, I trained the men in the uses of their farming implements as weapons. It would have been better to train them as archers, but I'd never made a bow either, and I wouldn't trust their lives to my first efforts. Once again I appreciated my army training. We were taught that anything can be a weapon when wielded correctly.

I spent time with small groups of men, those who chose the same weapons, rather than larger groups as I'd done when training soldiers. I taught Mullin, Neel Priven, and two others a circular style that took advantage of the heavily weighted hammers they chose. With proper usage, they would smash bones and provide a fairly effective shield for the wielder, but it would take practice.

Adin and several others chose shepherds' crooks or long staffs. None of them had Mullin's burly strength, but Adin at least had a quick hand with the staff and a good feel for his own distance and reach. A shepherd protects his flock from wolves, even bears at times, with his staff and a few good dogs. Adin was probably the best prepared of any of the men for combat, though in truth none would stand up to a trained warrior even after months of training. Not for lack of courage, for I wouldn't underestimate them so, but the skills a warrior needs do not come so quickly.

A few others chose sickles and flails, each requiring separate training. Hakan seemed thoroughly impressed by my knowledge, and I wondered what he thought a soldier's training consisted of.

The routine of childhood was etched in my memory. We were roused before dawn to run for an hour, all skinny legs and big eyes, hungry and silent except for our breathing. Cold in winter, heat in summer, there was always training. We tended the horses and chickens and pigs, milked the cows, picked the vegetables, did whatever chores the schoolmaster assigned.

We wolfed down bread and cheese and bacon at mid-morning, our stomachs growling, then it was time for our lessons. History, grammar in the early years and later literature, poetry, arithmetic, geography, logistics, tactics, strategy. Grappling. Weapons of all sorts, both on foot and on horseback. How to march and ride in formation. How to break a horse. Training your horse not to panic in battle at the noise and the smell of blood. Basic healing, how to stitch and bind a wound. Basic carpentry. Wilderness survival. Tracking. How to set snares for rabbits and humans. How to not be seen or heard when you didn't want to be. Lunch was in there somewhere, unless you were on field training, and then you ate only what you could find. Then more lessons in the evening, more chores, supper of milk and bread and honey, beef stew or pork roast, heavy and rich, and we collapsed into our beds too tired to cause trouble.

The life didn't suit everyone; some were more fragile than others, and they fell out somewhere along the way for easier jobs, funneled into the logistical corps, assigned to sew uniforms or work in the royal stables. But I might have been born for it.

I was never an archer. I trained most extensively with swords, the longsword, the scimitar, and the short straight twin swords. I'm large enough that I can use a longsword one-handed at need, though not for too long with any degree of skill. We also trained with hammers, sickles, whips, knives, boat oars, chains, horses' bridles, staves, and other more common items, as well as empty hand fighting. More importantly, we were taught a philosophy of fighting, a way of inventing effective moves at need with whatever implements might be handy.

The men took turns training, for they still had the work of farming and shepherding as well. I trained every morning myself, beginning in the cool grey blue light before the sun cleared the peaks to the east. I'd let myself get a little soft in the months of escort work, and so now I pushed myself harder, especially in my speed. Endurance is of little use in a fight if one is gutted in the first four seconds.

Hakan helped the men with the work of shepherding and farming. First he only observed them working, but soon he plunged into the work himself. He helped Thosin with some of the new foals. Adin taught him to milk the goats and sheep, and Adin's wife Anora taught him to make cheese and precious butter. Adin laughed at him for doing women's work, but Hakan took the teasing with good will. Though at first the men laughed at his inexperience with farming, his good humor and readiness to help made him popular. Adin was a born comic, and he and Hakan got on well. They joked and laughed, and Mullin joined in sometimes, his deeper voice a rumbling undertone among the others.

I wondered whether they had any idea he was the prince, but I heard no whispers about him. They seemed to think he was merely a city boy, and they shared their lives with him once they saw his eagerness to learn.

I trained him in the afternoons, and I pushed him hard. He did improve, though more slowly than either of us would have liked. Neel Priven watched us sometimes. Although he made Hakan nervous and self conscious, I think it was good for him to have an audience. He was less likely to show his frustration because he wanted to save face in front of the townspeople. It's an innate need of all men, to not show weakness or frustration before others. Yet I think it was even stronger for him, for though he'd been mostly hidden away in the castle by his father, he'd also grown up with the knowledge that he would someday be king.

A king is both the embodiment of his people and an example for them. His weaknesses are the weaknesses of the nation, and his strengths are the strengths of the nation. Hakan struggled in our training sessions, but he did not throw down his sword in frustration nor did I see tears again. He sweated and persevered, and I took care to note his progress and show my approval, especially when others were watching. A man needs his effort ac-knowledged, and though we both realized he'd never be an accomplished swordsman, I would not have him think his discipline was for nothing.

Despite our time spent training together, I tried to maintain my reserve. The fight for Hakan's throne, however it might occur, might cost either his life or mine, if not both.

I would give my life first, of course, because I'd already decided that he would be better for Erdem than Vidar. He was young and green, but he was also pure of heart. Erdem needed that, much more than she needed a strong military leader. His regard for me, his friendship, gave me hope for Erdemen Dari. His willingness to learn, to ask questions, had given me hope that he would be a wise and thoughtful king. A boy king, but one who would grow quickly into the heavy responsibility.

I wondered if the burden would make him sing less, whether he would smile less often.

That's why I kept my distance. When he and Adin laughed over some joke, when Mullin clapped him on the back in praise of his training, I smiled distantly. I'm not one to laugh often, but even so I might have laughed more than I did. Very occasionally, I even thought of a funny comment too, but I kept my few joking thoughts to myself. I tried to stay in the background, though I wasn't always successful. Hakan looked to me for guidance and I was so accustomed to command, to leadership, that it was natural to advise him. But I tried not to become his friend, at least not more than was inevitable. Removing the usurper would be dangerous, and if I died, I did not want Hakan to grieve too much.

My grief at Yuudai's death had been numbing. I'd been heartsick at the tragedy, at the uselessness of his death, at how quickly one of Erdem's finest heroes was forgotten. I'd needed time to grieve, and I would have been less than ideal as a commander during those first few months after his death. Erdem would demand all of Hakan's heart, all of his attention. She could not afford to have a boy king distracted by grief in those difficult times.

Eleven

I was training Hakan when the raiding party came one morning not long before noon. The townsmen had been practicing the moves I had taught them, still standing in the street. Many had weapons in hand already, mostly sickles and axes. But the men walking arrogantly into town were armed with swords and shields, trained warriors all. Four were on horseback, but the remainder, some twelve or so, were on foot. I sprinted to the front of the crowd, pushing men out of my way in my haste.

I spoke in Kumar because Rikutans do not often speak Common. "Go back!"

The man mounted in front laughed. "Go on with you. We only want some food, and two or three pretty girls." He pointed his sword at one of the younger girls, maybe fifteen or so, who was peering anxiously from an open door.

Her father growled angrily and moved forward. When I snapped at him to stay back, my voice was harsher than I had intended.

"Go back. If you're hungry we'll feed you, but you will take no girls." Hungry men are dangerous men, but perhaps with luck they would stand down.

He scowled and spurred his horse forward. "Stand back. We will take them whether you will or no, and the food as well."

"Then I challenge you to single combat!" My voice rang out. Better to fight him alone than everyone at once. He'd be shamed into taking the challenge, for his men all watched him. If I lost, the townsmen would have one fewer to fight; he would not escape me unscathed. They would never give up their daughters. Who could blame them?

"The terms?" He was dismounting now, deliberately turning his back on me as he did so. A terrible insult, but I was already furious enough that it made little difference.

"Single combat, any weapon you have on your person. On foot."

"And if I win we get our pick of the girls?" He smiled viciously, and a light colored scar at the corner of his mouth stood out with odd clarity.

"If you win, I'll not stand in your way." Take that how you will. I meant that I would be dead, but he apparently was satisfied, for he flung the reins to one of his friends.

I spoke in Common. "Stand back, everyone. If he wins, defend yourselves how you may." There was a grumbling mutter and I hoped no one would do anything too foolish.

The fight was short, as most are. He had a shield, small for suvari use, and I didn't, but I'm used to fighting without one. I prefer a knife in my off hand when I'm using a sword one-handed, but I didn't use it yet. I could tell from his stance he was a little afraid of me, though he hid it well.

He made a quick slash, I dodged, then another, I blocked and drove in, my left hand grasping the top rim of his shield to pull it aside and my right delivering the sword thrust from high down into his chest. It is a good move for me, since I'm so tall, and difficult for an opponent to counter. It also leaves my gut open, so I use it with caution, though often I can keep my opponent's shield between our bodies.

His death was quick. I hate to see a man die slowly. His friends muttered a moment and I stood, waiting to see if they would leave or if they would charge. Someone in the crowd retched. I remembered that sickened feeling after my first kill. It never quite goes away, but sometimes you have no other options.

I'd hoped one death would be enough, but it wasn't. They charged more or less in a group, but the three remaining horsemen hung back a moment. The men on foot did not use their advantage of numbers well, or I would have had no chance. A group must take advantage of its numbers, surround a lone fighter to strike from all sides. I had enough time to step back, to put the wall to my back. The first man left his shield a little too high, and I slipped my sword under it as I knelt, then swung it around again, higher this time, to catch another in the throat. By then my knife was in my left hand, and I moved automatically.

If it were not for the blood and the cries of pain, fighting would be almost like a dance. Not that I ever learned to dance, but I've seen it. The precision, the judgment. When can I have my knife there in his side, if I first block this strike? Where does that put my feet, and where can I move from there?

It was almost over when the three horsemen charged. I had not a scratch until then, though I was covered in hot blood. I would have twisted away, but my boot caught on a man's arm as he lay dead at my feet. The horse tripped and barreled into me before crashing headlong into the wall just behind me. The horse screamed in pain, the white bones of one broken foreleg glistening, and I gasped at the sharp, blinding pain in my ribs where its knee had hit me.

I rolled away from flailing hooves that narrowly missed my head, one hand slipping on the bloodied arm of the body beneath me. It was probably more luck than skill that enabled me to block the deadly thrust as the man leapt towards me, and then more luck still that he stumbled and I slipped my knife between his ribs, hard and fast. He fell heavily into me but I rolled away, sword still in hand, to face the other two horsemen.

"Go back." I wanted my voice to sound intimidating, but to me it sounded like a croak.

However, they gave me one final look of horror and galloped away, so I suppose it worked.

I'm always a little dazed after combat, the scent of blood metallic in my mouth, and it was a moment before I realized that everyone had moved forward to stare at me. Hakan pushed past Priven to stop in front of me.

"Are you hurt?"

I could not seem to find my voice again, so I shook my head.

"You're covered in blood. Come, let's clean you up."

I nodded. *Speak, fool.* "Right. Is anyone hurt?"

Several more men were around me, and they all seemed to be jabbering, though the voices blurred together. I felt light-headed from the pain in my ribs, which seemed to be growing rather than receding.

"No. Take off your tunic."

It felt odd to strip down next to the well, with dozens of people watching, but I did. Hakan poured several buckets of icy water over me, and my muscles tightened in the chill. I knelt, leaning my elbow on one knee, so that he could dump another bucket of water over my hair, which was stringy with blood. It would be a pleasant smell, coppery and warm, if it didn't also taste of fear.

"You *are* hurt."

"What?"

"Go get a bandage!" He flung the words over his shoulder to whoever would listen, and several people moved away from the small crowd. Hakan examined a deep cut on my arm. I didn't remember it happening at all.

I stood; or rather, I tried. My head suddenly whirled with the pain in my ribs and I clutched the edge of the well, feeling ashamed of my weakness. I wished everyone would stop staring at me.

Hakan looked me over and suddenly cried out, "Kemen! Your leg!"

"What?" I felt stupidly confused until I looked down. Blood was dripping steadily from a generous cut high on the outside of my breeches on the right, soaking through the thick fabric. That must have happened right at the end, when I didn't move quickly enough out of the horseman's way. His sword had trailed behind him, a poor move, hardly an intentional strike. He'd been off balance as his horse stumbled into me and then into the wall.

"Come on. Let's go inside. You'll need to strip down completely."

I blinked in surprise. Was he going to dress the wounds himself? Surely that wasn't part of a prince's education.

He put one arm about me for support as we walked the short distance from the well to the boarding house, but my pride would not let me lean on him until the end. Aye, there was a distant ache in my right leg, I started to feel it as we walked, but it was more a feeling of weakness than pain in the leg that made me limp. There was a growing cloud at the edges of my vision, and the ground seemed to rise steeply in front of me as we got closer to the boarding house.

"It's only a little farther. Come on." He hitched my right arm about his shoulders more firmly and the pain in my ribs exploded.

Everything whirled, darkness threatening to take me, and I stopped to lean over, putting my head down close to my knees.

I could hear the fear in Hakan's voice as he spoke to me. "Come Kemen, it's not much farther."

I couldn't seem to get enough air, and I closed my eyes for a moment as I took a deep breath. I coughed, and the sudden searing pain well nigh overcame me. Everything was spinning, and how I stayed on my feet I don't know. Hakan hauled me by my arm, stumbling and half-blind, into the boarding house and straight to a bed.

Flat on my back, the coughing eased a little, though the pain of each breath brought spots before my eyes. I tasted blood in my mouth after each bout of coughing. Hakan pulled off my boots and bloodstained breeches, swearing at the wound on my leg. I didn't know he knew some of the words he used, and I laughed until I gasped for breath and coughed up more blood.

"Hakan?" I felt as if I were underwater, breathing water, forcing it out of my lungs only with difficulty. "You have to kill the horse."

"What are you talking about?" He was not really listening.

"The horse. Its leg was broken." I coughed again, and my skin prickled with cold suddenly as spots whirled before me. I let my eyes close, but Hakan's working on my leg would not let me sleep. He cleaned the wound and started to bandage it.

"It needs stitches."

He looked up at me, his eyes wide and afraid.

158

"In my pack. A tin in the bottom." I coughed again. "Needle and sinew."

He dug around in the pack and finally pulled out the tin. "What do I do?"

"Sew it up."

"I don't know how." He sounded panicky.

"Then get a woman to do it." A woman's stitches would be more even anyway.

He disappeared and came back only a minute later with Twilling's wife. Lira Twilling was a calm and stolid woman, but now she looked nearly as frightened as Hakan did. She pushed Hakan down to sit in the one chair and knelt to examine the wound.

"Hold the edges like this." Her voice was steady, and I hoped Hakan heard it as reassuring.

Hakan's fingers were cool and I could feel them shaking slightly. She looked at me and I nodded. She and Hakan both held the edges of the wound firmly, as if they expected me to twitch away. I closed my eyes. The sting of the needle was distant and inconsequential next to the searing pain in my ribs. My left hand explored the damage gently. Three ribs broken, another possibly so. Cracked maybe. At least one of the three was broken in two places.

I had to cough between the third and fourth stitches, and swallowed blood. Hakan cursed, I think because my leg jerked a little, and then began to apologize in a manner entirely too courtly for a border town.

I interrupted him roughly. "Naoki, keep your tongue civil in a woman's presence." It was the

159

best I could do to cover his blunder, but even that left me gasping for breath.

"That must have hurt. I'll have to do that stitch again. When we finish I'll bring him some ale." Twilling's wife spoke quietly to Hakan.

I shook my head. "Only my ribs hurt."

"Where, what happened?" Hakan looked down at my ribs for the first time. I used my left arm to point. Raising my right arm caused flickering tongues of pain to shoot through my entire torso.

"The horse's knee hit me here."

He looked more closely. If my skin had been lighter, I suppose it would have been easier to see, but he must have seen something because he cursed again. I laughed but only for a moment; even tightening my stomach hurt. I clenched my jaw in an effort not to cough again, but I couldn't contain it, and when I took my hand from my mouth, it was spattered with blood. I heard his voice distantly, but I could no longer make out his words, and slipped into the warm darkness that had been beckoning for some minutes.

I WOKE ON my side gasping for breath, gagging and spitting blood. Lira Twilling brought a bucket, and Hakan insisted that I stay as I was, lying on my right side on the broken ribs, because I'd nearly choked to death before he turned me. It hurt, but he was right. I coughed and spit and tried not to groan at the pain.

Lira Twilling brought me brandy, which helped with the pain some. I told Hakan that the bodies must be burned out of respect for the dead. I didn't see it done, but I smelled the distinctive acrid scent of burning flesh. By nightfall I was exhausted, but I was breathing a little more easily and I could lie on my back without choking. Hakan asked me if I wanted dinner, but I shook my head.

Hakan ate dinner eyeing me worriedly. I let my eyes close, but I couldn't really sleep. Finally I had him help me sit up, pillowed against the headboard of the bed. I closed my eyes and thought, because I didn't have anything else to do. I didn't devise any real plans to help Hakan regain his throne, but it gave me something to contemplate rather than the pain.

Lira Twilling knocked on the door and said that several people wanted to see me. I nodded.

But Hakan looked at me oddly and asked, "Are you hot? You're sweating."

"No." If anything I was a little cold.

Lira put her hand to my forehead as if I were a little child. "I think you're feverish. How do you feel?" I remember it startled me that she touched my skin as if I were any Tuyet; she wiped her hand on her apron afterward.

"Well enough, considering." Talking was absurdly difficult and left me breathless, my vision fading at the edges.

She frowned, but she opened the door to let in the first of my visitors. There must have been a crowd, men and women, a few younger boys accompanied by older brothers or sisters. I don't remember much of what they said, but I do remember smiling weakly at them, wishing they would

161

go away, at least until I could speak properly. Their gratitude was welcome, though I'm not sure what I could have done differently, but it shamed me to be in bed while others walked around.

The last person who asked to see me was a young girl accompanied by her father.

"I wanted to thank you."

I didn't recognize her voice, but finally I realized she was the girl the horseman had pointed to when he said he wanted pretty girls. I didn't know her father either, he'd only trained with the sickle once or twice.

"What's your name?" Phraa, my voice was so weak.

"Bethla." She was pretty; the horseman was right. A round face with a shy smile, a turned up nose, blond hair with brown eyes and the comfortable figure of one used to working outdoors.

"I hope you didn't see the fight."

She shook her head. "No, I closed the door. My father told me how brave you were."

I smiled in surprise. "What else could I have done?"

She smiled back at me, shy and looking very young. I was already in the king's service at that age. "Father says you're a hero."

I smiled again. The darkness called and I didn't hear her leave, though I should have bid her farewell.

I woke sometime past midnight, thirsty and needing to relieve myself. When I sat up, with no little effort, the ends of the bones ground painfully against each other. The pale moonlight barely lit the room, and I stood still for a moment, trying to remember if there was a bucket close by or whether I needed to go outside. Was there water in the kitchen? When I moved toward the door, I stumbled over a dark mass and barely caught myself with one hand on the wall. Even that simple shock was nauseatingly painful.

"What do you need?" The dark mass was Hakan, rolled up in his cloak.

"To go outside. And a drink." I wondered distantly why he wasn't in his own room down the hall in a bed, rather than on the floor. Probably worried about me, though he didn't need to be.

"The bucket's in the corner." He leaned on one elbow. "There's water here, but brandy's in the kitchen if you want it."

"Water's fine."

"I'll get it for you if you want."

"Water's fine," I repeated. I just wanted to lie down again.

Lira Twilling was right; I did have a fever. I was cold that night, despite the warm weather and the thick blanket I pulled up nearly over my head. But it wasn't serious and I slept more deeply sometime near dawn.

Hakan wasn't there when I woke around noon, so I pushed myself up, swaying and weak, waiting for the pain to recede. My breeches were washed and folded, my shirt replaced by a new one. I supposed the old one couldn't be salvaged. Pulling the shirt over my head was a long and painful endeavor. I wondered whether I should sit down before venturing down the hallway, but that's not my nature. I buckled on my sword more out of habit than anything else; I wasn't fit to wield it.

Someone had repaired the slit in my breeches; the color was so faded it was hard to tell which stains were new. I followed voices down the hall to the dining room and pushed open the door to enter, hoping just to make it to a chair. Everyone stood, their faces swimming before me, and Hakan darted forward to guide me to a seat. I dropped into it and leaned forward, feeling the blood fill my head and clear it, the voices surrounding me becoming more defined.

When I straightened, there were dozens of eyes on me, and I nearly fled back down the hall. But a warrior faces his fears, and so I steeled myself for the onslaught.

I don't like being stared at. You would think, having taught fighting, that I'd be used to people's eyes on me, but the soldiers looked at the moves and techniques, not at me. I cannot say why it is different, but somehow it is.

Someone gave me a thick napkin, a bowl of steaming vegetable soup, rich black bread and goatsmilk cheese, ale and water, and a generous serving of the best lamb of the spring. I ate slowly. Everything seemed difficult, and I had to turn aside to cough frequently, the pain spreading in a throbbing wave from my ribs up to my scalp, making my skin tingle with clammy sweat.

The conversation flowed around me like river water around a rock or a fallen tree. I was surrounded by it, but apart, as I concentrated on guiding each bite into my mouth and on not dropping the mug of ale. Water tasted better, but ale eased the pain a little, and by the time I finished I felt noticeably better. I leaned back in the chair, resting my right arm on the table so it did not pull my side.

Hakan leaned over to speak in my ear. "How are you feeling?" His eyes searched my face, and I thought he looked older suddenly.

I smiled as best I could. "Better. How much did this dinner cost?" Probably all I had left, I imagined. At the time, it seemed a logical question, because I'd no longer be able to train the townsmen, but now it seems a bit thick-headed.

"Nothing."

I coughed, bringing the napkin up to my mouth as I leaned over. I could not conceal my gasp of pain, but the blood in the napkin was much less this time.

Hakan spoke quietly. "They want to sing you the Hero Song when you're ready to hear it."

I sat up in surprise. "What? No!"

Adin was sitting across the table, and he looked over at my exclamation. He leaned forward, placing both arms on the table to look squarely into my face. "Have you had enough to eat?"

I nodded.

"Then we'll sing." He smiled broadly.

"No!"

He stopped in surprise. There is an old tradition that the changing of dynasties comes when the father of a new line performs a great feat of heroism, one that is recognized as absolutely selfless and involves great personal risk, perhaps even death. Hakan's father's great grandfather became the first king of his dynasty by virtue of the heroism of his father, who died in battle defending a village from the Ophrani. Of course, there are many heroic deeds that are not the forerunner of a new dynasty at all. There are other conditions; a failing rule, a great threat to the kingdom, and of course the singing of the Song itself, among other things. I couldn't remember them all, and I was fairly sure Adin didn't either.

"We will sing the Hero Song for you."

More eyes turned toward me, and my answer fell into a suddenly quiet room.

"You can't sing the song for me. I'm not," I lost my breath and had to begin again. "I'm not the one to lead." Phraa, how hard could it be to see that? I cannot even read, much less navigate the maze of politics with kings and nobles.

"You can lead us. We would have you as our king." The voice rang out from the back, and was greeted by lusty cheering.

"No!" My sudden shout brought dizzying pain and I nearly retched. But they were listening and I forced out the words. "If you would follow me, I will serve at the pleasure of the prince Hakan Ithel."

There was a murmur of confusion. "The prince is missing, he's been gone for months. Vidar rules in Stonehaven."

I had their trust, and I would use it. "The prince has been among you. He's well-educated, well-prepared for his role." Perhaps I embellished a little, for he wasn't yet ready. But he would be by the time he attained the throne. A few people looked toward Hakan.

"Aye, Hakan Ithel. My friend and my prince. Soon to be my king."

Drama was needed. They were confused and didn't quite know what I wanted of them. I stood painfully, rising to my full height before dropping to one knee before Hakan and presenting him with the hilt of my sword.

"Hakan Ithel, I pledge you my devoted service and my life's blood for as long as you serve the people of Erdem." A much simplified version of the warrior's oath of service, but it would have to do. My vision was blurring and I couldn't seem to get enough air. I nearly fell as I stood again, using the edge of the table to steady myself. "Who is with me?"

There was a great rustling as they whispered to each other.

"Stand, Hakan."

He stood, awed and pale, beside me.

"This is your prince. Surely I'm not the only one willing to swear allegiance to him!" *Come, now is the time. Now, if ever.*

There was a hesitation, then Feo Priven stepped forward. "I will. If you trust him, I will too."

I will forever be thankful that good Feo led the crowd when he knelt. Another man followed him, and another, and in a moment the whole room was on their knees.

It was a great effort, but I managed to get the words out. "Do you swear allegiance to Hakan Ithel, your devoted service and your life's blood for as long as he serves the people of Erdem?"

167

The answers were a murmured flood. "I do." "Yes." "We do."

Hakan stared at me in shock as I nearly fell back into my seat. The men stood again, some going out into the street, bobbing their heads in respect as they walked by, some remaining for the warmth and the camaraderie that filled the room. I was well and truly exhausted, nearly blind with pain and dizziness. I tried to catch my breath, coughed, groaned, and coughed again. I vaguely remember Hakan and someone else catching at my shoulders as I slid to my knees on the floor, still coughing.

There was more blood. One part of my mind noted distantly that it was mostly dark and clotted, a good sign, but the searing pain took most of my attention. I finally choked out the largest clot of blood and gasped for breath, leaning against the leg of the table. Someone gave me a mug of water.

Hakan and Mullin helped me into the chair again. Once I could breathe, I felt reasonably clear-headed, and in a few minutes could stand with only a bit of help.

PAIN IS TIRING. I slept deeply that night, though I woke often. My coughing was much better, and near dawn I slept more easily. When I woke, the room was bright and warm. Hakan was sitting near the window working on something at a small table.

"What are you doing?" My voice came out a croak.

He spun around and smiled. "Some of the men helped me with the map. Would you like some lunch?"

"Lunch?" Had I slept that long?

"Aye, lunch." He imitated my tone on the word aye and smiled. "Priven sent his oldest son off south to Rysling with word that the village has sworn allegiance to me and asking for their support." He called down the hallway for my lunch before pulling the stool closer to sit perched looking down at me, sober and very intent. "Why did you do it, Kemen? You could have been king yourself."

I wanted to laugh, but it came out sounding rather strangled as pain shot through me. "I am no king, Hakan. That's your place, not mine."

Even if I had accepted the crown, the dynasty of Kemen Sendoa would have lasted for all of one generation. What woman would have me, and without a woman, how would I have an heir? And that beside my many other failures. Hakan had both the right and the better training, not to mention the chance at an heir.

Besides, if Hakan were alive, it was inherently unstable to have anyone else on the throne. The thought was terrifying.

What would happen to Hakan? When I died, who would succeed me? Someone would claim the throne and call himself king, with or without the Hero Song. Vidar. Taisto. Itxaro. Hayato. Even Priven. Anyone with the desire for power. There would be war.

Lira Twilling knocked at the door and entered quietly with a bowl of soup and bread melting into it. "Would you like water or ale? Or both?"

"Water. Thank you." I cursed my weak voice.

She returned in a few moments. Hakan helped me sit up, and I leaned forward a moment, letting my head hang down to steady the dizziness. Suddenly I grasped the thought that had been tugging at my mind for the past two days, fluttering just out of reach in my mental fog.

"Did you hear what they said before I challenged the leader?"

He shook his head.

"They wanted food. And girls. But the food was their first demand, I think the orders they received. What do you know of Rikuto?"

"Not enough." He was watching me closely now, and I took several bites as I thought.

"Girls are a common demand when men are riding about." Not one I agreed with, but common nonetheless.

Hakan was already thinking aloud, speaking my thoughts better than I could have expressed them. "Raiding on horseback is hardly an efficient way of providing food for a nation. They must be desperate."

I nodded and watched the bread melt into my soup. Breathing was difficult, and I took a sip of water and a few deep breaths to clear my head.

"Do you think we should parley with them? Crops were good last year, and we can spare some." He looked across at me seriously.

"Aye, we should. What will you ask in return?"

"No more raids of course, all along the border, not just here. I want to get back to the peace we had when my father was young. Our countries were not so opposed then, and I don't see why they should remain so now." He stared at the floor thoughtfully.

I nodded. "Give me two more days and I'll go."

He looked at me as if I had said I would fly across the mountains by flapping my arms. "You're in no shape to go. I'll go myself."

I shook my head. "No. You're the prince, soon to be king if all goes well. The king does not go about parleying with leaders of raiding parties." A deep breath hurt but helped clear the persistent fog about my brain.

Hakan's voice was flowing on. "We'll offer some food in goodwill, and then try to reestablish trade relations. They broke down years ago, but now is a good time to revive them. That was my father's fault; he demanded unreasonable prices. Rikuto has had several years of bad crops, but I didn't know it was so desperate yet."

He pulled the map from the table and put it in front of my face. "Here, this pass is wide enough for carts, and joins the Lobar Road here. It goes straight to Enkotan, more or less. If we could make contact with Tafari, I think we'd have a good chance."

"Tafari. Is that in the High Tongue?"

"Yes, it means 'he who inspires awe.' A good name for a king, don't you think?"

I nodded.

171

Names are important. My name, Kemen Sendoa, is a warrior's name, and I strive to live up to it. Kemen means strong, and Sendoa means courage or vigor, both in Kumar, the tongue of warriors. The prince's name, Hakan Ithel, is a kingly name. Hakan means emperor or king in modern High Tongue, and is a common one in the last bloodline. Ithel means generous lord in archaic High Tongue. His father was Hakan Emyr. Emyr also means king, but in archaic High Tongue. Not all names have such clearly defined meanings, and not all names fit their owners. But among warriors, we who live and die by honor, names carry meaning.

"What is his first name?" I knew it, but my mind was so foggy I could not remember.

"Ashmu."

It was in Kumar, odd for a king. It means 'just warrior.'

"Aye, I'll ride out in two days."

He was lost in thought, staring at the map. The soup was good, and I felt stronger, more clearheaded.

"The two that left, they haven't come back?"

Hakan looked at me absently and shook his head. I wondered what they would tell their commander.

TWELVE

"Kemen, you're in no shape to ride anywhere. It's absurd! I'll go."

"A king does not ride out to deliver his own messages!" I was frustrated. If we waited too long, Rikuto might well decide to send another, larger party. It would be much better to approach them peacefully before they made another attempt.

"Then I'll send someone else! Mullin or Adin or..." he stopped.

"A king does not send his messages by blacksmiths and shepherds. You must take care for your prestige, Hakan. If you want him to think you a king, you must act like one."

He cursed. "You can't ride."

"I'll strap up my ribs."

He raised his eyebrows.

"It will help the pain. I'll need to be able to loosen it at night."

Lira Twilling made the strap for me, a wide band of fabric with a buckle sewn on, so I could tighten and loosen it with only my left hand. When I stripped off my shirt to test it, she and Hakan flinched at the ugly bruising. They raised their eyes to me doubtfully. I almost blacked out when I tried it, but once it was on it was a considerable help.

Despite my best intentions, I did not leave until three days after the village swore its allegiance to Hakan. Thosin lent me a horse, a beautiful chestnut mare built for speed. Hakan wrote me a letter of authority to negotiate on his behalf. He also gave me a much better idea of how much food we could actually spare.

The night before I left, he sat at the little table in my room, chewed his lip, and stared at the parchment for some time. Then he wrote the letter in one frowning rush, read it over, and handed it to me. "What do you think?"

I shrugged. "I'm sure it's fine."

"You didn't even read it."

I swallowed. I should have told him then that I couldn't read. But I was tired, and my ribs hurt, and I wasn't brave enough. I glanced over the letter; I didn't pretend to read it, but I didn't admit that I couldn't. I shrugged again and handed it back. "Thank you. I'll do what I can."

I was ashamed.

I didn't expect to see Tafari himself, only the leader of the nearest raiding party. I was merely to deliver a formal letter from Hakan to Tafari detail-

174

ing Hakan's desire to reestablish trade relations and a mutually agreeable peace along the border. I would also offer the measure of food as a goodwill gesture for an immediate halt in the raids.

I took only a small pack with some bread and jerky and a long pole with a rough flag tied to the top. The colors were a little off, rough cloth dyed hastily the day before rather than the customary rich velvets, but it would signal my official intent. The path to the Ising Pass was easy to find, and I was seen off by a small crowd waving and shouting encouragement. It was an odd feeling, and I hoped they would cheer Hakan with the same enthusiasm. Hakan was worried about me, but I felt confident that I was healing well.

I'd rested the first two days after the town swore its allegiance to Hakan, but the day I left, I limped about the square, testing my strength. The pain in my leg was tolerable, my shoulder barely worth mentioning. The days of rest had helped my ribs considerably, though I was still troubled by bouts of coughing that brought spots before my eyes. The blood had mostly gone though, and except when I coughed, my breath came easily, though not without pain.

When I first opened the door, the street was mostly quiet. I chose the short walk toward the well, and I was glad it was short because I was unsteadier than I'd imagined. But no matter; I would be riding, not walking. Several women were drawing water at the well, and they smiled shyly at me as I approached. I reached the stone edge with relief and turned to lean against it, half-sitting with my eyes closed. I think they were cautious of me, but I had to either sit or fall on my face, else I would have shied away.

The air was cool, but the sun was warm on my shoulders, and my mind wandered a moment. The women finished drawing water, chatting all the while, though I felt their eyes on me at times. Always afraid of me, though they need not have been. One of them said Bethla's name, and I thought her voice was softer than it had been.

A girl cried out, and I opened my eyes to see a small boy hurtling toward me. He crashed into my leg, wrapping his arms about it in a tight embrace. His forehead bounced off the bandage on my thigh, and I winced, hiding it as best I could. A girl was running toward me calling him. I thought she was calling him because she was afraid of me, afraid for him, and it stung.

I reached down to pull him away from my leg. "What is this?"

He looked up at me, a laughing grin splitting his face. "You are the best!"

"What? What's your name?" I tried to shake off a feeling of unreality.

"Rihol. I want to be like you." He took a step back and flung out his hands wildly, holding an imaginary sword. "There! And there! And then they fall!" He spun around and fell dramatically, his legs flopping up toward the sky.

I laughed in spite of my confusion. "That's very good. You're well on your way. How old are you?"

He jumped up to come stand before me, clasping his hands together properly. It is a Common custom that I never learned; soldiers have different courtesies. But it was polite, and spoke well of his parents that he did it automatically. "I am four years and nine months old. How old are you?" That question was less proper, but I didn't mind.

"Ancient. I'm thirty three." I did suddenly feel ancient, aching and sober in the face of his innocent adoration.

His eyes widened. "Thirty three! That is old. But someday I will be old too." He spoke very solemnly. "And when I am, I want to be like you. Father says you're a hero, like the great heroes in the stories."

I smiled slightly as the girl drew up behind him.

"Rihol! Come away." She pulled at his arm as he tried to extricate himself. She was embarrassed, her face turning pink in frustration.

I gathered my courage and spoke. "Excuse me." Speaking to girls, women, takes nearly as much courage as battle. She was pretty, too, and it only made her more terrifying. Nothing can pain a man like the scorn of a woman.

She looked up at me in surprise, her eyes wide.

"He isn't bothering me. I don't mind."

She smiled and shrugged uncomfortably, and I knew I was right. She did fear me. I don't know why I said it, especially with Rihol still standing there, but the words came without thought.

"Do you think me a monster? Do you think I would hurt him?"

She dropped her eyes to the ground, and Rihol looked back and forth between us. "I suppose not." But she was not entirely reassured.

I gestured to the edge of the well beside me. "Sit. Please."

I stood, pushing away the slight dizziness. I bowed low, lower than would be normal for a warrior to a commoner, because I wanted her to trust me. Men are so weak before women, and the best women do not realize their power and use it against us. But I sat immediately after, saving my strength for the afternoon ride. "I would like to see more of Rihol's fighting prowess, and you are welcome to watch and see that I do him no harm."

She was more embarrassed, and I felt only a little guilt for it. However, she did sit carefully some distance away from me on the edge of the well.

"Rihol, will you show me again how you fight?"

He grinned with glee, jumping up and flopping down in the dirt as he imitated the raiders, thrashing his arms about as he supposed I must have done.

Suddenly I wondered. "Did you see the fight?" It was no sight for a child.

He pouted. "No."

"Good."

Rihol was happily rattling on. "But my father told me all about it. There was one of them who fought you first, then a hundred more all at once! And then a man on a horse who ran the horse over you, but you got up and won!"

I chuckled, rubbing my ribs absently. "More or less. I wouldn't recommend being run over by a horse when you're a warrior."

He played for another few minutes, until the girl stood. "Come, Rihol. We must go now."

I felt oddly saddened at their going, though the girl had hardly been happy to be there. But I smiled when she turned back to smile at me tentatively.

I ATE LUNCH at Twilling's before I departed that afternoon. I meant to set an easy pace; I don't have the foolish wish to injure myself out of pride. At least not often. But the horse made good time, and I was well into the mountains by nightfall. I didn't make a fire, supping instead on meat, cheese, and rich bread that Lira Twilling had packed for me. She'd also packed me a nearly full bottle of precious brandy for the pain. I had only a little because I didn't want to become inattentive, but that little was quite welcome.

I slept well that night, though I expected that the uneven ground would hurt terribly. I must have been too tired to care, for I woke with the early morning light streaming through the leaves onto my face.

I put the strap back around my ribs; I didn't want to sleep in it for fear of the bones healing wrong, but I couldn't ride without it. Thosin had filled the saddlebags with grain so I fed the horse, and in a few minutes we were off again. We crossed a small stream, and the horse drank long before we continued. In the morning we made good time again, but the ground became much steeper as we went farther into the mountains and our pace slowed.

The pass grew narrower, sometimes only a slim shelf on the side of the mountain, the ground falling away to my right. It curved around the side of Mount Crianuloku, which means something like dagger-clouds or blade-fog. I imagined it was named for the way the peak cut through the clouds; it made the sunrises violently beautiful.

I didn't expect to find the Rikutan camp so quickly, but it was still several hours before dusk when I heard voices around a corner of the rock-face on my left. I pulled the letter from Hakan from the saddlebag, the twisting in my saddle stretching my side painfully. I sat up straighter and took a deep breath before riding around the corner. The guards were surprised, shouting at me as I stopped my horse compliantly and dismounted at their command. I wondered whether they would honor the flag that proclaimed my official mission.

"Who might you be?" A man pushed to the front and addressed me courteously in Kumar, though the words of some of the others had been a little rougher.

"Kemen Sendoa." I bowed courteously, as a warrior does when he meets another warrior. It is the courtesy that signifies respect between equals who are both armed and both honorable. Courtesy that keeps your swords sheathed. "I would see your commander. I have a message for him."

He appraised me thoughtfully. He was tall, the top of his head just higher than my shoulder, and well built, with golden hair surrounding a handsome face. He bowed in return, graceful and appropriately courteous. "Kenta Isamu." Kenta, straight arrow, and Isamu, righteous warrior. A good name, one that might fit him well, if his clear gaze was to be believed. "Come. You will have to disarm, of course."

The camp felt much like an Erdemen camp. The tents were different colors, the flags were embroidered with brilliant red Rikutan lilies rather than golden Erdemen eagles, but it was not so different. The smell of the food was much the same, simple camp fare, venison and fowl stretched to go farther by the addition of onions, tubers, and mushrooms, all roasted together on skewers over the fires. The Rikutan horses were less proud, the men's weapons not quite as good as ours, but the camp was more familiar than alien. It gave me hope that Hakan's offer would be well received.

Isamu led me to the largest tent, a brilliant white, red and gold embroidered with red Rikutan lilies and the emblem of the Rikutan king. The fabric was more luxurious than I would have expected for an army officer, and I wondered if Rikutan traditions were more different than I'd realized. The men stared at me as they parted in front of Isamu to let us pass.

I saw two Dari soldiers among their number. It was all I could do not to stare at them. I felt their eyes on me as well, interested, evaluating. One was older than I was, with officer's stripes on his uniform, and the other young, probably not long out of training. I wanted to speak with them, to ask them how Rikuto dealt with the challenge of Dari-Tuyet relations, but it would have broken protocol. I was there as Hakan's representative, not for my own curiosity.

I disarmed at the entrance to the tent. If I hadn't already been well aware of the risk of the parley, I would have realized it then. Handing over my sword and knives with a courteous bow to Isamu felt like signing an agreement with my own blood. I hoped it was worth it.

I wasn't afraid; I was more than willing to die for Hakan's throne, for Erdem. It was more a feeling of humming tension, the weight of my responsibility to properly convey Hakan's message. If I failed, if I was not courteous enough, properly respectful and yet properly proud of my own country, noble and dignified enough to be a king's messenger, we might lose that tenuous grasp on peace. I wondered how many other soldiers were waiting beyond the next bend in the road. When the invasion might begin.

The tent was lit by a series of small openings between the pale white and gold walls and the dark red fabric of the roof, the light streaming in as golden bars. I nearly ran into Isamu, who stopped immediately inside the door with a deep, graceful bow much like our own.

He spoke in Rikutan to a man who was kneeling on a flat pillow behind a low table of polished dark wood. The man looked at me, and I bowed, taking care to convey great courtesy without bowing too deeply. Hakan's message should not appear as though it came from a supplicant. Isamu bowed again and stepped to the side. Other men stood behind the commander and in a line along the right side of the tent, apparently waiting for orders.

182

The commander stood gracefully, his eyes on me.

I bowed again. "My name is Kemen Sendoa. I bring a message from Hakan Ithel, Crown Prince of Erdem, Glorious and Free, to your king Ashmu Tafari, and a request for parley about the raids over our borders."

The man studied me intently, his eyes not leaving me as he bowed with utmost courtesy. "I am Zuzay Tafari. I will parley with you." His Kumar was accented but quite clear, his voice pleasant and neither too deep nor too high. He was not quite as tall as Isamu but more powerfully built, near to me in age. He too was light-haired, with golden brown eyes that were clear and honest. Zuzay, the Kumar word for pure. And the last name Tafari.

I looked at him more closely. "Are you related to the king, Ashmu Tafari?"

He nodded without taking his eyes from me. "Aye, he's my elder brother."

I could believe it; he bore himself with royal grace. One of the men standing behind him stepped up quietly and whispered in his ear a moment. It took me a moment to recognize him as one of the two horsemen who had fled after the raid. I wondered what he was saying, my stomach tightening. I tried to remain impassive and confident.

Tafari listened to him, his eyes on me, and finally nodded and motioned the man away. The horseman nodded tensely and stepped back, watching me with fear and a bit of what I took to be hatred.

183

Tafari stared at me in silence a moment, looking a bit perplexed and very thoughtful. I wondered whether he would order me killed immediately or want to question me first.

"Vorstin tells me you defeated the last party I sent out, except for him and one other. Alone. Is this true?"

"Aye."

He looked me over with interest, cool and inscrutable. "Were you wounded?"

"Aye." I nodded again. He stared at me again, and I wondered what he wanted of me. A detailed retelling? A look at my ribs, with the dark bruising and the uneven row of bumps where the bones had fractured?

"What was done with the bodies of my men?"

"They were burned the next day." It was the respectful thing, what any warrior would want done, and he nodded.

"Why did you fight them? The town has plenty of food. Risking death for a bit of grain seems foolish, and I don't take you for a fool."

I smiled then. "Did he not tell you the rest of what they demanded?"

He studied me curiously.

"Aye, they wanted food. They also demanded two or three young girls. I offered them food enough for the party for a peaceful resolution. But they refused to take only the food, so I challenged their leader to single combat to decide the issue."

He was staring at me intently now, his expression unreadable.

"I won, and I hoped that would be sufficient. But the men on foot charged me, and then the three remaining horsemen. The last horseman was the one that wounded me, and the other two, the two who came back, lacked the courage to fight with their friends."

I wanted to laugh at the absurdity. I wondered what he would think, whether he would believe me over his own man. Unlikely, at best, though by his look he would simply send me on my way, my mission a failure, rather than have me executed. He looked too honorable to execute an official messenger, despite the behavior of his men.

He glanced back at the man who had spoken to him and spoke quietly to him in Rikutan. The man stepped forward and bowed, glancing at me. I wished I could understand Rikutan. Tafari's voice rose in quick anger and the other man shrugged a little. In a moment, Tafari nodded curtly and the man bowed, then retreated out of the tent.

Tafari smiled politely at me. "Come, sit. You must be tired, and perhaps in pain." He knelt again with his knees on the pillow, sitting on his heels. At his motion, one of the men slipped a similar pillow in front of me, and I knelt on the other side of the low table. For me, the movement wasn't quite so effortless. The movement pulled on the stitches in my leg, but my ribs hurt more. I tried to conceal my wince of pain, but I don't think I was entirely successful, for he was studying me closely.

"Forgive me for the lack of chairs. They are not very portable."

I nodded.

"I did not order any girls captured. The men will be disciplined appropriately. Now, tell me about this prince, Hakan Ithel." He leaned forward

185

to rest his hands on the table as he spoke, and I warmed to his informality. It was not impolite, but simply less formal, as if we were two friends rather than representatives of two kingdoms nearly at war.

I licked my lips and began. "The prince Hakan Ithel and I believe that the demand for food by the raiding party was born of desperation."

He sat back, his gaze quite cool and a little angry at the word. No one likes to be called desperate.

"For this we cannot fault you or the king Ashmu Tafari. Any king will sacrifice another nation's men to save his own people. It is the nature of a king, or at least a good one. The prince is aware of the famine in Rikuto, and understands the need. He believes our kingdoms can and should be on better terms. He is aware that trade between Erdem and Rikuto broke down when his father the king Hakan Emyr was young because of his father's greed in asking unreasonable prices for food and other trade goods.

"He would seek to remedy this. He offers an initial delivery of grain as a goodwill gesture while we begin negotiations, which in turn will be aimed at reaching a permanent peace treaty and a reasonable trade agreement between our two kingdoms. In return, he expects that all raids across the border will halt immediately."

Tafari studied me at across the table. I handed him Hakan's letter to the king, neatly folded and sealed with wax, and then the letter of introduction authorizing me to speak on Hakan's behalf. He read this one twice, glancing up at me occasionally. Again I wondered what was in it.

Finally he put it down and smiled. He looked as though smiling came naturally to him, the corners of his mouth turning up agreeably even when he was quite serious. "It seems the prince trusts you implicitly. I also am authorized to speak on my brother's behalf, though I will not enter any binding agreements yet. Tell me more about this offer of grain."

Ah, so they were indeed desperate. I nodded. "The initial offer is ten wagonloads of various grains. It's past planting season, but some of the late barleys will still give you a crop this autumn if you sow them immediately. We would deliver them to you on the Lobar Road Pass, whereupon they would become your responsibility to transport."

My vision was almost blurring with my need for air, and I took a deep breath, thankful for the band around my chest. Even with it, I could barely hide the pain. "Our crops were relatively good last year, but we would need three weeks to gather and deliver the grain. It would come from the interior, closer to Stonehaven. The outlying villages most vulnerable to your raids have the least to spare. It serves neither of us to continue squeezing them for food." Another deep breath.

He studied me for a moment. "Vidar rules in Stonehaven now, I believe."

I nodded.

"How then will you accomplish this?"

The question had troubled me as well. I tried to sound completely confident, as if I were telling known facts instead of a shaky idea. "Vidar rules because the people fear your kingdom. The raids have made people uneasy. There have also been raids from the north, from the Tarvil. I imagine you have suffered them as well."

He nodded slightly.

"Nekane Vidar has credibility with the army and has already begun strengthening the northern border. Suvari and kedani may soon strengthen our eastern border as well." I could not stop the cough that interrupted me. "However, the army prefers the prince Hakan Ithel, not only because the throne is rightfully his, but because he was trained for kingship from birth. They hope Vidar will protect them, but if the prince can provide peace along the borders, they will support him completely.

"With this agreement—" I had to stop again to cough and continued with a deep painful breath. "With this agreement, Hakan Ithel stands to regain the throne that is rightfully his. He needs your co-operation. But you need his as well, for Hakan Ithel has much promise as a good king, though he is young. Vidar is aggressive and less forgiving, unlikely to reach any kind of peaceful settlement with your kingdom. He will seek to solidify his position by force, both against resistance within Erdem and against your kingdom.

"The prince believes our kingdoms can be at peace, and will pursue it. Peaceful trade will serve the needs of both our peoples and prevent much bloodshed." I coughed again and tried not to show how much it pained me.

His next question surprised me, for I expected him to want more details about Hakan's current situation, whether he even had the power to deliver what I had promised. But instead he asked, "How did a Dari come to serve in the Erdemen army?"

"I was a foundling in Llewton, southeast of Stonehaven."

He nodded. I had heard that in Rikuto foundlings were trained for the army also, and by his acceptance I imagined he understood. "There aren't many Dari in Erdem."

I shook my head.

"One of my best officers is Dari. Dari are more common in my kingdom. He's a fierce warrior, though I haven't heard of him ever defeating twelve men alone. Or was it fourteen? The prince Hakan Ithel is fortunate to have you serve him."

What was the proper response to that? Yes, he is lucky to have me? Certainly not. I bowed slightly. "I am honored to serve him."

He studied me a moment. "He is quite young, isn't he?"

"Aye, eighteen now. A good man, wise for his age." My mind felt a bit foggy as my ribs ached, and a deep breath helped clear my head, though it brought a more prolonged bout of coughing. He was watching me closely as I sat up straighter.

"You served in the king Hakan Emyr's army?"

"Aye. In the suvari for four years, then I was transferred to the kedani, where I served for eleven years."

"You have much experience as a warrior." It was a statement, not a question, and I merely nodded. "With leaders too, no doubt. Your army is much respected. Professional. Honorable."

I smiled. "I am honored that you think so."

He studied me a moment more before standing. I stood too. My right leg was stiff and painful, and there was no doubt he saw it that time.

"I believe the prince Hakan Ithel is more fortunate than he realizes that you stand at his side. You may tell him that his message will be delivered to my brother the king with all due haste. I will recommend that he take your prince's offer to begin negotiations. I cannot vouch for his answer, but he is a wise king and I think he will take it. I will send Commander Kenta Isamu with the king's answer to the village of Senlik in fourteen days, or as near as possible. If the king's answer is yes, then we will expect the grain three weeks after that at the place you specified."

I nodded. He stuck out his right arm and we clasped each other's elbows, a warrior's gesture of respect, friendship, and trust. He was smiling now, more lighthearted, and I imagined that he must have a woman waiting anxiously for his return.

He said, "There will be no more raids by my orders until we have received the king's answer."

I smiled in surprise. That was more than I had expected. "I'll convey your message to the prince Hakan Ithel. I thank you for your consideration of his offer and for the courteous reception today." I bowed to him, glad that the pain did not prevent me from doing him the honor of a deep and graceful bow. He returned the gesture with full respect.

I would have turned then to leave, but suddenly he smiled more broadly. "Would you share the evening meal with me?"

The request was phrased formally, not as a dinner between friends but as a sharing of food between emissaries. Yet I thought we might be friends yet, if the peace was made and then held. "I'd be honored." I smiled.

He asked several of the men to open the sides of the tent so that we might enjoy the fading light.

The meal was meager and simple, though the best they had, and I refused a second helping generously offered. The flavors were much like Erdemen campaign fare, and I thought again that our nations ought not be at war. We were too similar to face each other in battle.

It was near the end that I realized Tafari's purpose in opening the sides of the tent. I can only blame my difficulty breathing for my slowness in understanding, for it was quite obvious. Not only was he doing me honor, he was making the point to all his men that I was an honored guest, not simply a messenger. Perhaps the point needed to be made, at least to some of them, but I couldn't fault his leadership.

When we finished, he accompanied me to the door of the tent and then out into the growing darkness. Isamu and Tafari personally escorted me to my horse, where Isamu respectfully presented me with my sword and knives. I inclined my head toward them with a smile before heading off again.

THIRTEEN

I didn't go far that night. The quick darkness of the mountains made the path treacherous. But I was on my way early the next morning and sighted Senlik perhaps an hour before nightfall. The first person to see me was little Rihol, who had been watching for my return. He came sprinting up the path and danced about beneath the horse's hooves in excitement.

I dismounted to calm the mare, but Rihol's enthusiasm was unchecked, and finally I hoisted him to my shoulders to keep him from being kicked. Lifting him hurt, but carrying him was easy enough, though I nearly dropped him once when the heel of his flailing foot grazed my ribs. He hugged my head in apology and managed to restrain himself thereafter.

We made our way into town and someone took the horse's bridle from me as Hakan greeted me in the street. I lifted Rihol down and sent him off to his sister, who was giving me a very strange look. Twilling ushered us into the dining room and closed the door after us so we could speak in relative peace.

Hakan's first words though were not about my mission. "I didn't know you liked children." He was smiling as if I had done something very funny.

"Should I not?" I've never understood why some men seem to abhor the company of children. They're something of a fascinating and exotic species to me since I cannot remember being so innocent. They are pleasant, rather baffling at times, but certainly nothing to fear as many men seem to fear them. I'd always wanted children of my own. Most people got a little edgy if I even looked at their children, not to mention the sting when children shied away from me. Rihol's friendly smiles were a rare gift.

He laughed. "I just never expected it, Kemen. You do look rather fierce, you know."

I shrugged. "Your message was very well received. The leader of the raiding party here commands many of the raids down the border. His name is Zuzay Tafari, and he's the younger brother of the king Ashmu Tafari. He promised to deliver your letter to the king, and he will send one of his men with the answer in some fourteen days. He also promised no raids until the answer was received."

"Good! I didn't know you were a diplomat as well, but you seem to have made quite an impression. I didn't expect such good news." He smiled warmly and called for Twilling to bring me some dinner. "You look tired. How was your travel?"

"I had no problems." But pain is tiring and I was glad to be back in town with a bed waiting for me, though normally I'd consider it an unnecessary luxury.

He studied me a moment as Twilling brought the food. I hadn't realized how hungry I was until I smelled the rich bread and meat.

"I would like more of your impressions of them, but I'll not prevent you from eating now." He spoke quietly as I ate. "Priven's son returned the day after you left. Rysling and Fairsky have sworn their allegiance to me as well."

I nodded. Good. It was a good start, though far from enough. The population of Erdem is some four hundred thousand people, with some fifty thousand of those in and around Stonehaven. The others are scattered about in various smaller towns, with the port city of Pirketa being the next largest at around twenty thousand.

Farming and herding towns like Rysling and Fairsky often have no more than a thousand, with those spread loosely about a town center which may only have a few hundred people. Some twenty-five thousand men served in the army then, with perhaps half of those being foundlings or orphans and half volunteers. The allegiance of two or three little towns was hopeful, but hardly likely to sway the outcome of any fight for the crown.

Twilling opened the door after a hasty knock. "There is someone here to see you."

Hayato pushed past him with a quick nod, and Twilling closed the door when we stood to greet him.

"Hayato! I didn't expect you so soon." I smiled.

He smiled tightly. "I have news, and not all of it good." Then he looked closer at me. "Phraa, what happened to you? You look like death!"

"Come, sit. I'm having dinner and I don't intend to stop while you talk."

He bowed to Hakan and pulled out a chair, looking me over critically.

"Fight with a raiding party. I think we're on our way to an agreement with Tafari. What's your news?" I asked.

"I bet it was a fight! You're fine then?"

I smiled and nodded at his concern. I hadn't thought we were close enough for him to notice or care.

"I've left word with a few men I trust where I am, in case they find out anything else. Last week, Katzu Itxaro, you remember he's in charge of the kedani out of Rivensworth. Well, last week Itxaro received orders to march east to secure the border from the northeastern corner south to Tarman's Pass. They're leaving today."

What did that mean? Simple border security? War? A threat of war to secure a peace arrangement? Simply an excuse to get the kedani away from Stonehaven?

Hakan leaned forward, his eyes bright. "Who gave the order? Vidar or Taisto?"

"It was given in Vidar's name, but I haven't heard anything sure." Hayato addressed the prince for the first time, and I felt a little guilty. If he was to be king, I supposed I would have to let him take the lead occasionally. "The bodies have finally been taken down in Stonehaven as well, so that's some relief."

"What?" Hakan glanced at me and then back at Hayato.

"The bodies. The people from the palace, you know."

"What? What do you mean?" Hakan's voice rose.

Hayato glanced at me. "I'm sorry, I thought you knew already. It's been nearly a month." He spoke very quietly. "The royal tutor Tibon Rusta, his wife, the head groom Greso Torna, several menservants, a stable boy, and one of the cooks were accused of being part of an assassination plot. One which was presumed successful. They found a young man dead outside the walls of Stonehaven. He was disfigured, but wearing your clothes and carried your bootknife. The body was presumed to be yours. They were beheaded and the bodies have been on display in Stonehaven for over three weeks."

Hakan looked like he might be sick. "Who ordered the executions?"

"Vidar. Or Taisto. No one can be sure now."

"Who was the boy?"

Hayato shrugged slightly. "There are many young men of your age and build in Stonehaven. It could have been any of them."

Especially since those who knew him best were conveniently executed.

Fourteen

That night I stripped off my shirt and loosened the binding around my ribs. I tried to keep my breathing steady; breathing faster at the pain only made it worse. Hakan inspected me with a frown.

"How is it?"

"Could be worse." Could have been better, too. I carefully lay back on the bed and tried not to groan.

"Question for you."

I nodded.

"Were you ever going to tell me about these?" He held up the strip of cloth with my medals pinned to it.

I shrugged. "Why?"

"The Golden Eagle Regnant? The Iron Shield and the King's Silver Eagle? In the same year? The

Emerald Heart? *Six* bronze stars?" He was almost laughing. "That's incredible, Kemen. You might have told me about these at first. I was terrified of you."

I grunted. "Maybe you should have been. You were whiny and annoying." I was joking. Mostly.

By then he knew me well enough to realize it, and he grinned. "I was. I'm surprised you put up with me."

"So am I." I took another deep breath, which hurt immensely but also felt refreshing after the tightness of the strap.

He laid the cloth down on the table, inspecting each medal. "The army didn't offer to keep you on? The Iron Shield is a command award. There should have been a place for you, even if you were crippled, and obviously you weren't."

"No."

I'd wondered about that as well, sometimes in bitter frustration and sometimes only in hurt confusion. I'd given so much for my country, loved Erdem with everything I had. But I wasn't even allowed to continue my service.

When I'd walked out of the infirmary at Fort Kardu still unsteady on my feet, I'd been so dazed by my injury and so heartsick I hadn't even asked for my pension. Later when I could think a bit more clearly, it seemed stupid and greedy to request it, and I'd never pursued the matter.

I began my civilian life with a few golden eagles in my pocket, two weeks' worth of dried venison, a long line of medals pinned to a strip of cloth with officer's stripes cut from the breast of my uniform, my sword, my bootknife, and nothing else to show for my service except the scars.

FIFTEEN

I wondered how we were to fulfill the promises we had made to Tafari, even though we had not yet received his answer. But Hakan was not worried, saying that he knew several noblemen who would be glad to lend him money to buy the grain we had promised to deliver.

Hayato left early the next morning with some dozen letters from Hakan to the nobles he trusted. Hakan gave Hayato the authority to accept the money on his behalf and Hayato promised to send word to us about the nobles' responses.

The days until we received word from Tafari were restful and my aching ribs began to heal, but my mind was not peaceful. Four days passed easily in the clear warmth of late spring in the mountains. I watched the men practice their moves. They would be of little use against trained warriors, of course; there was no time for true training. In truth, I didn't expect they would need to fight, but they coveted knowledge. It gave them courage and confidence, and more than that, gave them pride because they didn't feel so helpless. I hoped they would never have to use what I taught them, and while we awaited Hayato's news, I hoped that peace would come.

Little Rihol scampered about my feet and imitated my every move, much to the embarrassment of his sister. The other girls and women were warmer toward me, though always cautious and carefully aloof. I supposed I couldn't blame them. The men they knew, fathers, brothers, and sons, were farmers and blacksmiths, shepherds, men of the soil. Despite their gratitude, which I confess warmed me, they never knew quite what to make of me.

I saw Bethla several times as she was drawing water, and she smiled at me. I didn't expect her to speak to me much. There was little to say and it wasn't entirely proper for a girl of her age to speak with a soldier, especially not a Dari soldier. But it was kind of her to smile as she did.

I did wonder why Rihol's sister was so cool towards me. Perhaps I hadn't been fair to her; maybe she feared Rihol's admiration of me. Though I'd never experienced it, I imagined that a sister's fear for a little brother is protective and sheltering. Maybe it was not that she feared me but that she feared that Rihol might choose to follow my path as a soldier.

PERHAPS A WEEK after I'd returned from the parley, I leaned against the edge of the low wall surrounding the well and watched Adin practice with his staff. The afternoon sun was warm on my shoulders.

I hurt. The ends of my broken ribs ground against each other with every breath. Earlier, before I'd moved upwind, I'd inhaled a bit of dust Adin kicked up and coughed, the pain searing across my chest.

Nevertheless, I was happy. Hakan was off helping Mullin with something, and I'd seen Rihol and his sister that morning. His sister smiled cautiously and Rihol pulled away from her to run to me. I knelt to speak with him face to face and he grinned. I was more than shocked when he wrapped his arms around my neck in a sudden laughing hug. He smiled like hay, dusty and fresh. I showed him how to clasp elbows as soldiers do. My forearm was more than twice as long as his and far too large for him to really hold, but he'd nodded seriously before grinning again.

A child's laugh can brighten a whole day.

Adin was doing something wrong with his feet and I was about to correct him when I realized the girl off to the side was approaching me. I bowed slightly to her, and she smiled tentatively.

"Sir?" She held out a basket with a cloth covering something in it. "My mother and I baked these for you."

"Thank you. What are they?" I took the basket and set it on the edge of the well. I was trying to remember if I should know her name, and finally

203

decided that I hadn't ever heard it, though I'd seen her speaking with Bethla a few times at the well.

"Nut cakes with cinnamon and honey." She bit her lip. "Aren't you going to try one?"

I smiled. When I pushed the cloth back, the smell was sweet, spicy, and warm. "Would you share it with me?"

She licked her lips and glanced away for a moment, then she nodded. I broke off a bit of one flat loaf and offered her the basket. She leaned on the wall an arm's length away, as I were some dangerous animal she didn't quite trust.

"My grandda said green eyes aren't natural." She didn't look at me.

I took a bite of the sweet honeyed cake. I didn't really know what to say, so I watched Adin mangling the form for the strike I had taught him earlier.

Finally, after the silence had become uncomfortably long, I said, "I'm sorry. I didn't choose the color."

She glanced at me. "Bethla's my friend." There was another long silence, and finally she said quietly, "Thank you."

THE ELEVENTH DAY after I returned, the twelfth after my parley with Zuzay Tafari, was bright in the morning, the air glowing in brilliance sunshine. But the afternoon brought clouds roiling from the west, ready to drop their rain as they flung themselves headlong into the sharp peaks of the mountains.

The rain arrived just before the messenger did, spattered with mud clear to his dripping hair, having ridden in the downpour all the way from the garrison at Rysig. Twilling opened the door at his knock with an exclamation of surprise and a kindly hand on his elbow as the young man stumbled inside.

"I bring a message for Kemen Sendoa from Commander Hayato Jalo."

Twilling pointed him toward the table where Hakan and I were standing, and the young man dropped to one knee in a bow deeper than he would have bowed even to a king at his coronation.

"Stand up! Come, sit, and give me the message." I bowed in return, though more properly, and pulled out a chair for him as I sat again. He was a young recruit, some two or three years older than Hakan, well built, fairskinned and blond-haired under the grime of the road. His uniform proclaimed him a suvari. He dropped into the chair with a sigh of utter weariness, inclining his head toward me in another gesture of respect, but pushed himself up to sit straight and formally, as if he were still in training before a high commanding officer.

He scarcely glanced at the prince, addressing himself to me. "Sir, I am Eskarne Desta."

Mercy Joy. A very odd name for a warrior, for clearly he was one, but the name made me warm towards whoever had given it to him. Mercy. There should be more that in the world. And Joy. Never enough of that either.

"Your fame has spread all the way to Stone-haven, and I am honored to be chosen to bring you this message from Commander Hayato Jalo. He gives you greatest respect and honor, and—"

I interrupted him. "Wait. What? Fame? What are you talking about?"

He bowed his head again. "Your fame, the tale of your great battle with the army of Rikuto. How you defeated so many, all alone against their champions! I am honored to meet you, sir."

I groaned and leaned forward to put my head in my hands, my side stretching uncomfortably. It was absurd. When we needed people to support Hakan they talked of my skirmish? Courage and skill in battle, though valuable and necessary, do not qualify one to be king.

"It was a raiding party, not an army." I sat up to stare at him, though I let myself rub my aching ribs. "It was nothing more than a raid, and there were no champions there on either side. Just a few Rikutan warriors and me. It was no great battle."

He inclined his head, speaking quietly as if he thought I would be angry at him. "Be that as it may, sir, the tale has spread rapidly, and reached Stonehaven some five or six days ago. It spread like wildfire. You are exceedingly popular there, a great hero of the people. The message from Commander Jalo is this: Because of your prowess and courage, and your unwavering support of the prince, the suvari has firmly cast its support behind the prince as well. They count you one of their own despite your years of service in the kedani, and they trust your judgment. This has not yet been made known to Nekane Vidar or Ryuu

Taisto, who still believe they have the entire army at their command.

"Commander Jalo says also that his friend Katzu Itxaro has sent him news of much division among the ranks of the kedani, some casting their support behind Vidar and Taisto, some behind the prince. He has had some difficulty in keeping peace among the men. The word of your great battle has swayed the balance toward the prince. Though you are respected by all without exception, not all have extended that trust and respect to the prince. Yet. Rumors of his death are still spreading, and many do not know what to think. They are already marching toward the border, and their news has been limited. Jalo's personal friendship with you availed much in the suvari, and he believes that a similar personal connection to Itxaro might assist in gaining the support of those in the kedani yet undecided." He bowed again.

I sat back to think.

Hakan's soft laughter startled me. The young soldier and I both turned to stare at him, and he grinned. "Kemen, really, you have to laugh. Did you ever think that one battle, gallant and heroic as it was, would sway the entire nation? As if I deserve the trust of the army more because of your heroism."

He smiled at Desta without affectation. "Kemen Sendoa is as noble a warrior as you will ever have the honor to meet. I'll do my best to live up to his trust and the honor of his esteem." His tone had turned quite royal to go along with his words, and he turned to meet my gaze seriously. "I'll be the best king I can, because you have trusted me to do so. I would not disappoint you, for I respect you more than anyone else in this world. I would not fail you after you've made such sacrifices for me."

I opened my mouth in surprise, but I could think of nothing to say.

Desta hesitated a moment, looking back and forth between us with wide eyes. "There is more to the message. Commander Jalo says that he has received affirmative responses from six of the men you sent messages to, as well as more than enough money. They are Vellorn, Kalyano, Tiniam, Rilhoma, Chastin, and Worthenson. He has not spoken to the others because he thought it wise to keep word that you were alive as quiet as possible. Those six send word that they are firmly with you and if you have need of anything, they are entirely at your service.

"Lord Kalyano sends an additional warning. He believes that Taisto knows you are yet alive, because he has some of his own men still scouring the kingdom for you. Lord Kalyano never believed that you were murdered. He was able to see the body Taisto produced before it was burned in the royal funeral. He urges you to take every precaution. He believes Taisto is much more dangerous to you than Vidar, but warns you not to trust either of them."

Hakan nodded. "That does not surprise me. Does Commander Jalo expect an answer immediately?"

"He desires confirmation that he should buy the grain. He believes he can use some of his men to deliver it without causing any suspicion. The suvari will stand by you to whatever end." He bowed his head again, and I wanted to smile at his overzealous formality.

"Aye then. Stay another four days until we receive word from Tafari, and then Hayato will have his answer."

The young officer hesitated but spoke again. "Commander Jalo also sends more troubling news. He has spoken with a friend in the kedani, Sverre Usoa, out of Stonehaven. Usoa made discreet inquiries on your behalf, since Commander Jalo told him that neither you nor the prince know much about Ryuu Taisto. It was difficult going, but he did find out two very interesting facts. Sir, you were the only survivor of the battle that retired you in the campaign against the Tarvil. One survivor, out of some forty-two experienced warriors, a group that would normally not have been sent out all together but split up to lend your expertise and courage to younger, less seasoned squads."

I nodded, wondering exactly what Usoa thought he had discovered. I could relive it in my mind if I wanted to, and I had a thousand times over. The sudden cries of agony, the courage of our men, the brilliant sun that mocked our tragedy.

Desta continued quietly. "With much effort, Usoa found that the orders for that foray came from Ryuu Taisto, who was then serving as deputy division commander out of Blackburn. There is no record that the division commander gave the orders for your patrols to be combined in that advance, nor that he approved it."

I frowned. Normally the division commander would have been involved in such an irregular decision. I hadn't questioned it at the time, because I wasn't commanding that patrol. Who had been? I couldn't remember his name, he wasn't someone I'd worked with before, but surely he would have noticed an irregularity in the orders.

"Who was the division commander?" I couldn't remember.

"Britlin Goroa. He died not long after, but I don't know how. Usoa believes that Taisto betrayed your group to the Tarvil in order to eliminate some of the most experienced soldiers who might oppose him and in order to gain credibility with the Rikutans by proving his influence. He believes that Taisto has been in the pay of the Rikutans for some years. Taisto has money that is unexplained by his pay from the king's purse." Desta bowed again.

I felt sick. Surely not. Surely an officer of the king's kedani would not betray his own men to the barbarians. I took a deep breath. That was the past. What mattered was the present. If the king Ashmu Tafari was false, what would be the result of my visit to his brother? How much had that cost Hakan?

I leaned back to think, though Desta almost seemed to expect an outburst of hot anger. Despite what people seem to expect, anger is rarely my first reaction to anything. Neither my nature nor my training encourages a foolish temper. I admit I felt a deep, cold fury at the utter futility of Yuudai's death, fury at the traitor who might have sacrificed him and other good men for his own gain, but that was hardly something I would hold against the young messenger. "Thank you for your message. Eat and rest now. Hakan will send his answer when we hear from Tafari."

He nodded and backed away, bowed more deeply to me than he should have, and strode off down the hall in search of Twilling.

Perplexing indeed.

Hakan stared at the table. "I thought you judged Tafari was honest?"

"Aye. At least the brother is; I cannot speak for the king. But Zuzay Tafari seemed to have a good opinion of his brother. I would be surprised if he was aware of such treachery."

Perhaps Tafari was not the culprit after all. The king Hakan Emyr had been a foolish king in some ways, but he wasn't false; he didn't send spies to corrupt the Rikutan army or send good men to their deaths for no purpose. He might have been stupid but he wasn't vicious. Yet men under him had been vicious and underhanded. Perhaps it was the same with Tafari.

I spoke slowly. "I wouldn't judge him false yet. Just as Taisto's misdeeds only mean that your father was unaware, not that he was corrupt, so too someone else under Tafari may be acting against his wishes and unknown to him."

Hakan nodded as though he wanted to believe me. "I suppose it is possible."

But it was also possible I was too optimistic, too trusting. How could I know what the king Hakan Emyr had done? He'd sent spies to gather information. He'd made many mistakes, only some of which I could have seen. I had served him without reservation, and he was hardly a model of a perfect king.

Tafari could be playing both sides of the conflict. He would need to be on good terms with whoever emerged as the ruler in Erdem. A man may be a good king and not entirely a good man, just as a good man can be a bad king. I wanted to believe that Hakan would be both a good man and a good king, and he was giving me reasons for confidence. But I hadn't met Tafari, and though I held onto my hope, I had to admit to myself that it was rather tenuous.

Sixteen

The fourteenth day I woke before dawn, nearly twitching with impatience to hear Tafari's answer. I was hopeful, but the stakes were very high. Hakan was even more nervous than I was, or at least not as practiced at hiding it. He paced back and forth in the dining room of Twilling's inn like a caged wolf. He looked painfully young and green, every line of his bearing taut with fear of failure.

Isamu rode in not long after noon, and I knew the answer before we were close enough to speak, for I could see the smile on his face. Hakan hung back, as I had advised him; I didn't think it wise for him to appear too eager.

Isamu and I bowed to each other, knowing that we were both glad of the news. He came into Twilling's inn to speak more privately, and Hakan received his bow with royal grace and noble composure. This, too, pleased me. I was glad Isamu could report back that despite Hakan's youth and inexperience, he was well-versed in the courtesy proper to a monarch.

Desta stood behind us as I had asked him to, lending at least a small air of formality to the meeting. I wanted Isamu to be honored appropriately as an official emissary, though there were only we two warriors and Hakan to do so. Diplomacy, like any conversation, is a dance of competing and cooperative interests, forces pulling two nations both together and apart, hidden agendas and open requests, demands and incentives, personal emotion and cool logic. Courtesy is both a measure of the respect one accords to another and a measure of one's own character.

Isamu bowed. "His Royal Highness the king Ashmu Tafari sends his respectful greetings to the prince Hakan Ithel. He wishes to open negotiations with you as soon as possible, and gratefully accepts your offer of grain, to be delivered as discussed."

Gratefully. A good sign there. A king does not want to seem too thankful, for gratitude implies need. It was well spoken, conveying appropriate appreciation while preserving Tafari's dignity.

"He has ordered that all raids across your borders cease at once while the negotiations begin. Of course, the borders will remain well guarded, but he trusts your men will respect the peace that both our nations desire." Isamu kept his eyes on Hakan's face.

Hakan nodded beside me. "They will once they receive their orders."

He and Isamu spoke courteously and seriously to each other, refining the specifics of how the negotiations were to begin. Despite his earlier nerves, he was proud and noble, supremely confident. Regal.

Isamu was greatly impressed by Hakan's royal bearing and generosity, and when he left he bowed with consummate grace toward a king, not just a boy who might one day have a throne. We saw him off with respect and he promised to take Hakan's answer to Tafari with all due haste.

When we entered Twilling's inn again, Hakan dropped into a chair and put his head on the table. He remained still a moment, eyes closed, and then raised his head to look at me. "Do you think it went well?"

"Aye, it did." I smiled. In truth, I was proud of him.

He called for Twilling to bring us ale, though it was not yet time for dinner, and glanced at his hands ruefully. Pale slender hands, despite the hours training in the sunlight, they shook almost violently.

"Are you ill?"

He shook his head. "No. They do this sometimes when I'm very nervous. Always have."

A man can't help some things, and I could not fault him for it. I've seen my own hands shake against my will after I've been wounded or in the presence of a beautiful woman. "You did well to hide it."

215

He shrugged. "I'd rather not have him know I almost vomited from nerves. It wouldn't exactly make me seem more regal, would it?"

I HAD EXPECTED to send Desta back with the answer to Hayato immediately, but Hakan insisted that we buy the grain and deliver it ourselves. I told him that a king delegates responsibility and that Hayato was quite capable of navigating a marketplace. He responded that he was not yet king, and he wished to personally see the fulfillment of the promises I had made on his behalf and that he had then confirmed to Isamu. I didn't argue too strongly. While learning to delegate is essential for a king, so too is taking responsibility for his word.

We left Desta in Senlik with instructions that he should receive any messages from Tafari on the prince's behalf and immediately convey them to Vettea, where we were planning to meet Hayato. Our travel southwest was much faster than our travel northeast had been because Hakan bought two very good horses from Thosin to speed our way. Despite his difficulty with the sword, he was a more than competent horseman, and we reached Vettea in only two days.

Hakan had never been in a market before, and Vettea's was far from Erdem's best. Nonetheless, he stared about him with wide eyes. Across the small square there was a Senga trader sitting atop his cart, and I nudged Hakan to be sure he saw the man.

"What's the mark on his face?" he whispered.

216

The mark was a series of darkened dots that arced around the Senga's left eye and down across his cheek, with a sharp upward angle to his ear. "It's a tribal marking. He's a Sesmerinal Senga, from the eastern desert. He's probably selling spices." I edged my way through the crowd to see if I was right. If so, he'd have evreok, which is a bit like cinnamon but with a sweeter tang.

"How did he do it?" Hakan was still staring.

I kept my voice low and spoke almost into his ear. "Small cuts with a knife, then ash or charcoal to darken the scars."

He grimaced. "That's horrible."

I smiled. "Don't let him hear you say that. They're very proud. It's a family marking, like bearing his father's name."

The Senga did have evreok, so I spent my next to last bronze hawk on a tiny bag. We used our borrowed money to buy all the grain we would need and carts to carry it. We also hired drivers, which was a bit more difficult since we needed ten men and mounts for them once the carts were delivered, but finally we had made all the arrangements necessary. Hayato had a small group of suvari to escort us on our way, some thirty men who bowed respectfully every time they saw me. Apparently my reputation had very much preceded me, although no one outside Hayato's group knew that my face matched the name of Kemen Sendoa.

I spent a pleasant morning listening to gossip and rumors about my prowess as we argued over the prices of grain, carts, and mules to pull them. I was unsure whether it was better to betray my identity and argue that the battle had not been the lone hero Kemen Sendoa against the entire Rikutan army, or whether it was better to remain simply an unknown retired soldier. Which was more modest, more proper for a warrior's denial of ego?

Of course, Hayato knew this dilemma, and he knew how I hate to be stared at. So it was a joke when he called out to me from halfway across the square with an impish laughter in his eyes. The entire crowd turned to stare at me, and suddenly everyone was talking to me and at me. They wanted to buy me ale and dinner, clap me on the shoulder, and hear of the skirmish in detail. I cursed Hayato inside, though I did manage to smile with some degree of courtesy at the crowd.

Hakan had laughed with Hayato when the crowd first recognized me, but later that night over dinner, he questioned me more closely. Hayato was eating with his men, giving them instructions, and Hakan and I were eating in a quiet corner of a small inn. With some effort I had managed to escape the stares earlier. Though the innkeeper bobbed his head respectfully every time he brought us food, we were otherwise able to eat in obscurity, which pleased me greatly. The food wasn't as good as Lira Twilling's, but the ale was better and there was a bit of music. I liked it, but Hakan winced when they hit the high notes, so I suppose the musicians were not especially good.

"Were you really angry at Hayato this afternoon?"

I shrugged. Anger over something so trivial does not become a warrior. There had been no affront intended. "Aye, a bit. I suppose I shouldn't have been though."

Hakan studied me, and I wondered what he saw. Sometimes I thought I understood him, for he was a boy and often quite transparent, but other times he utterly surprised me. "You really don't like the recognition then, do you?

"Every man likes a bit of recognition. But I don't like being stared at and made much of. It wasn't like they said, some great glorious battle." My emotion surprised even me; I'm used to being cool and logical. Emotion is dangerous, though pleasant and even beneficial sometimes, because it is unpredictable. "They glorify battle because they have never seen it. Watching a man die isn't a game. It isn't a nice story you tell over dinner."

You can smell a man's fear. You can taste your own fear. The air hums with the tension between two men. A sword cleaves through air and cloth and skin and flesh and sometimes bone, and you can feel the grinding crunch when a bone breaks beneath your blade. A man can die of infection days after a wound that looks trivial, a lingering painful death of fever and rotting flesh. Death is a bitter smell, but the rot that sometimes precedes it is sickeningly sweet. A man might cry for his mother, a brother, a friend, when he dies.

No man with a thinking mind is unafraid of battle. Courage faces that fear, but only foolishness pretends that it is glorious.

WE LEFT EARLY the next morning. Some of the people of the town watched us, and I hoped that Vidar and Taisto would not hear of our departure, though we had not given any information about our intended destination or purpose, and certainly not anything to indicate that the prince Hakan Ithel was in our little party. But if they knew I was there, surely they could guess Hakan wasn't far away.

The carts had some difficulty in the muddy roads at first, but as we made further progress the old roads were better drained and less used. We covered some nine leagues each day, camping just off the road. I pushed the group a little because the going would be slower once we reached the hills. The suvari sang as we rode, and sometimes I raised my voice with them, though my voice is hardly admirable. There is something stirring about battle songs, sung lustily on beautiful spring days, when the wind carries the scent of freshly plowed earth and green growing things.

Hakan smiled and laughed more than he had since I had known him. He must have felt the eternal hope of spring as well. He learned the songs we sang, and the suvari welcomed him as one of their own. His voice delighted Hayato, who was much more inclined toward music than I.

Once we reached the hills our progress slowed considerably. The roads fell out of repair as we moved farther from Stonehaven, and sometimes a cart would get a wheel stuck or even broken. One of the mules developed a limp that grew progressively worse. Though the driver removed the stone that caused it, the animal did not improve. We sold it and bought another at the next town, but it delayed us a little.

With no little effort and several very early starts, we reached the meeting place early on the appointed day. The mountain range narrows considerably there, and the Lobar Road Pass is the widest and, at least in the past, was the most traveled route between Stonehaven and Enkotan, the Rikutan capital. Roughly halfway between our two kingdoms there is a small plateau nestled between the mountains. It has often been a meeting place for traders, and it would serve us well now.

The Rikutans were not yet there, so our group settled around several small fires, cooking lunch and warming ourselves against the mountain chill. We waited only a short while before the Rikutan party arrived, led by Zuzay Tafari himself.

He waved a greeting and his men waited in formation while he rode forward to speak with Hakan and me. Hakan's first words, after a regally courteous greeting, were an invitation for Tafari's men to eat lunch with our men. I could see the pleasure in Tafari's acceptance of this courtesy, for it promised an ongoing cooperation. In minutes the men were mingling with cautious, friendly smiles.

Hakan generously offered the mules that pulled the wagons as a gift, though it had not been part of the original offer, which was only the grain and the wagons that carried it. I thought even at the time that it was an intelligent and perceptive gesture because it showed him as confident in his coming rule, generous because he could afford to be generous. Tafari and Hakan spoke quietly about the negotiations, initial expectations, desires, what each country was willing to extend in trust. Hakan carried himself very well, gracious and confident in every word. The interlude did not last long, but

Tafari bowed with respect and pleasure when he and Hakan parted.

Our party started again on the trail, the drivers mounted on the extra horses. We were nearly out of earshot around a bend in the road when I heard shouts and the clash of metal behind us. In a moment the suvari and I were galloping back.

The Rikutans had still been on the little plateau when they were attacked by a party of Tarvil raiders, descended from the north. We threw ourselves into battle as well on the side of the Rikutans, though the irony of that did not escape me even at the time.

I realized later that Hakan didn't even have a blade, only the wooden practice sword that I had made for him. I told him to stay back, but a skirmish is never predictable, and he was in the thick of battle before either of us knew it, swinging that stupid sword gamely. He was a hairsbreadth from being gutted by the time I reached his side again.

The skirmish wasn't long, for though the Tarvil had mustered quite a sizable raiding party, the addition of Hayato's thirty men had firmly tipped the balance in the Rikutans' favor. Hakan had a bleeding gash on one arm, but it wasn't serious. He gritted his teeth but did not complain when I cut a strip of cloth from the bottom of my tunic to bandage it. My ribs ached so badly that I felt dizzy in the middle of binding Hakan's arm and had to stop and lean over, rest my hands on my knees and steady my breathing.

Only one other of Hayato's men was even injured. Though his wound was a little more serious than Hakan's, it hardly looked life-threatening, though of course any wound can kill if it becomes infected. Some of his fellows were attending him, and Hakan and I made our way to Tafari.

"What happened?" I spoke before Hakan did, though I probably should have let him lead.

Tafari bit back a curse. "Attacked again. I should have known as much. They love this road. I lost several good men today. Many thanks for coming back. Without you we were outnumbered."

Aye, but they had acquitted themselves admirably, if the Tarvil bodies lying around were any indication.

Hakan's voice broke into my thoughts. "Have you been attacked here before?"

Tafari nodded. "Aye, we have, several times. That's why we had so many men to guard a few carts of grain. I'm surprised you don't know that, since your country has suffered the raids as well. You brought suvari too." His eyes were sharp on Hakan's face, but the boy did not flinch.

"Not so far south. 'Tis odd. Our men were more for protection against Vidar and Taisto than Tarvil raiders. I will question one of them, if there are any left alive." He hesitated, but asked Tafari again. "You've had convoys of grain here before then, do I understand correctly?"

Tafari nodded. "Aye, we've been buying grain from Stonehaven for months. I assumed you knew that."

Hakan shook his head.

"First from your father, then from Vidar. The prices are bleeding us dry, but we have little choice. This spring was the fourth of drought and already promises a scanty harvest in autumn. Raids cannot bring in all we need, and my brother is honest. He would prefer not to steal food, but he will if necessary. He will not watch the women and children of his kingdom starve to death."

Hakan looked as though he would say more, but suddenly turned away and began to walk among the bodies, kneeling to check the pulse of each one that wore Tarvil clothing. I followed him, wondering what he wanted with a Tarvil barbarian.

Finally we found one yet living, one of the leaders by the sashes about his arm and waist. He was lying on his back blinking dazedly, still stunned from a heavy blow that had left a growing lump over his left eye. He was bleeding from a deep wound in one leg, which he did not appear to have noticed yet.

Hakan knelt down to speak to him face to face. The man's face tightened and his right hand twitched toward his hip, where he no doubt had a knife, but I stepped on his wrist and pressed the point of my sword to his throat none too gently. His eyes flicked to me in naked fear. Hakan should have been more careful, but he was staring at the man intently.

"You've attacked the Rikutans before, haven't you?"

The Tarvil hesitated, glancing up at me again. I pressed the point into his throat a little harder, letting it prick the skin. A tiny drop of bright red blood welled up.

"Aye." He probably would have nodded but thought better of it.

"Why? What do you want?"

His eyes flicked about in panic, trying no doubt to figure out which answer would most satisfy the frightening Dari with the sword pressed close to the great blood vessels in his neck. Finally he settled on something relatively easy. "Grain."

"Why?"

I could not figure out what Hakan was thinking. Of course they would want grain; that made sense. So did we, and so did the Rikutans. But the Tarvil seemed even more nervous now, and Hakan repeated his question. "Why do you want grain? The Tarvil have never wanted grain before."

I knew little enough about the Tarvil, but I would ask Hakan about this later.

"We were hired for it. Can't blame me for following through on my word."

Hakan understood it before I did, for I heard his sudden sharp intake of breath.

"Who hired you?"

He shrugged as well as he could. "You should know. You're Erdemen. Ryuu Taisto. Paid good money for it too." Apparently the man had decided there was nothing to be gained by hiding information.

Hakan's jaw clenched, but his voice was very even. "What do you do with the grain after you take it?"

The man glanced at me again. "Take it back to Birchmere or Vettea. Taisto's men pay us then."

Hakan's eyes narrowed. "And what do they do with it?"

Again he shrugged, making a ghastly attempt at an ingratiating smile. "Don't know. I just do what I'm paid to do."

I balanced on my right foot, which was grinding his wrist into the dirt, and lifted my left foot to place the heel on the wound in his leg. He paled and gasped in pain. Hakan looked up at me in surprise, but I pushed my heel a little harder into the man's leg until his breath was quick and shallow, sweat beading on his forehead. His words came out in choking gasps, and I let up a little.

"I think they sell it. I don't know. I just do what I'm told. I get paid and I go back home. It's easy work."

I removed my foot from the wound on his leg, though I kept the sword point firmly against his throat.

Hakan stared at him in silence a moment. "What else do you know about grain convoys?"

His eyes flicked up at me. "Nothing much. But," he spoke quickly, his eyes on me all the while, "my brother's group burned a granary in Cherkasyo last week. Taisto paid them for it too. And last year he was in a group that burned the fields up by Vastilyo." He was pale with fear, and I tried to control my contempt for him.

Hakan stood, his face equally pale but with an absolute, cold fury that I had never seen in him. He walked away without a backward glance, stepping over the prone body of another raider on his way back to Tafari, who was speaking to one of his men quietly.

I looked back at the Tarvil and wondered if I should say something intimidating and fearsome, but settled for glowering at him before I followed Hakan. I was at his side when he called Tafari away from his men with an imperious tone that startled everyone but Hakan himself.

"You may inform your king Ashmu Tafari that it is due to the treachery of Ryuu Taisto that you have been so desperate for grain. He paid them to ruin your crops so that you would be desperate for any succor, and then he sold you grain at prices designed to bankrupt Rikuto. He paid the Tarvil to steal it back from you and then sold the grain he stole to my own people at exorbitant prices as well. All of this, to line his own pockets at the expense of both your people and mine."

His voice was clipped and cold, and Tafari's jaw set with anger when he heard the words. But Hakan was not finished. "If you doubt my words, go question the Tarvil over there, if Kemen hasn't killed him yet."

I shook my head.

"More's the pity. I hope this changes your king's view of Taisto. Despite his pretenses, he is no friend of Rikuto."

Tafari nodded.

"By your leave, we will depart again. I hope we meet again in better circumstances." He inclined his head with regal dignity, and in a few moments we were again mounted and on our way.

SEVENTEEN

We made good time back on the road back to Vettea. The suvari sang cheerily, and I raised my voice with them sometimes. Other times I rode in silence with Hakan, whose face remained set with grim cold fury. He scarcely spoke for some hours, but he questioned me in the afternoon.

"The suvari is more or less with me, is it not?"

"Aye, that's what Hayato said."

"Does Katsu Itxaro command the entire kedani?"

"No, just the division out of Rivensworth. It's roughly a third of the kedani. The others are commanded by Berk Havard and Yoshiro Kepa. They all receive orders from Taisto directly, but Kepa is stationed on the northern border and Havard on the southern border."

"Berk Havard and Yoshiro Kepa. Do you think they will follow Itxaro or Taisto in a conflict?"

Taisto was their commanding officer, but if they heard that Itxaro was serving the prince, they might defy Taisto. I waved Hayato forward, because he knew more about them than I did.

"Itxaro, most likely. Havard is a good friend of Itxaro, they were in training together. Kepa is a bit older, but has no love for Taisto. Taisto was promoted against his recommendations. He thought six years ago that Taisto was dangerously ambitious and possibly corrupt. He was the one who helped Usoa find the information about the betrayal of your scouting party."

I nodded. No love there.

"Good. The assassination parties that were sent after me. Who are they?"

I had no idea. No doubt some had been suvari, for Taisto's orders had not seemed so vile at first. But the others? Were they Tarvil barbarians? Erdemen rogues bought by Taisto's blood money? For blood money it was, gained by the starvation of innocents in Rikuto and the blood of good Rikutan and Erdemen soldiers and civilians trying to protect their crops.

Hayato spoke quietly. "Mostly suvari, but only a few of them really looked. Taisto has a few friends, snakes like himself, who can be bought."

Hakan glanced at me sideways. "We'll need men to remove Taisto from power. The kedani is mostly dispersed about Erdem, and there aren't many in Stonehaven now."

229

His voice had a slight question in it, and I nodded.

"Then we'll take the suvari. They are still available to us, right?"

Again I nodded.

"Much of the suvari is in Rivensworth now. We will go there immediately and take every man we can. Then we will march on Stonehaven before Taisto knows we are coming. Once we reach the gates, we will trumpet our arrival. You're popular there, Kemen, and that will help us. With luck, Taisto won't oppose us openly. The entire city will be on our side and he will be isolated."

He hesitated, as if he would say more, but subsided again into silence. The plan seemed so simple, so optimistic. I wondered if anything would actually go as we hoped it would. Surely Taisto would not be so agreeably easy to defeat, but given our lack of information I could suggest nothing else to do.

From Vettea, Hakan wanted to head directly toward Rivensworth, but I believed that it was a good opportunity to meet Itxaro, who had already cast his support for Hakan despite the difficulties among his men. His main camp was only half a day's ride north, and in truth, it had surprised me that we had not seen any soldiers patrolling the Lobar Road.

Hakan acquiesced, and so we paid and released the drivers and sold their horses before heading directly north. The headquarters of the kedani on the eastern border is located a bit north of the middle of the border since the roads in the south are faster to traverse. Here too we made good time, and in some hours were welcomed into the compound.

Itxaro himself came to greet us. He bowed low before Hakan and perhaps lower than he should have toward me, but the men were watching and he wanted to make a point of his respect and honor. The men saluted respectfully as we were conducted to his offices. Hakan looked very young in comparison to the kedani, but he carried himself well, and I believe that no man there faulted him for his youth. Perhaps for his inexperience, but his regal bearing helped him.

I liked Itxaro on sight. He had the characteristic erect bearing of a soldier, but there was not too much pride in his stance. His face was very thoughtful, more than that of most soldiers. My profession does not permit a man to be stupid for long, but neither does it encourage deep thought and introspection, which raise questions not easily answered. He was of average height for a Tuyet and a thick build, but not soft or fat. His eyes were a clear grey rather than the more common blue.

Hakan thanked him for his service and asked him what the men thought.

"Many are yet undecided, but word of Sendoa's support of you has tipped the balance. He has much respect among the men. Many remember him, and many more know his reputation." He turned to me with a smile. "I am honored to meet you at last. Everyone thought you dead. You are something of a legend, especially after that battle with Tafari's men."

I shook my head. "It was only a raiding party, despite what the rumors might say." I could only ride because I tightened the strap around my ribs every morning. It had been a little over a month, and any healer would have said I shouldn't be riding at all. But Hakan, and Erdem, needed me then, not in two months when my ribs would be healed.

Itxaro echoed Desta's words. "Be that as it may, you are a hero both among the common people and the soldiers. If you would address the men and take the evening meal with us tonight, I think you could do much to sway some of the undecided."

I glanced at Hakan before nodding. "If the prince Hakan Ithel wishes, I will."

I wondered whether Hakan resented the respect and honor that everyone seemed to be according to me. After all, it was his throne, not mine, that was under contention. But Hakan smiled easily and nodded, and after a few more minutes we stepped back out into the brilliant spring sunset.

Red and gold light flooded the simple exercise ground and gave it a glow no king's chamber could ever equal. Itxaro assembled the men in formation to await my words. There were some three thousand men here, and they formed neat squads as Itxaro commanded, with a man at the head of each group to repeat my words back for those who could not hear them clearly.

My stomach churned with nerves as I stood before them. I hate speaking in front of people with a passion I cannot explain. Their eyes on me make my gut boil. Sounds seem to come unevenly, voices fading in and out so conversations are hard to follow. I feel like vomiting, and my voice sounds squeaky and awkward in my ears.

This was the most difficult thing I faced for Hakan, though he did not seem aware of it at the time. Nevertheless, I realized my fear was foolish, and I faced it, for a man does not acquire more courage except by acting on what little he has. I stood on a small platform so that everyone could see me easily, and I clasped my hands behind my back to hide their shaking.

"Your commander Katsu Itxaro has asked me to speak to you in support of the prince Hakan Ithel. If you do not know me, my name is Kemen Sendoa." I waited my words to be repeated for the men in the back. My voice would have been stronger if it hadn't hurt so much to breathe, but at least it wasn't shaking.

"I served under Commander Ake Tallak in the suvari for four years, then I was transferred to the kedani under Commander Jetil Serhato during the campaigns against the Ophrani and then against the Tarvil. I served as an officer for eleven years until I was retired some four and a half years ago for injury. I have much experience with leaders, both good and bad. I've heard that some respect me, and that some of you might heed my voice. I have no call to command you; I'm no longer in active service. But I can say this. I've traveled with the prince Hakan Ithel for several months now. I vouch for his ability to lead Erdem."

I licked my lips and tried to look above the crowd rather than directly into the many pairs of staring eyes. "He's well educated, of course, and well prepared for his role as king. He knows much about the leadership of a country that neither Vidar nor Taisto can boast, despite their other qualifications. Things like economics and trade, diplomacy and philosophy. Things necessary for a king that both Vidar and Taisto are sorely lacking.

"He will not be quick to risk your lives in foolish wars, but neither will he allow the honor of Erdem to falter. He is well aware of the problems you face in the army and those that face civilians, especially in the border areas. Much better than his father was, and he has the knowledge and will to address those problems as his father did not.

"You served under his father honorably, despite his many flaws. I did as well. The prince Hakan Ithel is not only a friend I trust but a man I am proud to serve. I hope you will make the same choice, and pledge him your devoted service and your life's blood for as long as he serves the people of Erdem."

With that I was finished, for I could come up with no more words. I stepped down from the platform and tried to hide the relief that flooded me.

The kedani were silent. I had expected as much, but I wished I had some indication of whether my words had served Hakan as I wanted them to.

Hakan stepped up and spoke, at least as far as I could tell, with total confidence and complete poise.

"I'm honored by Kemen Sendoa's trust in me. I realize that I'm young and untried. You're justified in your mistrust of me. In truth, I doubted at first whether I ought to try to regain the throne.

Does that surprise you?" A few of the men in the first rows glanced at each other.

Hakan's voice rose. "I know that being a king, a good one, is a difficult task, and I feared it. I would not be the only one to suffer if I were to fall short of what it demands. I love the people of Erdem, and I would rather set aside the throne to someone better qualified than keep it for myself, if that person could better guard this country I love. You have heard some of the things I studied in my education as a prince, and they're good things, necessary things. But they're not the only things a king needs, and I still doubted.

"You might wonder now why I am opposing Nekane Vidar and Ryuu Taisto, since they both have no small measure of credibility. Nekane Vidar is a good man, but I do not believe he has the grasp on power that he believes he has. Some of you may have heard that groups were sent to eliminate me in order to assure that the coup was unopposed. Some of them were suvari, paid to act as assassins. These orders did not come from Vidar, but from Taisto, who supposedly follows orders from Vidar. Does that sound like the action of an honorable man?" He paused and looked over the crowd.

"From my friend Kemen I have learned more about honor than I've ever known before, and I would not have the Erdemen army of honorable men like him be led by a murderer and thief. Taisto stole from my father like a common thief years ago, and my father forgave him and trusted him again. Taisto and Vidar between them executed my tutor, his wife, and several other innocents for a plot to murder me, though I know they were not involved.

"Yet even this I could understand, if it was done for the good of Erdem. I would not, perhaps, agree with it, but I could understand. But then there is another fact that Kemen and I discovered yesterday. I assume you are aware of the famine that has plagued Rikuto for the last few years."

He waited until he saw a few nods among the men. "Rikuto has suffered both from bad crops and a great increase in Tarvil raids that have destroyed crops and killed women and children as well as men. The Rikutan king Ashmu Tafari has been buying grain from Erdem for over a year at prices that nearly destroyed Rikuto. I, in the palace, was not told of this. That grain, too, was often stolen by Tarvil raiders. What can you imagine was done with it?"

He paused again for one heartbeat. "It was sold in Erdemen marketplaces at absurdly high prices. The Tarvil raiders were paid by Taisto to destroy crops in Rikuto, then to attack the convoys carrying grain that Rikuto fairly paid for and bring it back to Erdem to be sold again in our markets. All this money was funneled directly into Taisto's pockets. The result, desperate raids by Rikuto into Erdemen border towns for food, was of no concern to him."

"I do not know yet whether Taisto's only purpose was gold, or whether there is more to his treachery than that. But I do know that innocent women, children, farmers, and soldiers on both sides of the border have suffered for his greed. I oppose Taisto and Vidar because they do not serve the Erdemen people. I care about Erdem more than I ever did when I lived in the castle, for now I have lived among farmers and soldiers, good men.

"I am honored by your support of my claim to the throne, as I'm honored to serve such a great country. I am young. I am untried. But I swear to you that I will serve Erdem before myself, and I will take the counsel of honorable men in doing so."

I noticed he assumed their support, rather than asking for it. Good.

Hakan's voice faded into a vast silence. He stepped down and glanced at me. Itxaro dismissed the men for the evening. The formations relaxed, and men began talking in the growing darkness. Someone on the far side of the training ground began to sing, and it quickly swelled to a roar, the song picked up by hundreds of voices. It was an old song, a song of love for Erdem, of a soldier's pride in the country he serves. The choice of that song didn't exactly promise anything. But it did give me hope.

EIGHTEEN

T he next morning we headed on to Relakato, some eight days away with quick riding. Hayato said his commanding officer, Sikke Bakar, who was normally stationed at Rivensworth, was meeting there with the local kedani commander. We didn't have many men, just Hayato's squad less the one man who'd been wounded in the skirmish, Hayato, Hakan, and me.

Every night I dismounted wondering why bones knit together so slowly. Hayato and his men prepared the food, and the first night Hakan brought mine to me before I realized it was ready.

I had taken off the strap around my ribs and was lying on the ground flat on my back taking deep breaths to ease the tension, trying not to grimace at the pain.

"Here." Hakan dropped to sit on the ground next to me, holding out a skewer of roasted venison, onions, and tubers.

We ate mostly in silence. It was late spring, and the country was beautiful, though most of the time we were riding too fast to pay attention to it.

"How much do you hurt?"

I shrugged. "It's fine. Why?"

He looked away. "In a couple days, when it's a bit better, could we practice with the swords again?"

I nodded. "You could practice with Hayato now."

He hesitated, but then nodded. He was nervous; he didn't trust Hayato the way he trusted me. That was good. He needed to practice against someone else, someone unknown.

I finished eating quickly and went to find Hayato. "Do me a favor."

He grinned. "Sure. What?"

I handed him my wooden sword. "Spar with Hakan."

"You think he'll have to fight? That's what the army is for." He frowned in confusion.

"I know." I nodded seriously. "Work on his parries and make him counterattack. He tends to be too passive, too defensive. Push him. Make him work. Give him confidence, too."

Hayato licked his lips. "Right."

Watching them train made me realize how much progress Hakan had made. He wasn't good, couldn't hold his own, but he was a hundred times better than he had been. With luck, he might last several minutes against an average kedani. I hoped we wouldn't have to test his skill, but I wanted him prepared for anything.

AT THE GARRISON at Relakato, we followed Hayato to the officers' quarters, where Hayato spoke with Bakar. After a few moments of conversation, Hayato invited us in and Bakar bowed deeply to Hakan. A solemn joy lit his face, and I warmed to him immediately.

Hayato told me later that Bakar, too, had been a foundling. Several years older than I, Bakar was then one of the highest-ranking suvari officers in Erdem, though not the oldest, by virtue of long years of service and a natural talent for leadership. He inspired men to greater heroism and loyalty and was known for his generosity in sharing his knowledge and expertise with younger officers. Hayato greatly respected him; he'd been one of Hayato's mentors and had taken great pains to give Hayato good command experience.

Bakar spoke to Hakan with respect and a fatherly sort of affection, though it was the first time they had met. He sent a messenger to Rivensworth to ready the suvari there to join with us in two days. The kedani commander offered his men, but Hakan shook his head.

"I want to be in Stonehaven before Taisto knows I'm coming. Kedani will take too long. Send word to all the garrisons to wait two days, as if I am still at the border, and then proclaim their support publicly."

We ate dinner that night with Bakar and Hayato. Hakan questioned them in detail about the raids over the northern and eastern borders. Though I'd heard of them for quite some time, he had not received much information in the palace. What we'd seen was enlightening, but hardly a comprehensive account of the border tensions.

I wondered what his father the king had been thinking to leave his son and heir with so little knowledge about the country he would rule. Trained, yes, and Hakan's natural intelligence and wisdom were becoming apparent. But he knew little about the true situation in his own country. Surprisingly, he seemed to have more information about Rikuto, I suppose as a result of the spies his father had in place.

Every nation has spies, and in some ways, I realize they're necessary. Information saves soldiers' lives. It prevents, or can help prevent, stupid decisions by a king or an army commander. But, though I realize its necessity, it leaves a bitter taste in my mouth. I prefer to fight my enemies face to face, blade to blade. Most soldiers I know feel the same.

I met a spy once, and he impressed me more than I would have expected. He was a man like any other. He had an easy and agreeable demeanor that distracted from the light of quick intelligence and relentless purpose in his eyes. His information about the Rikutan army's movements had guided our actions some two weeks before the battle that had retired me. I wished now I'd spoken with him more. His purpose was information, and that didn't strike me as underhanded in the way that a secretive strike or assassination would have.

I suppose I would have felt differently if he'd given information about our movements to the Rikutans. In fact, I suppose there is no reason to believe that he didn't give information to them as well, aside from the fact that we avoided a battle that would have gone badly by our numbers. The morality of spying makes my head ache, but Hakan seemed entirely comfortable debating the value of conflicting information he had received.

"I wonder what his purpose in this is. Surely it cannot be only gold." Hakan sounded puzzled.

I wondered if he underestimated the lure that gold carries for some people. Though I have many faults, gold has never tempted me unduly. It is beautiful, certainly, but the things it buys are not what please me most. Yet it can corrupt some men, leading them far astray into deeds they might have considered despicable in better times. Hakan had been thinking on the puzzle for days but still had reached no answers.

"His actions weaken Erdem nearly as much as they weaken Rikuto. I don't see the purpose."

Bakar spoke quietly. "Do you think he is working for Ophrano? His purpose being to weaken both nations for an invasion later?"

Hakan shook his head. "No. I mean, I suppose it's possible. But Ophrano has little to offer him, and I don't think he speaks Ophrani. He'd be at the mercy of a translator; I can't see him accepting that. Besides, he's been in Stonehaven almost continuously for four or five years. It would be difficult for him to receive orders from outside. Though not impossible."

No one asked about Irkamil to the northeast. Irkamil is weak and could never dream of invading Erdem. We'd been more or less at peace with Irkamil for two hundred years, and could have conquered it long ago if it had anything worth possessing.

Hakan tapped his fingers on the table as he thought, but that night we came to no answers.

FROM RELAKATO TO RIVENSWORTH is a four-day ride if you aren't in a hurry. We made it in two, and arrived late the following night in Esklin, a small village of no importance except that it had an inn. We could have camped or ridden through the night to Rivensworth, but Hakan looked tired and I wanted him strong for whatever would come when we reached the capital. My own aching ribs were not much of a concern; the pain tired me enough that by the time we stopped for the night I could have slept anywhere. Most of the men had to sleep on the floor, of course, but I wanted them near in case of any trouble.

The inn had room, so I did get a bed that night, though I didn't get to sleep in it. I was nearly asleep when the clatter of hooves jerked me back to wakefulness. I pounded on Hakan's door and waited until I heard an answer before running down the stairs. A young suvari was speaking breathlessly with the innkeeper. When he saw me, he dropped to one knee in a bow as deep as Desta's had been. I sat him down at a table, for he was clearly distraught, and he was already speaking when Hakan entered.

"Sir, I come from Relakato. I'm Rokus Serkan, a friend of Commander Siri Andar, in the king's guard. He's friends with Commander Hayato Jalo. I got a message from Siri a few hours after you left Relakato saying that Taisto had heard you were coming. Siri thinks he heard rumors from Vettea. Taisto knows your name, sir, and connected you with the prince even before the rumors of your triumph in Senlik reached Stonehaven. He sent me to warn you to move quickly. Taisto sent his men from Stonehaven three days ago to check every small town for you." He hadn't even stopped to breathe as the words tumbled out in a rush.

"How many men?"

"Thirty, sir."

"Who is their commander?"

"Baris Eker, out of Darsten. They heard you were at Relakato somehow and Eker guessed you'd head for Rivensworth. They're riding for speed, but they're kedani and won't want to fight on horseback if it comes to it. Two or three of them trained as archers for a while, though they're not serving as such now. There's a price on your head, but only Eker's squad took the bait, sir."

Of course, he would use official sanction for his revenge if possible.

Hayato entered then. "Rokus? What are you doing here?"

Serkan nodded toward him respectfully. "Message for Sendoa, sir, from Siri. There is more. Vidar was found dead this afternoon. Looks like poison. All the king's guards have been arrested on suspicion of murder and are to be held until trial next week if no one confesses before then."

Phraa.

I wondered if we would ever know what part Vidar had played. The young man looked down at the table. Would Taisto really wait until the coming week before executing them? Unlikely, unless it served his own purposes somehow. The men of the king's guard are almost beyond suspicion. Service in the king's guard is a reward for past honorable service. Commander Andar was probably older than I was, experienced, having volunteered for further service out of loyalty and pride in Erdem's glory.

Hakan spoke quietly. "We will do what we can."

The young man looked at him bleakly. "He believes Taisto ordered it done, so the real murderer will never be found. The food was not touched from the kitchen to Vidar's table, and Taisto has his own men in the kitchen. Siri will confess to the murder if it appears the other guards will go free if he is executed for it. He begs that you take care, for he is no murderer, and once he is dead, the threat still remains. It is to save his friends that he will do this, but he would have you know he did not poison Vidar."

Hakan nodded.

The young soldier stared at the table a moment before standing to bow again. "I am honored to meet you, sir. I should have been more courteous earlier. Forgive me for my haste and discourtesy."

"Sit down. Have some dinner if you haven't yet. We'll leave immediately."

Hakan nodded and ran upstairs to get his cloak. The innkeeper brought a bit of food and the young soldier ate quickly, as if he were out on a campaign. Good. A soldier learns to eat when there is food, regardless of emotional turmoil, for hunger can make one weak and slow one's reflexes. Hayato woke his men while I thought. When he returned, Hakan looked to me for direction.

I called the innkeeper in to speak with him. "There may be men hunting us. If they ask, say that we're moving west toward Llewton."

Then we mounted up and headed north on the road toward Stonehaven, and I saw the innkeeper staring out the door at us. Good.

Out of sight of the inn and well over a small hill, I led the group off the road to the east, stumbling through the dark woods until we reached a deer trail. That made our path easier, and we followed it for half a league until we reached the road going northeast, to circle around to Rivensworth and enter Stonehaven from the east rather than from the south. Rivensworth was not far.

If the innkeeper followed my instructions, Eker and his men would be off track, but if they threatened him, he would have something else to say and they would be full on the wrong path heading north before long. In the darkness they would have difficulty following our path; there was hardly a sliver of moon to light the way. It was all I could do; we had to go to Rivensworth to join with the men Bakar had commanded for us.

The night was cool and thick with fog which seemed to quiet the horses' hooves, and it would have been beautifully peaceful except that the fog preceded a light misting of rain. The mist turned into a drizzle and then into a steady heavy downpour that soaked through our cloaks, filled our boots, and turned the road to slippery mud. Our path would be washed away, which was good.

But one does not stay alive by trusting to luck, and it worried me that we could not have heard Eker and his men over the rain if they had been right behind us. I finally asked Hayato to take the lead as I fell back to make sure we were not followed.

The young messenger, Serkan, stayed with me, silent and dripping in the cool rain. I was glad summer was well started; even a month earlier the rain would have been much colder. After several minutes, I thought I heard something in the woods to our left, and I pulled Serkan off with me to wait and listen more closely. Indeed, there was someone approaching. Only one person by the sound of it, though the rain made it difficult to judge.

Rainwater ran into my eyes and down my back, between my shoulders and through my hair. My horse blew quietly. A twig snapped softly, barely audible under the steady rain. I dismounted and handed the reins to Serkan before making my way silently through the brush. I'm a better woodsman than most soldiers. It was so dark that I couldn't see clearly, but I waited and moved softly and finally he was within reach.

The edge of my sword at his throat brought a soft, surprised intake of breath, but he waited until I spoke. "What are you looking for?"

"I have a message for the prince Hakan Ithel." He kept his voice quiet and even, an intelligent move.

"I will take it to him." In the dim light, I could see the glint of the white in his eyes.

"I would deliver it to him personally."

I remained silent.

"Or to his friend Kemen Sendoa. I have heard the prince trusts him."

"I am Kemen Sendoa. What is the message?" I did not remove my sword from his throat.

"I was in a squad sent from Stonehaven to kill the prince. I didn't want to do it, so I left my horse to cut through the woods. I hoped I'd find you faster this way. The rest of the group has split, some going on the north road to Stonehaven, and some following the one that cuts around to Rivensworth and then enters Stonehaven from the east. Commander Eker did not believe you would go to Llewton."

"Why are you not with them, then? Surely you would be of help to the prince in a skirmish."

"I would rather join your party, sir. But if you do not allow me that, I still have information that may serve the prince." He stood very still and finally I removed the blade from his throat, watching him closely. I could barely see him incline his head respectfully. "Thank you, sir. I can't blame you for mistrusting me. But I wondered if you would be going to Stonehaven at all if you knew of the invasion."

"What invasion?"

He bobbed his head again. "I thought not. The word went out yesterday, and I heard it from a friend."

The rumors through the army were as bad as those in the marketplace. Gossiping soldiers are worse than gossiping old biddies over their knitting.

"Sir, Taisto sent word to Commander Katzu Itxaro, the kedani commander, to begin marching toward Enkotan immediately. The message will not be received for some two or three more days, but Taisto intends to bring down their capital. Word went out to Commander Yoshiro Kepa to march toward the eastern border and then to reinforce Itxaro's attack as possible when they arrived. Both messages went out last night."

Phraa. I wished there was more light so that I could see the boy's face more clearly. He was young, and his voice was very quiet. I wondered whether the tremor was from fear of me or fear of being caught by Taisto. "Have you any proof of this?"

"No sir, no proof. But you'll hear the rumors yourself when you reach Stonehaven. If you go on there." He hesitated. "I have friends in the kedani myself, sir. They don't see the purpose in invasion. Enkotan has nothing we want that we can't buy more easily than taking it by force. Their army is nothing to ours, but attacking over the mountains will be costly."

In that he was undoubtedly right, and though I still could not see his face I judged him honest. I cursed Taisto silently. What was he thinking now? What purpose would this serve?

"Sir? There is something else. The orders were
sent to Itxaro in the prince's name. Taisto knows
Itxaro has cast his lot with the prince, though I
don't know how, and he sent the orders under the
prince's name in order to ensure Itxaro's compli-
ance." He subsided into an unhappy silence.

No doubt Taisto would deal with Itxaro's loyalty later. The rain fell steadily as I thought. This
was interesting. Difficult.

Finally I spoke. "Follow me then. We'd best
get on."

He followed me back to where Serkan was
waiting anxiously with my horse. I had him mount
behind Serkan and we followed the road to Likur,
the next small town on the road. I had expected
that Hakan would be there waiting, but there were
only a few soldiers. Again I cursed inside. I wanted
Hakan's guidance. I am not qualified to make po-
litical decisions, but there was no time to follow
them.

The men informed me that Hayato had hurried Hakan hotfoot to Rivensworth for fear of
meeting Eker's squad on the road. They had been
worried. I'd disappeared for quite some time. In
the drenching darkness I could judge the passage
of time only with difficulty.

It was a good decision by Hayato to hurry on,
for there were few of us and in the darkness anything could happen. If Hakan was badly injured or
killed in an otherwise successful skirmish, all was
lost. But still it worried me.

NOW, IN THE TELLING of it, I wonder at my own readiness to trust such important news from unknown sources whose verity and loyalty I could not judge. I may have trusted too much in the uniforms they wore and my own experiences with so many good soldiers. We were fortunate. The messages were true and those that carried them were honest. This I count more as a testament to the honor of Erdemen soldiers than to my own wisdom. Later, when I more fully understood the extent of Taisto's treachery, I counted us more fortunate than I had realized.

At the inn in Likur, I used my last coins to buy parchment and quill, but I didn't sit down to write. Serkan waited anxiously as I paced about the room. "Write this letter."

He hurriedly sat down and pulled the quill and parchment to him. He must have wondered why I didn't write it myself, but it was better for him to think me insufferably arrogant than to doubt my competence if I revealed that I couldn't write.

"To Ashmu Tafari with utmost respect, from Kemen Sendoa, who serves the prince Hakan Ithel: I pledge you, on my honor and on that of His Royal Highness the prince Hakan Ithel, that the orders to march on Rikuto did not come from the prince. I beg you, as I have never begged before, to hold your men back in the face of this unforgivable insult to your great kingdom. Our soldiers have been given false orders by a false man, and desire conflict no more than your people do." I waited for Serkan to catch up.

251

"I go to Stonehaven myself to do what I may in Hakan Ithel's service and remove the poisonous traitor that now sits in the prince's throne. Neither the prince nor I expect you to leave your people unprotected, but I beg you to let the men pass unharmed as long as you can. I pledge to do all I may to counter their orders and recall them with all possible speed. His Royal Highness the prince Hakan Ithel is well aware of your honorable conduct thus far and looks forward to better relations between our nations in the future. With all respect and trust in your cooperation, signed Kemen Sendoa."

The boy hesitated.

"Sign it."

He shifted nervously and then complied.

"Make a copy of it, then seal them both." I walked back and forth, thinking as he wrote. Four long steps in each direction, five or six probably for a Tuyet. Two days for the message to reach the border, if we were fortunate, then how many to Enkotan?

"Now the next."

He nodded, quill poised over a new sheet of parchment.

"To Katsu Itxaro, with respect, from Kemen Sendoa, who serves the prince Hakan Ithel: The orders you received were not from the prince, as you must know by now. I trust that you support the prince over Vidar and Taisto, and now is the time to prove your loyalty. The king Ashmu Tafari is an honorable man, and wants no war with Erdem, despite whatever rumors you may have heard from Stonehaven. He did not send the assassins against the prince; that was Taisto's doing. The assassination plot was his, and those accused of it were merely conveniently removed before they could speak of his treachery. If you haven't heard it yet, the recent news of Vidar's death by poisoning should confirm this to you.

"I have begged that Tafari give you time to return to Erdem, though he has every right to send all his men against you now. Your division is strong, nearly as strong as his whole army, but there would be no purpose in spilling that much blood. If you would support the prince over the traitor, bring your men back with all possible haste, at least within our border but all the way to Stonehaven if you would be at the prince's side at this final conflict. I have no authority to order you to, but I believe this would be the prince's request were he here to give it. It would serve him far better than a pointless shedding of good men's blood against the Rikutans, who have no grievance against us aside from what Taisto and Vidar have done. I trust to hear your answer with all due haste. Respectfully, Kemen Sendoa. Make a copy of that one as well."

The boy sealed the two letters as I paced about the room wondering what else I should do.

I dictated a similar letter to Yoshiro Kepa, commander of the division that was to join Itxaro's.

"Give me the letters." In a moment I was out into the courtyard, where the soldiers were waiting. "I need couriers. Immediately."

Several men stood, and I chose the closest. "These go to anyone in the Rikutan army, to be

253

C. J. Brightley

taken directly to the king or to his brother Zuzay Tafari if he's close by. It's two copies, in case one of you meets with a delay."

The men nodded.

"These go to Katsu Itxaro, who leads the kedani now marching toward Enkotan. Again, two copies. And these two go to Yoshiro Kepa, heading toward the eastern border." Another nod, the men standing expectantly. "Kill the horses beneath you if necessary. Go now!"

Nineteen

We set off fast after Hakan and Hayato, but after only a few minutes on the road the rain grew even heavier. We were forced to slow the horses to a walk, picking our way through the deepening mud. I heard muffled curses sometimes from the men behind me when they lost the track and ran into a low hanging branch. I didn't mind the rain for my own sake, since I was already thoroughly soaked and it wasn't cold, but I hoped the messengers had outridden the heaviest of the downpour.

The first sign of trouble was the panicked scream of a horse behind me. Then there was much shouting, but the night was too dark to see much. I heard the twang of a bow more than once and bent low over the horse's neck. I worked my way back through the muddy jumble of men and horses. My horse stumbled, and I found myself pushed up hard against Baris Eker and his horse.

He shouted for his men, and some of them pulled back, though we were all still confusedly interspersed in the darkness. I heard several swords drawn, but in truth I doubted any of the men wanted to fight. It was too dark and too confused, and any of us could kill a friend just as easily as an enemy, or be killed by a friend. Besides, the men wore the same uniforms, the crest of the same kingdom upon them, and there is something sobering about that.

Eker pulled away from me, cursing as he wheeled his horse about. He called for the archers to shoot me. I could scarcely see him in the darkness and I doubted the archers could see me clearly either, but I heard bowstrings stretching taut.

"Sir, I don't think he's even drawn his sword."

That voice was off to my left. If arrows did start to fly, I would drop to the right side, keep my horse between the archer and me.

"Phraa! Shoot him! He's more dangerous than any ten of you!"

Still they hesitated.

I smiled then, hoping they could see it. I was cool and calm to his hot temper, and any soldier would respect that. "Why, Eker? Because I support the prince over a traitor?"

He cursed and kicked his horse forward, though still well out of easy reach. "There's a price on your head, Sendoa, and I intend to collect it." He raised his voice. "And I'll split it with any man that helps me!"

"A price set by a traitor! A usurper who sits on the throne rightfully belonging to the prince Hakan Ithel!" I wondered if any of his men were listening.

Eker must not have trusted them, for he suddenly kicked his horse toward me, cursing and attacking wildly. My sword met his, but I did no more than parry before the archers let fly. They apparently made different choices, or the darkness hampered their shooting, for two arrows thudded into Eker while one hummed past my ear and a fourth cut deeply into my right shoulder. Eker slid off his skittish mount with scarcely a sigh.

I leapt after him, but my sword at his throat was unnecessary. He was dead before he hit the ground.

"Eker is dead. If any man would collect that price for my head, take your chances now. I've an arrow in my shoulder." I heard nothing but the horses moving restlessly in the steady rain.

Finally there was a voice out of the darkness. "No, sir. I have no wish to fight you."

I kept my head well down as I listened, my left hand exploring the damage on my shoulder. The arrow had not lodged in my shoulder, for it had come from an awkward angle far off to my left, but the sharp iron head had furrowed a dangerously deep gouge through the muscle. I couldn't tell how much blood there was as it mixed with the rain, but the hot smell of it stung in my nostrils. The rain felt oddly cool when it flowed into the wound. I should have been faster to drop to the right, but Eker's horse had been in my way.

"No one wishes to collect the prize?" I took care not to sound too strong, even letting my voice waver a bit.

"No sir."

"No."

"I'd rather serve the prince, sir."

I tried again. "Not even the man who shot at my head? It was a good shot in the darkness." There was silence except for the rain. I waited a moment more before mounting again. "Then any man who wishes to cast his lot with Taisto had best get on. I've cast mine with the prince and will not change it now." I wheeled about and let the men follow as they might.

I HALF-EXPECTED AN ARROW in my back as we rode slowly through the darkness. It wouldn't have been difficult for one of the archers to work his way close to me. But no arrow came, and the men stayed soberly quiet in the drenching downpour. I eventually enlisted Serkan's aid to bandage my shoulder, and he made a good attempt given the darkness and rain.

We finally reached Rivensworth not long before dawn. The guards opened the gates to us and Sirak Zhurbinar, Bakar's deputy, greeted us himself. Sirak means "support," and in my weariness I found that comforting.

Hakan, Hayato, and his men had arrived some hours before, mostly ahead of the rain. The men with me were shown to the barracks and fell into bed to sleep before we set out again. Zhurbinar showed me to a nicer room, which he said was

Hakan's request when I arrived. Until then we had been walking and speaking in the darkness, but he lit a lamp to show me the room, and suddenly he cursed. "Why didn't you say something? Come, man, let's take a look at that."

"What?" I looked down at myself as he set the lamp down on a little table. "Oh. It's not as bad as it looks." The front of my shirt was covered in blood, bright red streaks diluted unevenly by the rainwater. "If I could have a clean bandage, it will be fine. The rain made it look much worse than it is."

He nodded and sent a guard hurrying for clean water and bandages. "Let me take a look. Take off your shirt."

I peeled off the dripping bloody shirt and let it fall to the floor with a wet slap. I'd wash it and hope it dried, for I had nothing else to wear for the morrow.

I sat while he untied the bandage. I wondered that he didn't call for the healer instead, but he explained it before I asked. "I trained as a healer as well as a soldier. I always thought it should be part of every soldier's training, but my superiors never seemed to take that suggestion seriously."

I would have, for I've seen several men die who could have been helped with just a bit more knowledge. My own knowledge is limited, so I cannot fault others for the same lack, but I can see the value of it all the same.

"Good. You're right, it's not as bad as it looked at first, but I wouldn't begrudge you a few complaints. Looks like it hurts. You can bite this while I wash it if you want." He handed me a roll of cloth, but I didn't need it. I sat close by the table so he could see in the flickering lamplight. He cleaned the wound and washed it with wine, then powdered it with some herbs he said would help prevent infection. Then he stitched it and bound it more securely.

He gave me the news in uneven spurts through his concentration, and I wished we had more men like him. When Hakan was king, I would advise him to spend more money and more effort on training of healers, for the army did not have enough of them.

"I'd like a longsword, if you'll lend me one." I also wanted a bath, because I was covered in mud and grit, but there wasn't time for one.

"Of course. Why? Something happen to yours?"

"No, mine is fine. Hakan doesn't have one."

"He doesn't?" He looked up in surprise. "He's not armed?"

"No." Of course he had a bootknife, but there was no way to get a good sword for him out in the hills where we had been for months. "But he will be."

"Of course." He finished on my shoulder and stepped back. "Much better. It's not pretty, but you'll have good use of your arm, I think. How does it feel?"

"Well enough. Thank you." In truth, my broken ribs still surprised me at times with pain much sharper and more immediate, though that skirmish was nearly six weeks past. Six weeks isn't long for broken ribs, but I had more important things that demanded my attention, and it was frustrating.

"What'd you do there?" He nodded at the strap around my ribs for the first time, though he'd noticed earlier.

"A couple broken ribs. They're healing."

He frowned more severely, but only unbuckled his sword and handed it to me. "I'll use a standard issue. Give him this one, it's the best we have here."

I examined it closely. It was finely made and very serviceable, though it had not seen much use. It was an officer's weapon, certainly more beautiful than a standard issue longsword. "Standard issue is fine. I'm giving him mine. I trust it best. Whatever you give me will be for my use, not his. If you'd rather not lend a mercenary such a beautiful blade, I won't be insulted." I wouldn't have blamed him if he'd been offended at my mistrust of his weapon, taken it back and sent the guard for a standard issue, but he smiled suddenly.

"Good. I'm glad you're with him. Take it."

He gave me a clean shirt, and I left the old one hanging over the back of a chair to dry. When he left, I washed as best I could and fell into bed for well-deserved rest. But the sun rose in only a few hours, and I was up with it. I consider myself very collected and not easily excited, and in general it's true, even before battle. But I was tense and restless, and I believe it was because my fear was not for myself but for Hakan. My shoulders were tight and I went outside to sweat out my nerves.

I exercised in the grey light of dawn. The sky had cleared though the ground was still wet and muddy. I watched the company go through their exercises together. Hakan met me when the morning exercises were nearly finished, standing quietly as he watched the men practice their sequences.

Finally he spoke. "I take it you had some trouble last night?"

"Aye. A bit. Baris Eker is dead, and some of his men have cast their lot with you."

He looked up at me seriously. "And the others?"

I spoke so only he could hear me. "Half of them took the north road to Stonehaven. I know nothing about them. I'm not sure about some of the ones that fell in with us. You haven't asked, but I'd recommend that we leave them here in training under Zhurbinar when we continue on to Stonehaven. Not under arrest, for there is no proof of anything, but out of your way until your throne is assured."

He nodded slowly and eyed the white bandage on my shoulder. "How bad is it? What happened?"

"It was an arrow. It's not bad, just a cut." I felt strangely awkward, but now was as good a time as any. I unbuckled my scabbard and handed it to him. "Here. You'll need a sword."

His mouth dropped open in shock as he looked up at me. "I can't take this." He held it uncomfortably.

"You can't ride in to Stonehaven with a wooden practice sword. I hope you won't need it, but you'd best have a sword. Zhurbinar lent me his. It's more kingly looking. You can choose between them if you like." I walked quickly back to my room and presented him with the commander's sword.

He glanced between them.

"His is more royal, without a doubt. But I haven't used it, and cannot vouch for its soundness. My own blade is humble, but it has served me well, and will do the same for you if you take it."

He licked his lips and glanced up at me. "I'm honored, Kemen. Are you sure?"

I smiled. "Every soldier needs a sword, Hakan. A king most of all."

He bowed to me, as I had taught him to bow, but more deeply than he should have. He took my sword and began to belt it on.

"If you'd prefer, we can switch scabbards. This one is more handsome."

He shook his head and smiled. "I'm not ashamed to wear your sword, Kemen. It's an honor, and I won't hide it."

"Take the grip of it, feel it. The weight is different from the wooden ones we've been practicing with. I should have given it to you earlier, so you'd be more familiar with it."

He drew it carefully and moved it about experimentally.

"Taisto sent word two days ago to Itxaro on the eastern border to march on Enkotan."

He scowled as he sheathed the sword. "Why? We were doing so well. Relations were improving. I'll send word to him immediately to turn around, and an official apology to Tafari."

"I took the liberty of doing so in your name last night, as soon as I found out. Speed was crucial."

He nodded and looked at me oddly, as if he were evaluating me.

"I hope you will forgive my presumption," I added. He was the prince after all, and I wouldn't have been surprised if he'd been angry with me, though I could have done no differently. The lives of too many men depended it, soldiers, men I had trained with and taught.

He hesitated, biting his lip and glancing away, as if he didn't want to look at me. "How did you send the order?"

"Letters. One to Itxaro to turn around immediately and one to Tafari, apologizing and begging his forbearance until Itxaro turned back to the border." I wondered what he was aiming at. "Also one to Yoshiro Kepa, who was sent to reinforce Itxaro, requesting that he turn toward Stonehaven instead."

"You wrote them letters?"

I swallowed. "I sent them letters." I wondered if he would notice the subtle difference.

He nodded. "I see. Thank you." He hesitated again as if he would speak, but then turned to go. He abruptly turned around again. "You know, you've seen enough of my weaknesses, and yet somehow you still trust me. You've honored me with your sword, of which I'm unworthy. We both know it. You might do me the honor of trusting that I would do the same for you."

I swallowed hard again. "What do you mean?"

He stared at me a moment before I dropped my eyes. "I can teach you to read, Kemen. It's not hard."

I shook my head, feeling very stupid and wholly inadequate. Shamed. I pushed down the anger I felt, for he did not mean to shame me. "You cannot. Others have tried, Hakan. It's not for lack of teaching that I cannot read." I turned away, thankful that my dark skin mostly hid the heat I could feel in my face.

He stood in silence a moment before saying, "I'll try to teach you if you like. But I think no less of you, and I will think no less of you if you can't learn it. Not everyone has every gift. Clearly, it is no lack of intelligence that prevents it. I count you a friend, the best I've ever had, and friends take each other as they are, not as they would want to be."

He nodded abruptly and left me staring at the floor, my throat tight.

TWENTY

W e set off that morning with most of the men of the garrison behind us, some five hundred armed suvari. The men sang rousing marching songs, and farmers along the road cheered us and waved encouragingly. As we rode, I thought about Taisto's invasion. I wondered what he thought it would accomplish. Did he truly think to rule both nations from one throne? He scarcely had a grasp on the throne of Erdem, much less that of Rikuto. Erdem's army is much stronger than that of Rikuto, and perhaps, if we threw our entire might into it, we could indeed conquer it.

But there would be no purpose. The Rikutan people would not consent to Erdemen rule. The arm of the Erdemen king is not long enough to enforce obedience in Enkotan, much less the Rikutan countryside. We don't even share a language with the common people, only Kumar with the warriors. On a map, if one were to look at Erdem and Rikuto as two halves of the same country, the Sefu Mountains would divide it almost impassably, a vertical line through the center of the kingdom. How could one king hope to rule both sides? Erdem is richer and more powerful, but the mountains would make such a kingdom impractical, completely aside from the difficulty of the invasion itself.

Hakan was silent until we were nearly at the open gates of Stonehaven.

"Kemen." He didn't look at me. "I imagine at least some of Taisto's men will be willing to fight for him. We'll be outnumbered in the palace, and I don't want a siege outside it. I want to change their minds. I want to confront him in front of everyone."

My shoulders tightened. "We will fight for you. The army is yours. Use it."

"I don't want a fight. They're good men, at least most of them are. Many of them probably don't even know I'm alive. They might support me if they knew." He took a deep breath and kept his eyes forward. "Truth. I will tell them the truth about Taisto and what he has done. Then they can decide."

The silence between us drew out, broken only by the sound of hooves on the road. He was pale, nervous, and my ribs ached with tension. Fear for him.

"I left a letter with Bakar at Relakato. It says that if something happens to me, I have formally named you as my successor and that the letter stands as my personal singing of the Hero Song for you. I've recommended a few changes in the ministerial staff if you take the throne."

It took me a moment to be sure my voice would be steady when I replied. "If there is a duel, I will fight for you, Hakan. You should not cross swords with a traitor." He wasn't ready and we both knew it.

"You told me once I needed to earn the trust of the people. I don't deserve their trust if I'm afraid to fight for them."

"He's a murderer. You don't have to do it." My voice sounded flat and hard in my own ears, but in my heart it was a plea.

He swallowed and nodded once. "I know."

I don't know when he grew from a boy to a man in my eyes. But that ride was when I realized it.

A boy must be protected, even from himself. A man has the right to risk death for his beliefs, and a king has the right to fight for his people. I did not have the right to deny him that, regardless of how I might fear for him.

All the way to Stonehaven I wrestled with my fear and the questions it raised. He had the right to face Taisto, the right to risk his own life. But for Erdem's sake, I would sacrifice much. My own life. My honor, perhaps, depending on how you define honor. I had sacrificed men under my command before, and would do it again. I felt torn, shredded, because by then I respected Hakan too much to needlessly tread on his rights as a man and a king, but I could not bear the thought of watching him fight a duel, watching him die, and with him watching Erdem's hope die. I could not be the king Erdem needed, and no one was more aware of it than I was.

Outside Stonehaven we gathered a small train of cheering commoners drawn by the songs and the distinctive bugle call of the musical corps announcing the royal presence. The gates of the city were already open for the day by the time we arrived, and we entered the city at the head of an impromptu parade. Women and girls threw flowers on us from upper windows and people followed us singing and even dancing to the spirited songs. What they would do when we reached the palace, I had no idea, but the feeling was more than pleasant. The song rang from the stone walls and preceded us into the grand empty space around the palace itself.

The palace was surrounded by a high stone wall which itself was separated from the nearest buildings by some distance, the better to give defenders space to breathe. Guards were stationed along the top of the wall as well as at each gate, and I wondered whether they would let us in. The army could have besieged the palace, but it would take time to get more men and longer for the palace to concede.

Again we were fortunate. The men at the gate saluted respectfully and stood aside. I was glad to find that they had not betrayed their vow of loyalty to the king. Surely only a very few of them could have recognized Hakan personally, but those few were the highest officers. That, and we were accompanied by five hundred suvari in uniform. They bowed low before Hakan, who returned their courtesies with a nod and trotted briskly into the palace grounds.

Hakan strode up the grand front staircase as though he owned the palace already. Hayato and I followed, the suvari following closely behind us. They were suvari swordsmen, and I thought suddenly we would have been better served to have some archers with us. I hoped it would not come to that, and for a while I almost thought we might be so fortunate. We were unopposed at first.

The men at the grand door at the front of the castle also bowed respectfully and backed away. Aside from those few, the halls were deserted, and Hakan hesitated a moment before turning to his left and walking through the great entry hall to a smaller room. It was darkly luxurious, deep green tapestries lining the walls with scenes of the great battles of the past. I recognized one of the most famous scenes of the battle of Liriankano, when the king Piakarto himself defended Fort Kuzeyler with some few picked men from the raging Tarvil barbarians. The white horse was quite distinctive, though who knows what color the horse really was, or whether the king was truly there at all. That was the legend, and it was an inspirational one, for it embodied the idea of great Erdemen kings, the sacrificial love for their people, the great courage that gave them the right to rule, the loyalty that they demanded and received of their brave soldiers.

The suvari followed us in uneven formation through the halls. They were distracted by the luxury, and I hoped they would not become inattentive and careless. I half expected Taisto to have archers along the raised walkways in the great hall, but there was no one. The halls were empty and our steps echoed on the marble floors. I could see the slightly worn paths that feet had made through the centuries. Hayato set groups of twenty men in several key points to prevent Taisto from fleeing if he were inclined to do so.

Hakan stood in the middle of the smaller hall and thought a moment before continuing to the end and turning down another hall. I wondered at the lack of servants. Surely a palace of this size would have servants to handle the horses and cook the food, clean the floors and light the many candles and lamps at night. Taisto must have eliminated many of them as well; they would not be eager to serve him after seeing his treachery.

There was no one in any of the rooms, and Hakan led the way to the king's suite of planning rooms, where the real work of ruling is done. The throne is for ceremonies and royal events, but for administration and planning, the king works at a desk like any common administrator.

We found Taisto sitting behind a desk in one of the king's planning rooms. He looked up and smiled when we entered, a cold and confident smile with no little scorn.

TWENTY-ONE

R yuu Taisto was some eight or ten years my senior, an age past the prime of speed in one's reflexes but not yet weakening in strength, a trifling slowness counteracted by greater experience and cunning. He was tall, Hakan's own height, though still shorter than I, and fairskinned with curling blond hair beginning to grey and eyes of a clear icy blue. He was lithe and muscular yet, though there was some slight thickening about his middle as most men acquire as they age.

He stood as he spoke to Hakan. "Ah, so you decided to come back after all." His voice was very even, almost pleasant.

"You are under arrest. Place your sword on the desk and step away from it at once. Take him to the throne room for trial." Hakan's voice sounded terribly young, but he held his chin high, his face taut and very white. Of course, it would not be so easy, but he would try to remove Taisto peacefully. It was not in his nature to deny Taisto that chance.

I stepped toward Taisto with several of the other suvari, and his men stepped forward as well, providing a human shield. I wondered if they knew of his treachery, what they thought of him. Whether they were willing to die for him. The tension was like a humming in my ears.

Taisto smiled again. "I think not. You are not worthy of your father's throne. Nor was he worthy of it. You know this just as well as I do."

I almost struck him then. I could have done it. But I waited for Hakan's command. He'd said he wanted the truth to be known, and I would honor his wish.

Hakan paled and his lip trembled almost imperceptibly before he steadied himself.

"It will be better for everyone if you leave now. Take your Dari and your few pathetic soldiers and leave ruling to someone who knows what he's doing." Taisto's voice was smooth and cool. Confident.

I gauged the faces of the men ranged about him. Most were very young, raw recruits with no experience to guide them, no ability as yet to see through Taisto's treachery. With luck, for one can never discount the danger of bad luck, I could handle somewhere between three and ten. The fight would probably go in our favor, even without the suvari outside, except for the one most vital factor. If Hakan were killed, all was lost, and it would matter less than nothing if everything else went perfectly.

Yet I had no desire to fight them. They were boys that I might have trained myself in any other circumstances, young men that I might have led into battle in other times. I would have guided them, trained them, driven and encouraged them. I felt slightly nauseated at the idea of drawing my blade on them. Hakan could easily have stepped out of the room, commanded us to fight for him. Outside, there were nearly five hundred more suvari ready to fight for him as well, and the city for him beyond the palace walls.

My fingers curled around the hilt of my sword. My mouth tasted sour, but I readied myself. For Hakan. For Erdem.

Hakan spoke very clearly, his voice slightly raised so that everyone might hear him. "I suppose you mean to you? You, who killed my tutor Tibon Rusta and his wife and other innocents for a plot to assassinate me? When you sent the assassins yourself? Killed an innocent boy to provide a body?"

"Come now. Can you deny I would be a better king? Better for your people?" Taisto's lips lifted in a smile, white teeth glinting in the light coming from the window. He was handsome, but for the light of cruelty in his eyes. Born for leadership, with a cunning, beckoning voice, seductively touching on Hakan's insecurity.

"I would have given you that. Until I found that you were selling grain to the Rikutans and then stealing it back from them to line your own pockets. Paying barbarians to destroy their crops to drive up the prices. Little children starved because of you! Men died for your greed! I wouldn't have to be a very good king to be better for Erdem than you." Hakan's voice rose in anger.

Some of Taisto's men glanced back and forth between Hakan and Taisto. Good. Let them question their loyalty to him.

Taisto smiled coldly. "What do you care for Rikutans?"

"I care for my own country! You betrayed our soldiers to Tarvil barbarians. You can't pretend that you serve the interests of Erdem. You serve only yourself."

Several of Taisto's soldiers narrowed their eyes at Hakan's words.

Taisto's arrogance cost him, because he did not try to deny this. "They were problematic. Wouldn't you sacrifice those who kept you from a greater goal? I would be a far better king than a foolish, untried boy. Better for your country, better for the glory of your kingdom. I won't pretend that I wouldn't enjoy it. Just like Rusta and the others, they stood in my way. Just like you now stand in my way. In the way of my rule, in the way of greater glory for Erdem than has been seen in a thousand years."

He smiled again, handsome and cruel. "You don't understand, do you? Of course not. Rikuto is weak now, I have assured that. Tafari has no money and no food, and his army has been employed hunting rather than training for over a year. The time is ripe to invade, and indeed the invasion has already begun. Soon there will no longer be Rikuto and Erdem on opposite sides of the Sefu Mountains, but one great kingdom, united under one king. Me. Ryuu Taisto."

Hakan was wise enough not to admit that we hoped we'd forestalled the invasion, though I saw his mouth open in quick anger. Finally he spoke. "I should have expected such a base plan from a base and dishonorable man."

Taisto's eyes narrowed in anger, but Hakan continued. "I didn't expect much from you. Even as a child, I could see your greed and contemptible nature. I had expected a little more loyalty to my father despite his many faults, but your treachery should not have surprised me."

Hakan was very pale, standing rigidly straight with his chin held high. I wondered whether he was deliberately baiting Taisto, and finally decided that he was, for such discourtesy doesn't come naturally to him.

He lifted his chin. "One of my father's greatest mistakes was trusting you after you were caught stealing from the king's treasury like a common thief. It was foolishly optimistic of him, but it was a mistake that showed his character as much more noble than yours, despite his failures."

Taisto's voice was high and tight with anger. "You may insult me all you wish, but I will not give up the throne so easily. You believe it is yours for the taking. I do not. It seems there is little to do but fight for it, but I doubt you have the courage."

"I can muster the courage now." Hakan's voice rang out clear and strong.

Taisto's face was white with anger as he drew his sword. He studied Hakan as he slowly wiped the blade with a white cloth that had been sitting on his desk.

I spoke quietly. "It is not fitting for a prince to duel a common thief and traitor. I offer my sword in your service, if you care to command me, Prince Hakan Ithel."

The corners of Hakan's mouth twitched in what might have been a smile if he had not been so nervous. "Thank you, Kemen. But I will cross swords with him. Some have doubted that I own the courage to rule, and I would prove them wrong. If any man doubts me, take heed now."

Again my voice was quiet in my attempt to be calming. "Perhaps you both would be better served to take the fight to the great hall. There's more room."

Hakan nodded, but Taisto shook his head.

"There's no need for that. It will be over soon. If all but five men of your men and five of mine go out into the hallway to wait, we'll have plenty of room in here, and plenty of witnesses for your cowardice." He was smiling again, a cold confident set to his lips.

I saw Hakan's jaw tighten, but he only nodded in reply, and Taisto motioned his men out into the hallway. Hayato sent out the suvari as well. When I glanced back into the hallway outside, they were staring tensely at each other, and I wondered whether they were really on different sides at all. Taisto's men looked shaken and unsure of their loyalties.

Those of us left pressed ourselves against the walls, leaving a large clear space in the middle of the room, bounded on one end by the heavy wooden desk. I ached to take Taisto's head myself, and my stomach twisted with fear for Hakan. He was not ready for it. All our training, hours and hours of grueling training, for I had pushed him very hard, had come to this.

He was young and he was brave. He was very smart. But he was only one step above mediocre with a sword. He had neither the speed nor the strength necessary to defeat Taisto, who held his sword with the familiarity of long use.

Every muscle in my body was taut with fear for the boy. I wondered how dishonorable it would be to kill Taisto myself. To my mind, Hakan had earned the throne already through honorable conduct, his education and wisdom, his agreements with Tafari. He would be best for Erdem. Surely a man could do something dishonorable, on the surface, for the good of Erdem? I wondered if Hakan would think me despicable if I did so. For his life, and for the good of Erdem, I might do it anyway.

Hakan drew his sword, the one I'd given him, and Taisto smiled coldly when he saw Hakan's hand shaking.

"Still afraid of swords, aren't you, boy?"

"I'm not stupid. If you're not afraid, you're less clever than I'd given you credit for."

They took their stances as for a formal duel. Taisto's bow was graceful and mocking, not nearly as low as it should have been. Hakan's was perfect in courtesy, and he remembered not to take his eyes off Taisto. I had taught him never to look away from an enemy.

Then the duel began. Taisto attacked and then retreated, testing Hakan, not yet interested in killing him. In and out. Hakan's form was abysmal, worse than it had been in months. He was afraid, licking dry lips in a pause in the action while Taisto studied him. Taisto arrogantly left him several openings, but Hakan did not attack, and I cursed myself for not pushing him harder.

I had drilled him over and over again on parries and blocks. One must first stay alive before one can counterattack. At least Hakan was doing that well, for despite his shoddy footwork and his sloppy form he blocked every strike. Taisto grew more confident as they circled, and I could see the lust for blood in his eyes. Blood and power, for his ultimate goal I believe was not murder but power.

Taisto glanced at me periodically, though he did not look at any of the other soldiers about the room. He spoke coolly, though both he and Hakan were breathing harder now.

"How much did you pay for your Dari dog?"

"He's a friend. A good one." Hakan's voice shook with anger and fatigue.

Taisto could have killed him several times over, but he was toying with him. Whether it was for his own amusement or for some other purpose I never knew, but I wouldn't have been surprised if he meant to use it for his glory in front of the soldiers watching. I wished Hakan wouldn't show his fear, wouldn't show that he was weary. He'd put on the façade for Tafari, he could have done it again. Taisto would take advantage of his weakness.

"Kemen Sendoa, is it?"

"Aye." Hakan blocked another strike by Taisto. His footwork was barely good enough to keep him moving, his form scarcely better than an utter beginner.

"I thought I killed him once. He's trouble, along with his friends. Though they were not so difficult to dispose of."

My jaw tightened in anger when I thought about Yuudai, and suddenly I realized what Hakan was doing. He wanted to be underestimated.

Taisto was directly in front of me some distance away, his right side facing me, Hakan far off to my right. I stepped forward, my footstep deliberately loud and ringing, my hand on my sword.

Taisto swung wildly at me, taking his eyes from Hakan. In that moment Hakan lunged forward and buried his sword into Taisto's belly, ducking under the weak swing of Taisto's sword back at him as he pulled away.

I'd twisted away from Taisto's sword, which, instead of spilling my guts on the marble floor as he had intended, merely grazed my arm. I stepped in again to grab Taisto's wrist, bringing his sword down and forcing it from his hand.

Hakan stepped away and watched, very pale, still holding his bloody sword.

Taisto dropped to his knees, clutching weakly at his stomach, bright red blood pulsing out in a fading rhythm. His face was terrible to see, but mercifully, his death did not last long. He collapsed sideways, an awkward and undignified way to die. I could find in myself no pity for him.

Hakan turned away and dropped his sword. It fell with a great clatter that rang in the room, and when the sound faded, there was nothing but silence.

Everyone's eyes remained on Hakan, and he must have realized it, for he drew himself up stiffly. "Take the body away."

Taisto's men stepped forward quietly, took the body by wrists and ankles, and carried it out through the hallway. The blood smear on the marble floor looked vulgar, almost profane.

The scratch on my arm stung more than I would have expected. Hakan was shaking visibly, and he walked to the end of the room to lean half-sitting against the desk. I followed him. He looked very young and very overwhelmed, grieving, though I cannot imagine it was for Taisto. More likely it was for the time in which he had taken no one's life, drawn no blood. It is a form of innocence you can never return to, and I mourned it as well.

I sat beside him in silence and inspected the cut on my arm. It was burning like fire, and the edges were an angry red, though the cut was scarcely more than an inch long and not at all deep. Odd.

Finally I spoke. "You did well. Don't regret it, Hakan. You had no other choice." My mind felt fuzzy, and I was thirsty.

Hakan looked at me and I blinked. His face suddenly split into two, the double images wavering before me.

"What's wrong?" His voice sounded very distant.

I felt light-headed, and suddenly I understood.

"His blade was poisoned." That's what I intended to say, anyway. I am unsure if the words came out clearly, for I heard Hakan speaking and could not decipher his words anymore. My tongue seemed very large in my mouth.

I remember sliding down to sit leaning against the front of the desk and Hakan's voice shouting, and after that everything was unclear for some time.

Twenty-Two

I f the darkness after my ribs were broken was warm and welcoming, this one was hot and feverish and entirely unpleasant. My skin pricked with chill while I sweated through the sheets. Every muscle in my body ached and I shook violently with fever. I felt cool hands on my forehead and I choked on honeyed wine at times, but I lived more in dreams than in reality. I watched Yuudai die again. I relived the campaign in the south, but only the horrifying parts.

I watched Hakan's duel with Taisto over and over. Once I was Taisto, and I watched my own hand plunge a sword into Hakan's body. He writhed in pain, blood coming from his mouth, his eyes huge and reproachful on mine. Another time I watched Hakan kill Taisto, but then collapse in grief himself, cursing me for teaching him violence.

I suppose I should have died. That was no doubt Taisto's intent, though I imagine the poisoned blade was meant for Hakan. That I was there was only a happy coincidence for him, a chance to remedy that earlier failure to eliminate me. I am much larger than Hakan, larger than nearly any Tuyet man, and the scratch was so small I had not received much of the poison. An unpleasant death it would have been, too. I count myself very fortunate.

When I was aware enough to appreciate my surroundings again, I was amazed. I'd been inside the palace only once before, on taking the oath of service before the king Hakan Emyr. That took place in the great throne room, and didn't last long, for we were hurried back out to duty. I'd been fourteen years old, tall, gawky and painfully shy, awed by the king's grandeur and the beautiful age of the palace. Even the Golden Eagle Regnant had been presented outside on the palace lawn. A Dari, even a soldier serving the king, wasn't entirely welcome in the palace.

My room was luxuriously appointed, but much smaller than the great throne room. It was warm and richly inviting, elegant. The bed in which I lay was covered in gorgeous green blankets with gold and silver threads woven into them. The outlines of the royal crest glinted in the light. The walls were covered in tapestries, and large windows all along one wall let in streams of golden light. The windows were open, and I could hear the stamp of horse hooves outside far away, birdcalls, and distant voices singing and laughing. The air carried the scent of flowers, and I wondered if there was a garden behind the palace.

There was a small table in front of the windows with two matching chairs carved of dark wood, intricately beautiful with the curving lines of classical Erdemen design. On it was a gleaming silver tray with a light breakfast of tea, fluffy brown bread, grapes, goat cheese, and some sort of little pastries that I had never seen before.

I was terribly thirsty and so I struggled from the bed, feeling the edges of fever not entirely receded. I ate sitting at the little table. The tea was still quite warm; I thought I recognized the smell of an expensive tea from the south that I'd wanted to try when I was there but had never been able to afford. The pastries had some sort of honey and nut mixture inside, and I wondered whether Hakan ate like this every day as a child. I'd never seen such luxury.

I was dressed in a rich silk robe, though I didn't remember changing clothes.

How long had I been ill? I searched the room until I found my own clothes neatly folded on a trunk at the end of the bed. Good.

Wearing familiar clothes, I felt a bit more like myself, though my arms and legs still felt hollow and weak from fever. I opened the door and looked out into the hall. There was a young girl walking quickly toward my room, and she startled in surprise when she saw me.

"Where is the prince Hakan Ithel?" My voice was rough from disuse. "What day is it?"

She swallowed and curtsied politely. "It is Nelja, sir. You have been ill for three days. The prince Hakan Ithel is in his working office. Would you like to see him?" Her voice was high and clear, still childish. She must have been no more than fourteen or so. She spoke very courteously, her eyes cast down in respect.

"Please."

She curtsied again. "This way. Are you feeling better, sir?"

"Aye. Thank you." I followed her.

She walked quickly, and I cursed the weakness that made me stumble in the long hallway. I had to pause and lean against the wall a moment when my head whirled.

She was back at my side immediately. "I'm sorry I'm going too fast. Father tells me I walk too fast. Do you want me to get someone to help you?" Her eyes were very wide, no longer quite so afraid. I must have looked awful, and I felt very self-conscious. Even a young girl can cause a man to stand up straighter.

"No. Thank you." I was too proud to ask her to walk more slowly, but she did anyway. We walked through several halls until we reached a very ornate door.

The girl knocked quietly, and at a sound from within, she opened the door. She stepped inside and I heard her speak. "Your Royal Highness, Kemen Sendoa is awake and wishes to see you."

In a moment, she opened the door wider. Hakan was already on his feet striding toward me, and he stopped in surprise. "Kemen, you should be in bed! Come in, sit down and rest."

I nodded my thanks to the girl and stepped inside. She closed the door behind me. I sat, but I didn't really feel any more comfortable. The chair was of rich red velvet and ornate wood, and I felt very out of place. Hakan sat across from me, smiling with pleasure. He seemed totally at ease in the rich surroundings, and though it should not have, it startled me to realize that the palace was his home.

"Are you feeling any better?"

I nodded. "Aye, thank you."

"I suppose you'll want to know what happened then. It's Nelja. The fight with Taisto was on Edella, so you've been ill for three days."

I nodded.

"Katsu Itxaro received your message and turned around immediately, sending his own apology to Tafari and request for safe passage back to the border. Tafari granted it, and they were escorted courteously to the border. This of course is due to the respect they both have for you, so Erdem and I are again in your debt."

I looked down at my boots. Though they had been neatly cleaned, they were still only a soldier's boots. They looked rough and uncultured on the ornate rug.

"You did well in the duel." I didn't know what else to say, but he did deserve that.

He smiled. "You thought I'd forgotten everything you taught me."

I nodded. "At first."

"I wanted him to underestimate me. I'm not good with a sword, and I never will be. I had to do it that way, let him think me helpless."

287

I nodded.

"Thank you for giving me the opening, though. You know I've never been good at making my own."

I nodded again. In truth, I had done it almost without thinking.

"I've planned the coronation for Seitsema, in three more days." Something was familiar about that date, but my mind was still cloudy.

"It's five months to the day since my father died and the three hundredth anniversary of Hiraku's victory at Silverhill." Yes. Tarmo Hiraku, one of the great heroes of Erdem, had won his greatest battle on that date while leading the united eastern Tuyet forces against the Tarvil. I must have been more ill than I realized if I hadn't remembered that.

Hakan's voice broke into my thoughts. "Traditionally the king, if he is yet alive, crowns his son. If the prince is a minor when the king dies, the regent crowns the prince upon his majority. If the king dies before crowning his son, and the son is not a minor, the prince crowns himself."

This I knew.

"Kemen, I would be honored if you would crown me king in three days' time."

My jaw dropped in surprise.

Hakan smiled. "Don't protest. It makes perfect sense. If a prince crowns himself, the implication is that he has taken the throne himself. You have earned this throne for me, and if you want it, I will give it to you without protest."

I shook my head, as he must have known I would.

"My father would have done it if he were alive. I would be honored if you would serve in his stead."

I had to swallow before my throat would make a sound. I dropped my head in respect, for he was not only Hakan, but soon to be king. "I would be honored to serve you in whatever way you wish." It was true, for he would be a good and wise king.

He laughed gently and put one hand on my shoulder for just a moment. "No. It is I who am honored by your friendship. I would ask, most humbly, if you would continue to serve me as advisor. I have great need of good men. Trustworthy, honorable, wise, and brave. A king cannot ask for more than that."

"Aye." I smiled at him when I looked up. My arms prickled with chill. The fever was rising again; I could feel it in the tingling of my scalp and the odd hollow feeling of my arms and legs when I rose to bow formally to him. He deserved that honor, though, and I was glad to give it.

There was a knock at the door, and I was able to sit again without Hakan realizing how much the bow had taxed me. "Your Royal Highness, Commander Yoshiro Kepa is here to see Kemen Sendoa. Should I tell him to wait or send him in?"

Hakan glanced at me and I shrugged. Hakan answered, "Send him in. And bring some wine when you come."

It was a few minutes before there was a knock on the door. The girl entered and curtsied as she introduced Commander Kepa, and he bowed deeply to Hakan and then to me. He was older than I was by some ten or twelve years, with the erect bearing of a lifelong soldier. Hakan motioned him to a chair, and he sat uncomfortably, his back rigidly straight. I knew the feeling. A soldier does not sit in the presence of a king, even a king not yet crowned.

"Your Highness, I am honored to serve you. Yet I hope you will forgive me now, for what I have to say more closely concerns your friend Kemen Sendoa."

I sat up even straighter. Even my bones felt cold, and I hoped that my slight shivering wasn't noticeable.

Kepa studied me a moment before speaking again. "I am honored to meet you at last, Sendoa. Our paths have crossed before, but I didn't have the honor of meeting you in person then. I wanted to express my regret for the way you were discharged from the kedani. It was on my orders, but it was not my will."

I stared back at him, wishing I did not feel so achingly cold. My feet seemed clammy and icy in my boots. I wondered what he meant, but he spoke more plainly.

"I ordered you discharged as soon as you could stand, though you deserved much better. I suspected Taisto even then of betraying your squad. That battle was never meant to happen, and he was the only one who could have betrayed you. I sent messages to the king Hakan Emyr, a dozen messages, at least, some before your group was betrayed and some after, warning of my suspicions about him. I don't know whether the king Hakan Emyr never received them or whether he did not believe them, but in any case, nothing was done. I had it recorded that you died of injuries received in battle."

I could no longer control my shivering, though I still held myself very upright. What is the difference between courage and stupid pride, when it comes to showing weakness or pain? I've never been able to tell. Hakan poured me a glass of wine.

"I hoped even then that you would elude him, for I knew your reputation as a man of honor. Did you never receive my message?"

"What message?" My voice betrayed my deep shivering, and Hakan looked at me sharply.

"Are you well?" Hakan asked.

"What message?" I stared back at Kepa and did not answer Hakan. What could I say? The fever would have to run its course.

Kepa sighed quickly. "I thought not. I sent a message with the orders for your discharge, an apology and the advice that you should live under another name. I wasn't sure Taisto would believe you died and he might have been looking for you. You were the only survivor of your squad, and Taisto had already eliminated many of the best officers."

"What of you, then? You're older than I, with greater experience. Surely you would have been a greater threat than I was?" I shouldn't have asked it. It questioned his competence, an open insult. I can only plead that the poison and fever had eroded my courtesy, for I realized the affront a moment later. "Forgive me." I ducked my head in a seated bow, for I no longer trusted my legs enough to rise as I should have.

"No, you're right. He didn't judge me much of a threat. You may have been unaware of your reputation, but you were well known, very much a rising star and destined to replace Taisto if the king had his way. I have no great gift for strategy and was never much of a warrior, but I do what I'm told, most of the time anyway, and don't cause problems. On the northern border, Taisto thought me out of the way. I offer my most humble apology, Sendoa. You deserved better, without a doubt. I did what I could for you, and through you for Erdem, because I knew you to be an honorable man though I hadn't met you. I am honored to meet you now."

I smiled and pushed myself up to return his bow, though my head spun as I did so. "I am honored by your trust. Thank you." I would have said more, but I could think of no appropriate words.

I let myself sit again and could not help hunching forward in my chill, shivering violently. I scarcely heard him speaking with Hakan. I heard my name more than once, but I could no longer make out the other words.

Someone put a thick blanket around my shoulders, and I tried to stand. Even with help I stumbled and fell to my knees, shaking so hard that even my jaw ached with tension. The tightness in my muscles made my ribs ache more than they had in weeks. No doubt they could have carried me to the sleeping chamber, but Hakan and Kepa helped me to a couch in Hakan's study and piled another thick blanket around me.

I don't know if I slept, but I wasn't aware of much for several hours.

THE FEVER RECEDED again more fully by the late afternoon. Hakan took me to a bathing room, where a boy heated water for me. I'd never had a hot bath, but Hakan assured me that it was much more pleasant than icy river water. He left me to it, with instructions to the boy to keep a sharp eye on me in case the fever returned. The boy heated the water until it nearly scalded my skin off.

I removed the bandage from my shoulder and let the water enter the cut from the arrow. It stung, but the pain was bearable and almost pleasant because it kept me clearheaded. The fresh tender scar tissue on my leg and arm from the skirmish in Senlik itched in the heat and I rubbed it gently. I sweated and soaked in the warmth, and when I finally dragged myself from the water, I felt much better.

The heat sweated out some of the fever, and though I had a chill again that night, it was much less severe. After the bath, the boy handed me a thick robe rather than my clothes and ran off. In a few minutes, Hakan was back with a servant woman old enough to be my mother. He gave me my clothes, which had been washed and were nearly dry, warm from the sun outside. I dressed quickly behind the corner.

"This is Lika. She's going to take your measurements for your new clothes."

"I'm getting new clothes?" I raised my eyebrows at him.

"Aye, you're getting new clothes. You can't crown me wearing that."

I wondered whether Hakan would expect me to pay for the clothes. Surely not. I couldn't have, in any case.

I stood still while the woman moved me about, measuring me in every possible way with a thin strip of cloth. She wrote her measurements on a bit of parchment. Even a seamstress can read and write numbers.

Hakan spoke quietly. "I received a message from the king Ashmu Tafari today. He requested that I send you as my official representative in the negotiations. His brother spoke very highly of you."

I blinked in surprise. "Really? That's interesting." How would I serve in that capacity if I couldn't even read?

"If you want the position, it's yours."

I glanced at him.

"Of course, you would have assistants, scribes and historians and such, to assist you in the minute details."

"I will serve in whatever way you wish." I smiled.

There was not even a trace of condescension when he nodded. "I trust you best, and it serves Erdem to send a representative that Tafari trusts as well."

The woman tried to measure my shoulders, but she could not reach them easily. I would have knelt, but Hakan pushed a chair closer.

"Stand on this."

She bobbed her head and murmured quiet thanks. She finished in another few minutes and curtsied on her way out.

"I haven't the money to pay for new clothes, Hakan." The words slipped out quietly, for I felt almost ashamed of the fact. Though I don't know why I should have been ashamed. A soldier is never rich.

"Don't be ridiculous. I don't expect you to pay for them. Why would you think that?" He looked baffled, and I shrugged. If my mind hadn't still been so fuzzy, I would have realized it myself. Hakan was nothing if not generous, and my worry about the expense did him a disservice.

"There is no precedent for a friend and soldier to crown the king. You cannot be dressed as my father would have been, nor would you be comfortable in a nobleman's attire. Your clothes will be similar to what you're wearing now, only better quality."

I swallowed. Right. I would have to speak in front of a crowd, no doubt. He must have seen that in my face, for he smiled suddenly.

"I can give you the words tonight, if you want to study them. You can practice. It's meant to be an honor, Kemen, not a torture session."

I nodded, my throat feeling tight with nerves.

He wrote the words himself, and read them to me several times. They were simple and direct, for which I was grateful. Most of them were traditional, the same words used at every coronation, and these were familiar from stories told by every soldier since the beginning of Erdem itself. I've always had a good memory. I suppose I've exercised it more than most people since I can't read the words in front of me. I'd committed the words to memory soon, but I resolved to add in a little more praise of Hakan than he'd written.

I slept very deeply that night until I woke with a chill in the early morning hours. But it passed quickly, and I slept again until the sun was well above the horizon. I felt lazy and frivolous for sleeping so long, and the luxury was welcome. My old clothes were gone, and there was a new set on the table near the foot of the bed. A shirt of soft white linen, a dark green tunic, dark breeches of a soft cloth I couldn't identify. They were thinner than the canvas ones I was accustomed to, comfortable and cool. The clothes were much like my old ones in design, better cloth but not the formal attire I would wear for the coronation. The seamstress must have worked overnight, or worked her girls overnight, to finish them so quickly.

Again, there was an exquisite breakfast prepared for me. I ate quickly, for though I was still a little weak I felt much better than before.

When I finished eating, I opened the door to the hallway. There was no one there, and I wandered through the halls and rooms for some time without seeing anyone. I saw the great dining hall, a richly luxurious room with three great fireplaces along one end and a smaller version of the throne at the other. Above the throne was a great tapestry with the crest of Erdem, a smaller version of the one in the throne room. It is an eagle grasping an olive branch with one foot and a sword with the other. The colors of Erdem are green and gold, with silver used to define the edges.

My heart beat faster at such a magnificent representation of Erdemen glory. A soldier serves Erdem in dusty or muddy combat and the cries of dying men, when the flag may be torn and despoiled in the confusion. I hadn't seen it so beautiful in many years.

The eagle represents strength, power, honor, and triumph. His great golden eyes hold the wisdom to use that strength well. The sword is for military might, and the olive branch is both the richness of the land and the great pure hope of peace. The green of the background is the color of the richness of the crops in spring and the pride of Erdemen kings. The gold is the color of the harvest and of the great wealth of Erdem, both in the metal gold and other temporal things and in a rich and beautiful history. The silver that edges the great crest is for purity and selflessness, a reminder to all kings of their purpose in serving their country. I gazed at the crest for some time. It warmed me inside.

TWENTY-THREE

The day of the coronation was almost blindingly bright, the sun glittering on the golden accents on the palace gates. The grounds had been prepared the day before, and the coronation was set for mid afternoon. Huge green banners with the royal crest were hung on either side of the great steps that led up to the grand doorway. A green carpet woven with gold and silver threads defined the path up the steps that the army officers would take to swear their allegiance to Hakan after he was crowned.

The nobles arrived first, their clothes like jewels in the brilliant sunlight. The men escorted ladies wearing velvets, silks, and satins, with feathers and flowers in their hair. The highest-ranking nobles were accorded the honor of the positions closest to the stairs. I reviewed my words in my head as I waited, studying them from a shadowed nook just behind the stairs. I took no great pains to hide myself, but I did not want their attention either.

The noblemen were all on the soft side to my eyes, although from their stride and bearing I could see that a few of the men had served in the army at some point. That was good. Though I do not believe that being a soldier necessarily qualifies one to lead, it can provide a perspective that many noblemen probably need. The mood was very festive and I was glad to see them smiling for it promised little resistance to Hakan's rule. Of course he could earn their resistance soon enough, but at least it would not face him without reason.

The women were like flowers dancing in the wind, their laughter like the sound of many small streams. They were very different from the women of the border. I could not have said which I preferred, for they were like different species, but if I had to choose, I thought the calm kindness of a simple farm woman would be more to my taste than the sparkling laughter of those bright and cultured ladies. But perhaps I did them an injustice, for I can't say that I knew them to be less than kind. I had no call to be judging either kind of woman.

Behind the highest ranked nobility there were lesser nobility and some of the richer merchants of Stonehaven. Those of other regions had not had time to hear the news yet nor to travel to Stonehaven, but Hakan was right not to delay the coronation longer. High ranking suvari officers formed a line on one side of the green carpet, the highest ranking closest to the top of the steps. Sikke Bakar was near the top, while Hayato was a few steps from the bottom.

The kedani officers formed their own line on the other side. I saw Katsu Itxaro near the top of the steps. I hadn't thought he had time to ride to Stonehaven, but he must have ridden hard ahead of his men. Yoshiro Kepa was also there. The officers gathered in small groups to speak to each other, for there was some time yet before they would have to be in position. Among the military men, the feeling seemed to be of great relief, and I suppose it was justified. Though I hadn't seen much of their side of it, they had been on the verge of a war with Rikuto that none of them had wanted, pointless bloodshed narrowly averted.

Inside I changed into the clothes that the seamstress had brought me, the ones prepared for the coronation itself. There was a shirt of fine silk, and over that a tunic of rich green brocade edged in gold. The breeches were a darker shade of the same green and a thicker, sturdier cloth. I was glad they weren't the same shade; I had a momentary vision of myself as a tall stern vegetable, a broccoli or a bean of some sort. For Hakan's sake, I would wear the clothes, but I felt rather ridiculous.

I liked the boots much better. The deep brown leather was beautifully soft and well sewn, with an intricate design about the top stitched in subtle brown thread. They fit perfectly, and I supposed the bootmaker had taken the measurements during the days I was fevered. The belt was of the same dark leather and muted the green, which made me feel less absurd.

The cloak was beautifully made of a heavy cloth that was more than serviceable, though far too beautiful to risk dirtying. It was edged with a wide border of gold, the threads woven into an intricate design of vines, and between my shoulders was the royal crest in gold and silver threads. The gold on my clothes was worth more than I'd ever held before, except for the one time I held Hakan's little bag of coins for a moment.

There was also an exquisitely made longsword, the hilt wrapped in dark leather. A flowing script ran up the blade like a tongue of fire. It was a beautiful weapon, far better than any I'd ever held, made by a true artist.

The actual coronation I remember almost as a blur. I stood well back from the steps, and I doubt many in the crowd even noticed that I was there at first. Hakan was regal and commanding in his address. He spoke first, which was a bit unusual, but in the absence of a sitting king it was unavoidable. He praised me more than he should have, and my throat tightened until I feared I would be unable to speak myself.

His voice carried well in the warm afternoon air. "My father cannot be here today to crown me king. As you know, I could have chosen to crown myself. Instead, I have asked my friend Kemen Sendoa to crown me king, as my father would have done if he were alive. Kemen Sendoa embodies everything that is noble and honorable in Erdem. I could ask for no better friend and no better ally as I serve Erdem as your king. I have been honored by his trust in me and his support thus far, and as king I shall endeavor to be worthy of the trust he and you have placed in me."

301

I stood in front of the great crowd and let my voice ring out, my hands clasped tightly behind my back to hide their shaking. Hakan stood beside me, young, proud and very handsome. His smile was very solemn and very regal when he bowed his head to accept the crown that I placed on his head.

Then I knelt to swear my allegiance to him as king. I presented him with the hilt of my sword, and he took it and bowed in respect before handing it back to me. He caught my eye with a warm and gracious smile as I rose, and he thanked me quietly and very seriously before he turned to accept the oaths of the officers who came before him.

Each knelt in turn and presented his sword, swearing the oath with head bowed in respect. I stood well back while the men walked up the steps each in turn. I could see the hilt of his sword, and I was relieved to note that he was wise enough not to use my sword for the final part of the ceremony. The king's sword symbolizes his protection of the people, and the same sword has been used for generations at the coronation.

When the last of the officers had vowed their loyalty, Hakan drew the royal sword and held it upright before him to take his own oath. The words were familiar to me from history, but they acquired a new solemnity when I saw Hakan's eyes glistening with his emotion.

"With the sword I will defend my country. With the shield, I will defend it. My learning, my wisdom, my gold, my blood, and every treasure I possess shall be for the protection of the people of Erdem. On the honor with which I stand before you, I swear to serve the people of Erdem until my dying breath."

He knelt and bowed his head, the golden crown glittering. We knelt to give him full respect for this great oath. My heart fluttered with awe, and my own eyes were not dry when I rose.

THE END

THE ERDEMEN HONOR SERIES

CONTINUES IN

A COLD WIND

When retired Erdemen army officer Kemen Sendoa helped the young prince Hakan Ithel reclaim his throne, he thought he was happy. He had shaped the future of his beloved country and earned a place of honor and respect.

In the shelter of the palace, he finds peace and the promise of a life he'd only imagined. Yet his own choices, and brewing border troubles, may force him to make a final sacrifice.

A tale of love, honor, and forgiveness, A Cold Wind follows The King's Sword in the Erdemen Honor series.

C. J. BRIGHTLEY

C. J. Brightley lives in Northern Virginia with her husband and young daughter. She holds degrees from Clemson University and Texas A&M. She welcomes visitors and messages at her website, www.cjbrightley.com.